A ROVING EYE

Also by Gally Marchmont

WILD GRAPES

Gally Marchmont

A ROVING EYE

A Cordovan Chronicle

ORION

First published in Great Britain in 1997 by
Orion
An imprint of Orion Books Ltd
Orion House, 5 Upper St Martin's Lane,
London WC2H 9EA

A CIP catalogue record for this book
is available from the British Library

ISBN 0 75280 489 8

Typeset at The Spartan Press Ltd,
Lymington, Hants

Printed in Great Britain by
Clays Ltd, St Ives plc

For Von

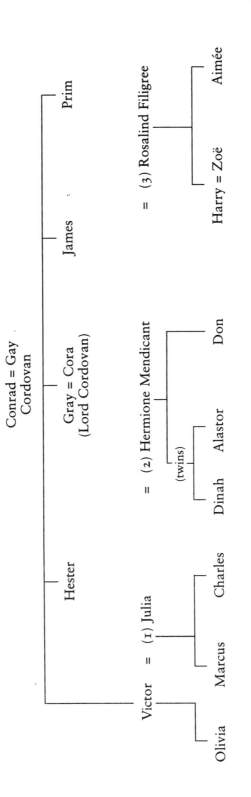

CHAPTER 1

'He'll live.'

'Ah.'

Lisa had known he would live. Philip was tough. Philip wasn't about to set off on his journey to eternity. Not just yet.

'Good,' she added, feeling that the doctor had hoped for a more joyful response.

He was a thin, wiry, intense man, with sandy hair. He looked as though he knew what he was doing.

'You'll want the consultant to confirm that.'

'Why?'

He gestured towards the closed door. 'He's a fat cat, isn't he? Bundles of medical insurance. Into the private ambulance, and straight round to the London Clinic, is that it?'

Fat cat?

Yes, Lisa could agree with that. At least with the cat part. Philip was definitely like a cat. A prowling, arrogant, oriental cat, compact of muscle, domineering in his territory in that way cats are. Not, though, very ethical, was it? Calling a patient a cat. Then she realised what he meant.

'Rich, you mean.' She wondered why the doctor was so angry.

He told her.

'He gets the same treatment as everyone else here, and it couldn't be better. Not anywhere in the country, not if you paid, oh, tens of thousands of pounds.'

'I'm sure,' she said.

He looked even tougher and leaner. 'No doctor could have saved that eye. A lot of doctors couldn't have saved his life. We did. He's very, very lucky.'

'I know.'

'Perhaps, when he's discharged from his posh clinic, he might like to make a donation to our hospital.'

'I'll see that he does.'

He gave her a strange look. 'He won't be going anywhere just yet, though. You do understand that? It isn't a small thing, to lose an eye. He has to stay in intensive care until we're quite sure there'll be no complications.'

'I know he can't be moved.'

Lisa's calmness was worrying the doctor.

'You are his wife? That *is* right? You are,' he glanced down at his notes, 'Mrs Philip Maffick?'

'Lisa Maffick.'

She hated being called Mrs Philip Maffick, although Philip didn't mind. He could never see why she objected to it.

'Do you know how this happened?' The doctor was looking at her intently, his pale grey eyes a great deal too sharp.

Best to sound nonchalant. 'A fencing accident, I believe.'

'Were you there?'

Lisa stared at him. Was she likely to have been there while her husband tried to kill his best friend?

'I was not.'

'How do you know it was a fencing accident?'

Her eyes flickered down the shiny grey passage to the distant waiting area which lay through two sets of swing doors. 'I saw Rory. He told me. He and my husband often fence.'

'At home? In the hall?' He was incredulous. 'Unprotected? No helmets?'

'At the club, usually,' she said.

He gave up. 'The police have been informed,' he said, suddenly very formal and wirier than ever.

He's tired, she thought, noticing the drawn skin under his eyes.

'They'll take a statement right away from,' and he glanced at his notes, 'Mr Rory MacLehose. And from your husband when he's well enough.'

'Yes.'

'I have other patients to attend to,' he said abruptly. 'Sister will need some details from you. Through there.'

'Can I see him?'

He looked surprised. 'Do you want to?'

Lisa shrugged. 'Not if he's better off alone.'

'He's unconscious,' he said, exasperated.

She stared at him. 'Yes, I suppose he would be.'

2

'From the anaesthetic,' he said with a sigh. 'He might like you to be there when he comes round.'

'How long will that be?'

'Couple of hours. Maybe less.'

'I've got a lunch appointment,' she said.

He gave her a contemptuous look, and went away, calling to a passing nurse for information about how the motor-bike crash in bed two was doing.

'Thank you,' Lisa called after him.

He stopped, and turned round. He gave her a last, hard look, and then pushed through the swing doors. She could hear his voice, chopped up by the chunk chunk of the door as it swung backwards and forwards. 'Callous cow . . .'

That's me, she thought, leaning against the gleaming wall. The faint smell of polish, of disinfectant, of air-conditioned air, was nauseating. Sister emerged from a door along the corridor, on the other side, and eyed her unenthusiastically. The muscular nurse had a surprisingly full mouth, which was as pursed as it could manage.

Then a professional air came over her. 'Shock,' she said briskly. 'I'll get someone to bring you a cup of tea.' She guided Lisa along the corridor, and thrust her into a little room. 'Sit in here, and then I'll be back to ask you some questions.'

What the sister took for shock was fury.

Fury at the two of them for fighting in that ridiculous way. Fury at Rory for so nearly killing Philip.

How dare they.

There was her summer turned upside down in one flash of an anachronistic blade.

She'd known for sure that Philip wasn't going to die. She'd seen Granny Paget only three days before. Granny Paget would have told her if Philip had been going to die. Not one to pull her punches, Granny Paget.

'An accident, luvvie,' she had crooned in her mock-cosy way. 'A terrible one, in strange circumstances. Not to a little one,' she added quickly, knowing that she would immediately worry about Alec. And Polly, too, of course.

'Philip Maffick.' The sister wrote it down with deliberate neatness. 'Just Philip? No other names?'

3

'Henley.'

'Like the rowing?'

'Like the rowing,' Lisa agreed.

'D.O.B.?'

'What?'

'When was your husband born? Date of birth?'

'Sorry. Twenty-third October, nineteen forty-five.'

'Nationality?'

'English.'

She looked at Lisa, affronted, as she wrote down 'British'.

'Religion?'

Easy. 'None.' None that he'd admit to, at any rate.

The list droned on. Allergies? Illnesses? Operations?

'He seems a fit man for his age,' she said dispassionately. 'What a pity about his eye. It'll spoil his looks.'

Oh, no, it won't, Lisa said to herself. She considered Philip no great beauty at the best of times. His attraction lay in his vitality and brains and cussedness. He already had a scar across one cheek, from a youthful prank. His dark, watchful, knowing eyes; yes, they were arresting. Well, he'd have to use a single eye to double effect. No problem for Philip, in her opinion. He had never been conventionally good-looking, and was certainly not beautiful the way Rory was, even at forty-five.

'We don't call men beautiful.' Lisa could hear Emilia's icy tones. 'We say handsome, or good-looking. Or charming, if you must.'

'Can I make a phone call?' Lisa asked.

The sister looked disapproving. 'We haven't finished.'

'It's important. I need to phone my mother-in-law.'

She beamed. 'Mr Maffick's mother? Of course.'

She would be on the side of mothers-in-law. 'And the children.'

Her face took on extra sympathy. 'Is someone looking after them? Do you need to contact a neighbour, a friend, anything like that? Sometimes, when one is shocked, one forgets about that kind of thing.'

'They're all right.' They would be, she'd left a message for Mrs Juniper.

'Mrs Juniper?' said the nurse, her hand on the door handle.

Lisa hadn't realised she'd spoken out loud. 'She looks after the house. And the children when necessary. I work.'

'I see.'

Lisa remembered the tussle of earlier years.

'Polly's too old for a bloody nanny,' Philip had said. 'Seven, at school all day, old enough to move on.'

'To an attractive au pair?'

'Why not? Anything's better than that bun-faced woman you have now.'

'She's very highly-trained.'

'Time she was off, using her training somewhere else. Get a Swede,' he said grandly. 'Or someone from Switzerland. Get the girl going on a language. Could help Alec with his German, too.'

So Mrs Juniper had come into their lives. Not Swedish or Swiss, not young, not at all glamorous. A disappointment to Philip from an aesthetic point of view, with her bony body and face, but indefatigable, reliable and full of common sense.

Emilia's voice on the telephone was always a decibel or two beyond comfort. 'Accident?' she said piercingly. 'Nothing serious, I do hope.'

Emilia blamed Lisa. At once, without asking for any details. She was convinced that Lisa longed for Philip to die, so that she could become an immensely rich widow and live the life of Riley. Such a strange idea, thought Lisa, as she gazed out of the glass telephone dome at the tide of humanity swimming past. Men like Philip didn't grow on trees.

'I'll come straight to the hospital. *Where* did you say he was? Good gracious, why?'

'It was the nearest casualty department.'

'We must get him out of there immediately. Have you arranged it?'

'No.'

'Why not?'

'Intensive care, Emilia. You don't drag ill people out of intensive care. He's all tubed up, wired to beeping machines, that kind of thing.'

Sharp intake of breath at the other end of the line. 'Wait for me at reception. I suppose they do have a reception?'

'They do, yes, but I won't be there.'

'You'll be at his bedside,' she said with grudging approval.

'No, actually, I'm going out to lunch.'

'You're what?'

'I'm lunching with Iain Stirling. The designer.'

'I know perfectly well who Iain Stirling is, nasty little pervert. Your place is with Philip.'

Must be the first time she's ever thought that. 'No, I didn't say anything, it's the line.'

'Are you ringing from a public phone?'

Emilia hated public anything. Lisa didn't think she'd used a payphone in years, all those germs from common people lingering on the mouthpiece.

'He's all yours,' she said. 'He's out for the count, you see, after the op. I'll be back in time to hold his hand when he wakes up.'

'Have the doctors told you when that will be?'

'Nope.'

'There you are, then.'

'They don't need to. I'll know. I'll be there.'

Ha, that touched her on the raw, Lisa thought, knowing that Emilia considered she was a witch. Lisa would like to have been a witch, because there were a great many spells she wouldn't have minded using from time to time. Such as now. And there was no point in telling her mother-in-law that telepathy was just a knack, or a genetic inheritance. Lisa had the gift, Emilia didn't. So she'd know when Philip was surfacing from his druggy trance, and Emilia wouldn't.

The bustling restaurant was a haven of peace after the hospital. Although Lisa could still hear Emilia's voice dinning in her ears.

'How will you know?' Iain fixed her with his knobbly eyes.

She pulled at the bone with her fingers. 'I just will.'

'I wish you wouldn't do that.'

'What?'

'Eat with your fingers.'

'I always do.'

'Yes, but it's embarrassing.'

Lisa couldn't care less. If people hadn't got anything better to do than notice her eating with her fingers, then she felt sorry for them. And as for Iain, he needed a bit of reality in his bubblegum life. She told him so.

'You're very hard. Everyone thinks so.'

She swirled her fingers in the finger bowl and a waiter darted forward to whisk away the glass bowl with its single floating flower. Lisa dried her hands on the thick white napkin.

'You sound like Emilia. She's endlessly moaning about how hard I am. Meaning, I don't do just as she says.'

Iain gave his unbecoming giggle. 'When Philip first met you, she was *so* horrified. "It won't last," she told everyone. "She isn't his sort."'

Typical Iain. He loved to remind her that he'd known Philip much longer than she had. Practically cradle sharers, according to him. Philip was the first of a long line in that case.

It was the first warm day in a summer which had been late and chilly after a miserable spring. As the sun came out and the temperature rose, so did the traffic fumes and the pollen count.

Lisa dawdled in a rectangle of cars, three lanes of them, stretched out like a carpet. All hot and smelly, inside and out. The driver in the car next to her started sneezing. The traffic jam didn't bother her, but oh, Lord, she thought, I hate people who sit in cars and sneeze.

Another contortion, another spasm, and another.

And another.

Just expire quietly, she said to him through the glass. He didn't notice, too busy snuffling into a grubby handkerchief. Hay fever. Where did the pollen come from, in the wasteland that was the centre of London? Or did he bring it in from his suburban garden, his country retreat? Did it cling to the wheels and upholstery of his gleaming car?

Lisa had told Philip once that a sneeze was a spontaneous and uncontrollable spasm, just like an orgasm. He was furious.

'That's it,' he said, thumping the pillow and dragging the covers over his back.

'Don't stop,' she said sleepily.

'How can I not stop when you say things like that?'

'Try sneezing,' she said helpfully. 'Maybe that'll firm things up a bit.'

That was Philip off to the spare room for the rest of the night. It wasn't usually a problem with Philip, he was rarely put off his stride.

The wodge of traffic edged forward. No more flirting with Rory, she told herself. Fair was fair, and if what was only the mildest of encounters with an attractive man had got under Philip's skin, then so be it. Although Lisa wasn't sure that she had got to the bottom of the fight. On balance, it was almost as though Rory had been trying to hurt Philip. If not actually to slay him.

Extreme, thought Lisa, letting in the clutch to slide forward a few more feet. The little street where she turned off was in sight now, and then she could put the car away and get back to work until she felt it was time to return to Philip.

Later, Lisa walked to the hospital. She walked a lot in London. It was exercise; she could think and plot and plan while walking, and it was usually quicker than taking the car. Philip didn't notice how she got about, as long as she was where he wanted her at exactly the right time.

Philip was a punctual man.

Emilia hated her walking, and she expressed her disapproval at great length, as soon as she had bestowed an insincere butterfly kiss on Lisa's cheek. For the benefit of the nurses, Lisa supposed, nobody else was watching. And Emilia was old enough not to worry about impressing people.

'It isn't safe.'

'London in broad daylight is quite safe, Emilia.'

'I sometimes think you've never quite got out of old habits, Lisa.'

By this she meant her being brought up in a grim northern city, and slouching off to a common grammar school on foot, and going out with a rough crowd on Saturday nights.

'I can look after myself, Emilia. I don't dress ostentatiously, I don't wear a lot of clanky jewellery and I don't look as though I've just come out of Harrods' beauty parlour. To sum up, I don't look worth mugging.'

'Exactly,' said Emilia in triumph, looking at her baggy trousers. 'Not very smart, if I may say so.'

One general moan was enough.

'How's Philip?' Lisa asked, moving off towards his room.

'Still asleep,' she said, lowering her voice to a whisper.

'He's not asleep. He's out cold with anaesthetics and drugs. He'll come round in a few minutes,' Lisa said, sitting down on a plastic covered chair and taking a book out of her bag.

Emilia wouldn't sit down. Not on a horrid green shiny seat. So she prowled, getting in the way of passing personnel, and driving Lisa mad as her heels went tap, tap, tap along the corridor.

A nurse approached, a genuine smile on her face. 'Mrs Maffick? Your husband is just coming round from the anaesthetic.'

Lisa got to her feet. 'Want me to hold the bowl?' she asked.

The nurse grinned some more. 'That won't be necessary.'

Emilia surged up. 'How is he? Is he awake? Can I go in now?'

'Only his wife, I'm afraid.'

'Don't be absurd. I'm his mother.'

She was a nurse of character. 'Not yet, I'm sorry. Strict instructions from the doctor. Could you come this way, Mrs Maffick?'

Lisa hated seeing Philip lying there, motionless, in a maze of medical paraphernalia. And that bandage over his eye; God, what a fool he was.

She told him at once, about the eye. He had asked, as soon as he'd taken in his surroundings. Difficult to speak when you're full of tubes, but he managed it.

'What's the damage?'

And then, when she'd told him, ignoring the rustlings from the nurse, there was quite a long silence. 'Could be worse,' he said. 'Thought he was aiming at a different part of my anatomy.'

'All quite untouched.'

Good thing too. Apart from the personal inconvenience, Lisa couldn't see Philip as the Fisher King.

'We'll soon have you up and around again, Mr Maffick,' said the nurse brightly.

There was a nurse who liked the look of what she'd seen, that was clear.

'Gone altogether?' he asked after a while.

'I believe so.'

'Now, don't take on, Mr Maffick. They do wonders these days, you'd hardly know.'

Lisa doubted if Philip would agree to any cosmetic touches; she couldn't imagine him with a glass eye. She suspected it would be a dashing piratical eyepatch, or a scarred nothingness, and damn *your* eyes if you don't like it.

'Emilia's here.'

'No,' said Philip. 'I'm going back to sleep.'

He did, for about thirty seconds, and then he remembered something. 'Nurse,' he said, sounding very woozy. 'Accident. It was an accident. Okay?' And then he sank back into what Lisa hoped was a dreamless sleep.

'Has he had plenty of painkillers?' Lisa asked.

The nurse looked affronted. 'He has everything. We're watching him every second, and we wouldn't want him to have any discomfort we could spare him.'

Discomfort. One way of putting it.

'Don't tell him about the painkillers until you have to. He'll refuse them.'

The nurse eyed Philip admiringly. 'That kind, is he? I like a brave man.'

CHAPTER 2

Emilia had given Lisa a lift home. Lisa wasn't too keen; she knew Emilia would have a go at her.

She was right. Emilia had decided to take the children off Lisa's hands. Or, at least, one child.

'You'll have so much on your plate,' she said. 'To and fro from the hospital, keeping everyone in touch with how Philip is. No, no, I insist. It's much better this way. I'll look after Alec.'

'And Polly?'

That gave her a fright. 'Can't Mrs Juniper look after her? Of course, if she's going to be a problem, then I'd love to have her.'

Liar.

And you only want Alec so that you can bend his ear with poisonous thoughts about me, Lisa thought. Emilia was always trying to kidnap Alec. She felt she'd done such a wonderful job bringing up Philip that there was no one better able to look after the next generation. Tough.

'I don't suppose I'll be spending much time with Philip,' Lisa said, waving a red rag. 'As soon as he's himself again, which knowing him will be about two days, he'll have all his minions summoned to his bedside.'

'Work is one thing,' said Emilia. 'Family is another. He'll need company. Someone to talk to.'

'Perfect job for you, Emilia.'

Emilia knew that she and Philip didn't talk to each other. They argued.

'And you can use your dinky mobile phone and ring everyone up to tell them about Philip.'

It amazed Lisa that formal, out-of-this-century Emilia was so devoted to all the electronic trappings of late-twentieth century life. She despised her daughter-in-law, because the only kind of phone she would use was one which stayed firmly in one place.

She didn't spend hours on the phone to her friends; if she wanted to talk, she would go and see them. And if she was driving or sitting at the other end of the garden or by the lake at Maffick, then she didn't feel any need to talk to anybody. If it was urgent, they could try later.

Fortunately, Emilia was on the gad that evening. Going to have a good moan to all her cronies about how bad a daughter-in-law Lisa was, and poor Philip, lying there, neglected. And how he deserved a better wife, what a pity he never married that nice Youdall girl, thought Lisa as she threw herself into a large and comfortable chair. Who had been well past thirty then, for heaven's sake; girl, indeed! And was long since married and living in Scotland with five red-headed children.

Lisa was grateful to have an Emilia-free sitting room, and with a cup of strong black coffee to help her concentration, she turned her mind to present problems.

First, she had to think about the summer, now that Spain was no longer possible. Oh, bother Philip, why did he have to do it?

Alec had no doubts about the best way to pass the summer weeks. 'Let's hire a yacht. Then we can get shipwrecked, or attacked by pirates.'

'Stupid,' said Polly. 'Daddy will need to be near doctors.'

'Take one with us,' said Alec grandly.

'He and Daddy would argue all the time.'

So wise, so young, was truly irritating.

'We are not going on a yacht.'

Alec flung himself dramatically on to the huge sofa, his great feet scuffing at the covers.

'Take your feet off the sofa,' Lisa said automatically.

Alec gave her a look from under his lashes, assessing how serious she was. He swung his feet away from the cushions. He was a very good judge of her moods.

'So?' said Polly. 'We can't go to Maffick, because Iain prissy Stirling is there with all his young men, doing up the big room.'

'Yes,' said Alec. 'Stripping all the wallpaper and giving little shrieks of dismay all over the place.' Alec was an excellent mimic.

And hadn't that infuriated Emilia. 'Maffick is perfect.'

'Maffick is shabby, it needs endless work done on the roof, the leading is in a dreadful state. And the drains, too. So while some of the most urgent work is being done, Iain can do his stuff.'

'The expense! I sometimes wonder whether you remember what it was like to have no money. You've got so used to it, you never think about it. What would you do if you were penniless again?'

Manage, as she did before she married Philip. And how Emilia would love to see me penniless again, thought Lisa. But Emilia couldn't quite work out any way that could happen, however, without Philip being penniless, too. She devoured the divorce reports in the papers, sucking in her breath when she read that a millionaire's wife had been awarded a settlement of so many millions of pounds. She would wince, as though it all had to come out of her own pocket.

Just as she read the engagement notices every day, and sighed over the excellent matches other people were making. 'Look, Lucy Tinhul's boy, marrying the daughter of that shipping man.'

They must have put Lucy's boy on drugs to get him anywhere near anybody's daughter, thought Lisa. And you'd imagine that after fifteen years of me, she would have given up the sighs.

She hadn't.

She had never approved of Lisa. When she was first going out with Philip, and Emilia met her for the first time, she looked like a student, which was what she was. A mature one, but still a student.

A poor student, with no Daddy-allowance to pay for the flat, the car, the designer clothes. Lisa had her own ideas about clothes, and would turn up with Philip in some very original and striking numbers.

'Bohemian,' Emilia would explain to her friends with a thin smile. 'It's a phase,' she would add, although the friends were uncertain whether Lisa's clothes were the phase, or if Philip could be expected to grow out of his unusual girlfriend.

Emilia lived in hope as long as Philip and Lisa lived together, but in the end she had to concede defeat and watch Lisa sailing up the aisle looking, so she furiously said, for all the world as though she'd just stepped out of a gypsy caravan.

A further grievance was that Lisa looked foreign as well as arty. Since Lisa's father had been Viennese, this wasn't surprising.

Emilia had no time for foreigners, except rich ones, who were automatically honorary Englishmen and women. Oh, and the French were all right. That came from too many trips to Paris, and feeling at home among everyone being so rude.

'How about America?'

'How about we stay in London?'

'We are not staying in London. Your father will work if he's in London, and it's no place to convalesce. We will find somewhere in England, in the country. I don't know where, but we will find somewhere.'

'No point arguing with her,' said Alec, afflicted by a stab of hunger. He hadn't eaten for an hour, and was heading for the kitchen. 'If Ma feels in her bones that we're going to spend the summer in the country, then we will.'

'And I bet it'll be really, really boring,' said Polly. 'With some boring, boring friends of theirs, and nothing interesting will happen the whole time.'

'Wait and see,' Lisa said.

CHAPTER 3

Visitors to Heartsease Hall, a fine manor house in the county of Heartset, often found the family passion for a substantial tea at five o'clock hard to take. The Cordovans loved it, and whoever was about the house or the estate turned up to have a good argument with some other member of the family, discuss the evening's plans, and catch up on the gossip.

'News,' said Harry, coming swiftly in from the garden and helping himself to a large piece of coffee cake.

Victor was standing in front of the fireplace; tall, dark and bearded, he dominated the room as he always did. He had been eyeing that particular piece of cake, and he glared at his youngest son. 'News? What news?'

'Haven't you seen the Turnip Times?' asked Harry, whisking a copy of the *Heartset Gazette* from behind his back. 'Look.'

Victor's sister, Hester, handed Harry a cup of tea. 'I put the paper in Victor's study,' she said. 'For later.'

'No good trying to keep it from him,' said Harry, reaching out for an egg and cress sandwich. 'Wonderful tea time, what would we do without you, Hester?'

Victor read the front page with growing fury.

'Wait for it,' said Harry.

'Calm down, Victor,' said Hester, who was looking at her brother with a weary expression on her face.

'Five, four, three, two, one . . .' counted Harry. 'Explosion!'

'What!' thundered Victor, pat upon his cue. 'A Roman find! Of importance!' He took a gulp of tea, and then set the cup down with a terrifying crash on a nearby table.

He biffed the paper with the back of his hand. 'It's nonsense of course. Local reporters, they haven't got a clue. A few pieces of Roman pottery, I dare say; well, we're always ploughing those up. And we don't make a song and dance about it and rush bleating to the local rag.'

Harry gave his father a quick look. 'No, Pa, more than a few bits and pieces. Quite a find. Everyone's talking about it.'

'Gossip and rumour. That's all it is. Why should there be a major Roman find in somebody else's house? There's been nothing major about that house or anybody in it for generations.'

'The TV people are coming, so rumour has it,' said Harry, stirring things up.

Hester was not pleased. 'Harry, that's enough,' she said. 'And Victor, don't be ridiculous. Just because a neighbour's made an interesting discovery at the bottom of his garden, there's no need for you to get into a fret about it.'

Victor glared at his sister. 'Fret? Of course I'm not in a fret. Load of rubbish, for one thing, and what's a kiln, for another?'

'That's the spirit, Pa,' said Harry.

'Harry, take that plate away from Victor before he grinds it to dust,' advised Hester, removing the cucumber sandwiches out of her brother's reach. 'Victor, your blood pressure must be sky high. And Julia isn't here to dose you.'

Julia was Victor's first wife, who had returned to Heartsease Hall after the departure of his third, happy to renew the delights of married life.

'Thank goodness she isn't,' said Victor, collapsing, a broken man, on to a handy sofa. 'She would be shocked at the vulgarity.'

'What's vulgar about a Roman find, Pa?'

'Nothing, but announcing it to the world at large is extremely vulgar,' said Victor. 'In any case, they know nothing. It'll turn out to be Elizabethan, or from the last century.'

'More news, Pa,' said Harry, giving his father a quick look from under his slanting brows and timing his next little morsel perfectly.

'What now?'

Hester sighed.

'Your chum Philip.'

'Philip who?'

'Philip Maffick.'

'What about him?'

'Had an accident,' said Harry, this time in a muffled voice as he took a large bite of buttered toast.

'Car?'

'No. Much more dramatic than that. Fencing, with unbuttoned foils.'

'Harry, no!' said Hester.

'Fact,' said Harry, scattering crumbs. 'He was fighting Rory MacLehose, do you know him?'

'I do.'

'Thought you would, you know everyone, Pa.'

'Why was he fighting Rory like that?'

'They were duelling, I expect,' said Harry. 'Over some woman, the buzz is.'

'What, Philip? Nonsense, Harry. He's got Lisa, and I know he still sees that old flame of his, what's she called? Titia, that's it. No beauty, but a nice woman. Apart from that, it's work, work, work, with Philip.'

'Mid-life crisis, possibly, Pa. He's coming up to fifty, isn't he? It takes some men that way.'

'Fifty?' said Victor furiously. 'Crisis? What crisis? Fifty is an excellent age, positively youthful, men of fifty, these days.'

'Is Philip badly hurt?' asked Hester.

'Lost an eye,' said Harry.

Hester made tsk-tsking noises of shock and horror; Victor was unimpressed. 'Could be worse. Got another eye, he'll manage.'

'They were going away this summer, I heard,' said Hester. 'They won't be able to if Philip is recovering from an injury like that. Poor Lisa, she was so pleased that she was dragging him away from work for a few weeks. He hasn't had a break for years. She'll be furious.'

'They can go to Maffick,' said Victor.

Harry shook his head. 'Can't. They've got works on. Scaffolding and decorators everywhere.'

Victor snorted. 'That makes a change. It's disgraceful, the state Philip's let that house get into.'

'It's very comfortable,' said Harry, who never took much notice of his surroundings.

'Comfortable! Maybe it is comfortable, but that doesn't make up for everything falling apart and the wallpaper peeling off the walls. Yes, and a bucket catching the leaks in one of the lavs, last time I was there.'

'That was some time ago,' said Hester mildly.

'Worse now, probably. Buckets in *all* the lavatories, I bet you.

Anyway, you're quite right, Harry. Philip can't go there after an accident like that. He'd get an infection.'

'Pity Zoë and I are installed in the Lodge,' said Harry. 'Otherwise they could have stayed there.'

'How is Zoë?' said Hester. 'Didn't she want tea?'

'She's waddled off to see Sybil.'

'Harry,' said Hester sharply.

'I speak as I find.'

'She can't help waddling, not at her stage of pregnancy.'

'I don't blame her for it. In fact she looks more wonderfully blooming every day. However, heaving that bump around makes for a strange walk. That's all. I'm to pick her up at six sharp.'

Victor was lost in thought. 'Hester, why don't we let them have the Tower? After all, Julia's put in that extra bathroom and so forth, guests can't complain.'

Bathrooms at Heartsease Hall were in short supply.

'James usually stays there,' pointed out Hester. 'He said he'd be down this summer.'

That was irrelevant as far as Victor was concerned. 'If he comes with Cora, they'll stay with Prim; that's what Cora likes. If he comes on his own, he can stay in Harry's old room.'

'I don't think he minds where he is, as long as he's near the horses,' said Harry.

'All right, that's agreed,' said Victor. 'That's a good idea, I'm glad I thought of asking them here. I haven't seen Philip for a while, and Lisa's always good to have around the place.' He downed his chilling cup of tea in a single draught and held it out for Hester to refill.

'You mean her bosom is,' said Harry.

Victor ignored that. 'Excellent, excellent. And the youngsters, as well. What's the boy's name?'

'Alec,' said Harry. 'He's very troublesome at the moment.'

'Isn't there a girl, too?'

'Polly,' said Hester.

'Must be, what, ten now?' said Victor. 'Nice little creature, from what I remember. Pretty child, is she, Harry?'

'Hideous,' said Harry. 'All scowl and heavy brows. Takes after Lisa's mother.'

'I never met her.'

'She's dead.'

'Ah,' said Victor. 'That reminds me.'

'No, Pa,' said Harry. 'Philip's mother is all too much alive.'

'I don't suppose she'll want to leave London,' said Victor hopefully.

'Dream on, Pa,' said Harry. 'Too high a price for friendship?'

'Of course not,' said Victor. 'She's probably much improved,' he added, his optimistic nature getting the better of him.

'Oh, Pa!' said Harry.

CHAPTER 4

Lisa remembered her mother's funeral as though it had been last week, not ten years ago. The howling wind, the driving rain, the flapping robes of the clergy and Canon Urquhart's black cloak turning him into Dracula as he tried to hold the graveclothes down with his foot.

Funerals always made you think of other funerals, Lisa reflected, until it seemed that you spent days of your life going to them. She hadn't intended to come north for this one. She only heard about it by chance, when she got a letter in neat round writing from Mrs Daly.

Mrs Jenson passed away sudden Tuesday night. The funeral is on Monday and I take the liberty of writing knowing you will want to pay your respects.

Yours truly, E. J. Daly

Lisa had taken a bundle of post in for Philip, and this one had slipped in among them.

'Who's Mrs Jenson?' asked Philip. The wiry doctor's predictions had come true, and he was installed with maximum comfort and facilities in a private room.

'My godmother.'

'Didn't know you had a godmother. Didn't know you'd ever been christened.'

'Lots are.'

Philip gave a snort. 'You must go.'

'No, I hate funerals.'

'Your godmother, you should go. Or did you never see her after the font?'

'She was always very kind to me,' Lisa said. 'I do mind, you know.'

'Then go. Where is it, up north, I suppose?'

'Yes, and you see, it would mean not visiting you for a day.'

'Someone can drop the post in for me.'
'Emilia will gloat.'
'Go.'

Lisa was glad she'd come. Not to the funeral, because she found them ghastly affairs from beginning to end, and cremations especially so, but because she met up with Fanny again.

'I'm sorry about Amy,' said Lisa, giving Fanny a hug. 'Gracious, you've grown up. How long has it been?'

'Fifteen years. At your wedding.'

Lisa looked at her, seeing a tall, pale young woman. Lovely reddish-brown hair, she thought. It's a colour which can look stunning when properly looked after. Since Fanny had tied it back in a thick plait which hung on a level with her wide shoulders, it didn't look its best.

'Why are you wearing those peculiar clothes?' Lisa asked.

Fanny looked down at the baggy skirt, heavy black shoes and ill-fitting jacket with surprise. 'It's what I always wear.'

'What do you do?'

'I work for a charity,' she said. 'Greensleeves. I do administration.'

'Have you got a boyfriend? Several? Or are you married?'

'No, but I'm going to be.'

Lisa could hear the pride in her voice.

'Tell me about him.'

Once you got used to the strange garb, Lisa thought, Fanny was okay. She had been an intelligent, impulsive child, and she hadn't changed much. Her boyfriend sounded most unappealing, Lisa decided, as Fanny talked, but Fanny clearly thought the world of him.

'Where is he?' Lisa asked, looking round the room, which was crammed full of people eating and drinking and talking nineteen to the dozen. That was just as it should be; Amy Jenson's house was always full of talk. 'Comes of having an Irish grandfather,' she used to say.

Lisa had never forgotten Amy Jenson's front room; it had been an oasis of her childhood. It had always been used, which was not the case in most houses in Getley when she was a girl. It had a comfortable sofa, a comfortable armchair and a lot of fat cushions. It also had white walls, a pale grey carpet and a painting by Harriety on the wall beside the door.

It hadn't changed, although someone, Fanny presumably, had moved the cushions and armchair out and some hard chairs from the kitchen in. To make room for the throng.

So why didn't the throng include Fanny's boyfriend?

'He's very busy at work,' Fanny said. And then she went on to tell Lisa about their plans. They were going to sell the London flat, buy a house with a garden some way out of London – possible, because of all Gerry's hard work – so that she could have a baby.

Babies are a risky enterprise, and Fanny didn't look to Lisa as though she had any idea what she was letting herself in for.

Lisa knew about babies. Babies grew into fractious, rebellious children, and then became difficult adolescents. Or they were dull and uninspiring, doubtless in training to take their future places in society as boring adults.

Like this Gerry, Lisa thought. She didn't like the sound of Gerry. Why hadn't he come to Amy Jenson's funeral?

Fanny had another glass of wine and confided that Gerry and her mother had never hit it off.

I'm right, Lisa told herself. Gerry is a no-hoper. Never mind, perhaps he'll be run over by a bus while Fanny's up north doing her grieving and saying goodbye to the mortal remains.

'How was it?'

'Grim, as far as the funeral bit goes.'

Lisa was trying to cut Philip's toenails, which was a tricky business. He was exceedingly ticklish, and heaving with laughter wasn't good for a sore eye socket.

'Leave it to the nurse,' he said.

Lisa suspected that Philip was enjoying this idle life. The sooner she got him out of there and back to reality, the better, she thought.

And she meant reality. Eye or no eye, she resolved, she was going to tear Philip away from his computer screens and fluctuating currencies for a few weeks. He could enjoy some fresh air and consort with normal people.

That's why she'd arranged for the family to go to Spain. To a village in the hills, few mod cons, plenty of pleasant people around, no Emilia, and good food. Philip liked his food.

Philip wasn't keen on abroad these days. He travelled for work, but reluctantly. He could speak German and some Spanish, but preferred not to. So the house in Spain had been a triumph for Lisa; trust Philip to bugger it up with this eye business, she thought bitterly. She suspected that he was delighted; getting back to work as soon as he was fit was what he had in mind.

She was wrong.

'Victor got in touch with me yesterday,' he remarked.

'Victor Cordovan?'

'Yes.'

Vibrant, sexy, unreconstructed Victor, who adored breasts, thought Lisa. And other womanly bits as well. She'd never known him well, but her old friend Anna had ended up in bed with him, and was loud with enthusiasm. Plenty of oomph, she said. 'One's never had a session with a bull, of course, but that's what it would be like.'

Was there such a thing as a Pasiphae complex?

'Not crude,' she'd added, lest Lisa should have the wrong idea. 'Plenty of finesse there. Very more-ish.'

Anna never had the chance of more, because Julia, jealous, eagle-eyed Julia, got wind of it and saw her off pretty smartly.

'What's Victor up to?' Lisa said.' Did he ring to commiserate?'

'No, he wouldn't know how. Hester wrote a sympathetic letter, though.'

'How is Hester?' she asked. It made Lisa feel happy just thinking about Hester. Every home should have a Hester, in her opinion, although Lisa didn't make the mistake of taking her domesticity at face value. Beneath the genuine warmth, Hester was one tough cookie.

'She sounded fine. She and Victor ask, do we want to spend the summer at Heartsease.'

What a wonderful thought, but there was a hitch. 'No bathrooms,' Lisa said, remembering past visits.

'Nonsense, plenty of bathrooms. Besides, Julia's been busy, put a bathroom and shower in the Tower. Hester says James won't be using it, so would we like it.'

'Um.'

'So I said yes. We're going next week.'

It could be worse.

Lisa knew Philip had no intention of convalescing in any serious way. He wanted to go to Heartsease because of the horses. Apart from his currencies and the economies of far-flung places,

Philip's passion was horses. There were plenty of horses at Heartsease; the place was awash with them. James, Victor's brother, bred Arabian horses. Philip could whicker and snort at them for hours at a time and would doubtless be riding them long before it was good for him to do so.

It wouldn't be restful, Lisa was sure of that. The Cordovans weren't restful.

Ever.

They were always up to something. In her experience, the Hall seethed with intrigue and complicated family and neighbourly feuds and alliances. The youngest Cordovan daughter, the divine Aimée, wouldn't be there, she remembered. She was in America. Just as well; she wouldn't trust her near Alec. Lisa considered there was plenty of time yet for him to find out what the Aimées of this world had to offer.

All in all, Philip could have had worse invitations. He would have fresh air, good food, and Hester's excellent attentions. The children would have acres to roam; she could take a heap of work, and have plenty of time to think about this and that.

A rare luxury.

CHAPTER 5

If the local paper had hit Victor hard, he was devastated by *The Times*. 'Headline news,' he said, waving away Hester's offer of toast to round off a large breakfast. 'How can I eat a morsel, Hester, when I have to read such appalling rubbish?'

Don, Victor's son by his second wife, had dropped in for breakfast. He took after his mother, not after Victor, and so wasn't tall and domineering like his father. He was of medium height, with a face that revealed a sense of humour and an enjoyment of the good things of life. His business was vines, and he ran a thriving vineyard on the edge of the Cordovan lands.

'Don't read it, Pa,' advised Don, wiping a big white napkin across his mouth and rising from the table. 'I wouldn't have come for breakfast if I'd known you were going to carry on like this.'

At the sideboard, Guy deftly slid the plates into a pile. He'd read *The Times* before bringing it to Victor, and he had been just as indignant.

His indignation had fallen on deaf ears in the kitchen where Maria was presiding over the presentation of bacon just so, rings of apple cooked to precisely the right texture, eggs of exactly the right firmness and softness.

'Roman kiln? Ha, this is nothing,' she said. 'Roman remains in this country are little, unimportant. I, who come from the land where is Mérida, aqueducts, amphitheatres, ruins everywhere, I give you that' – a dramatic snap of her fingers – 'for a Roman kiln.'

'Victor won't like it.'

'Victor is jealous.'

Victor raged out of the morning room, seeking whom he might devour. He raked the gardens with a wrathful eye. 'Ha, Jarvis,' he shouted. 'What are you doing?'

Jarvis was mowing the lower lawn into precise stripes from the back of a tractor mower. This garden tractor was Victor's pride and joy; it was a toy he was, however, only allowed to use in the orchard, where he annoyed the pigs but could do little harm to the ground.

Jarvis sighed and switched the engine off. 'What?' he shouted back, in a most unservile way. Jarvis knew that you had to stand up to Victor, or you were steamrollered into schemes you wanted nothing to do with. Victor might pay his wages, but he had a job to do, and keeping this place in order was enough for any man.

'Get a spade,' shouted Victor. 'We're going to do some digging.'

'Oh, no, we aren't,' Jarvis said to himself, raising his hand in acknowledgement. 'I'm off to the kitchen for a coffee break,' he added out of earshot. That should give Victor time to forget about spades. He sighed, jingling the keys to all the garden sheds which he kept in his pockets. Hester had the only other set, and she wouldn't go handing them out to Victor for him to run amok among the flowerpots and pruning snoots.

'Pa,' shouted Harry.

Victor took no notice.

'Hester,' said Harry, putting his head in through the kitchen window. 'What on earth is Pa up to?'

'I think he's being a Roman.'

'A Roman. I see.'

'Did you read *The Times* this morning?'

'Aha,' he said. 'Not only *The Times*, but a lot of the other papers, too. They've gone to town about it.'

Hester raised her eyes to heaven.

'Ha, Harry!' said Victor without enthusiasm as his son bounded into the rose garden.

'Looking good, your roses,' said Harry.

Victor glowered.

'I came to bring you up to date on the find. Did you see *The Times* this morning? And it was on the news last night.'

'You know perfectly well I never watch the local news, the people on it all look like kippers.'

'Oh, it made the national news, both channels.'

Victor tore a few roses off their stalks.

'Ah, dead-heading, I'm a great believer in that. Although those didn't look dead to me.'

'They are now,' said Victor, tossing the blooms away.

Harry followed his father between the rose bushes, sniffing the heavy-scented air with exaggerated appreciation.

'I thought you might care to pop over with me and have a look at it. In a day or two, when the press have gone.'

'I've seen plenty of Roman remains in my time,' said Victor.

'This is an exceptional discovery, so they say. Professor Salvatore Buonamici is coming down from Cambridge to have a look.'

Victor stamped viciously on a centipede which had been unwise enough to stray across his path.

'Thank you, Harry,' he said. 'I'm a trifle busy just now, so I don't see myself getting over.'

'Never mind,' said Harry, enjoying Victor's rage.

Harry tweaked a branch of a nearby rose down, buried his nose in a glowing pink bloom with appreciative delight and then released the thorny bough which flew back towards the wall.

'Don't *do* that, Harry.'

'Feeling tetchy this morning, Pa?'

Victor ignored the remark, and gazed round the walled rose garden with a calculating air. 'This is the spot,' he said. 'I feel it in my bones.'

'Planning to bury one of the neighbours?' enquired Harry. 'The one who discovered the kiln, perhaps?'

'Why aren't you at your office?' said Victor crossly.

'Come on, Pa, you know I work a lot at home now.'

'You'll regret it if your business starts going downhill.'

'It won't, Pa. Business is booming.'

Victor, the concentrated look still on his face, set off at a cracking pace towards the house.

'Where's Jarvis?' he demanded as he strode into the hall.

'He's gone to the village,' said Guy.

'And taken all the keys with him, I suppose.'

'Probably,' said Guy. 'He does usually keep them about his person.'

'I won't be thwarted like this,' grumbled Victor. 'Guy, where's that silver spade?'

'Silver spade? I don't . . .'

'Yes, come along, don't be so dense. You know the one, it

belonged to my father. It's here somewhere, I know it is.'

"Have you really got a silver spade?' said Harry, who had come in on his father's heels.

'Yes, I have. It was used to cut the first turf of some coal mine or other. Ah, I know where it is. Guy, get it for me. It's in the downstairs cloakroom, behind the fishing rods.'

'Is it?'

'Yes,' said Victor. 'I hid it there years ago so that my father wouldn't find it.'

'Pa,' said Harry. 'What are you going to do?'

'Dig,' said Victor.

Jarvis couldn't believe his eyes.

This was his rose garden, tended and coaxed into perfection with much mulching, spreading of compost, digging in of manure, application of rose food, spraying against fungus and other pests . . .

And there was Victor, his panama on his head, calmly digging a trench through it.

'My roses!' cried Jarvis. 'My roots.'

'Ah, Jarvis, good,' said Victor. 'Nip along to the shed and get another spade, and then you can give me a hand. Bring me a proper spade, too, this silver one isn't very practical.'

'Why are you digging up my rose garden?'

'I've got this feeling. Instinct. I know that if I were a Roman, then this is where I'd build.'

'A Roman? I'm not having Romans in my rose garden.'

'No, no, ancient Romans. Long ago, Jarvis. Quite deep, it would be. Time piles earth on top of ruins, you know.'

Jarvis stood his ground. 'There aren't any ruins here,' he said. 'I've dug every inch of this soil, and there aren't any Roman anythings.'

'You won't have gone deep enough.'

'I dug deep enough when that new drainage went in, ten years back.'

'I expect you weren't digging in quite the right place. Now, hurry up, get those spades, and then we can really make some impression here.'

Speechless, Jarvis retreated. Not to the shed where his well-maintained tools were kept, but to the house, to find reinforcements in the shape of Hester.

'The rose garden?' said Hester in surprise. 'Victor hardly ever goes there.'

'He's there now. Digging.'

'Digging? Victor?'

'Yes.'

'I can't think why,' said Hester, 'but if Victor wants to dig, we could find plenty for him to do.'

'This isn't serious digging,' said Jarvis, exasperated. 'This is digging for Romans. He thinks they're buried there maybe, or I don't know what. But he's attacking the ground like he's crazy, and my roses won't stand it. Before you know where you are, he'll be hacking into the roots. Let alone disturbing those new ones I put in last year.'

'Of course Victor mustn't dig up the rose garden,' said Hester calmly. 'I'll come and have a word with him.'

Victor was implacable. 'I tell you, Romans lived here. On this very spot. I can feel their ancient presence brooding among the roses.'

Hester was unimpressed. 'Victor, if there were any ruins here, they would have been found years ago. There can't be a spot of the gardens that's been more dug over than this. It was used for vegetables during the war, or have you forgotten?'

He had, but he wasn't going to admit it. 'It's just a matter of going deep enough,' he said. 'I'm going to go on until I find something.'

Hester gave him a cold look. 'In that case I'm going to get hold of Julia in Sweden and tell her to come back, that you need medical attention.'

Victor looked at his sister, a thunderous expression on his perspiring face. 'You wouldn't,' he said finally.

'Of course I would,' said Hester. 'And if I didn't, Prim would. She's put a lot of work into this rose garden, as well as Jarvis.'

Victor was nervous of getting on the wrong side of Prim, another sister. A keen farmer and gardener, she was a force to be reckoned with.

'Women,' said Victor, jamming the spade into the earth so hard that the blade buckled. 'I can't even do a little digging in my own grounds; this simply isn't a free country any more.'

CHAPTER 6

Lisa was sitting in her office on the ground floor of her London house. She looked up from a pile of artwork as Toby came through the door, carrying a manuscript as though it were a tray resting on his hands.

'Lightweight,' he said, putting it neatly on his desk so that it lined up with other papers. 'Lightweight, but delightful.'

Lisa looked at him over the top of the specs she wore for reading. Her mind wasn't on work. 'Can you manage on your own for the next three weeks or so?'

Toby flicked an errant sheet of paper into place and switched on his computer. 'Okay by me,' he said. 'I'll be able to get some work done if you're all away.'

'Could you look after the house for us as well?'

'What about Colonel Juniper?' Toby didn't like Mrs Juniper; he said she reminded him of his pottery teacher at school. 'The sadist,' he added, thinking of hard times in the art class.

'Nonsense, Mrs Juniper is not a sadist.'

'She's just biding her time. Lulling.'

'She's taking her annual holiday while we're away.'

'Very well, so you want me to feed the parrots and plump up the cat,' he said in his facetious way. 'Will do. Can I have a friend to stay?'

'As long as it's not that unpleasant truck-driver.'

He looked appealing. 'Now, would I?'

'No, because if you do I shall get to hear about it, and there'll be trouble.'

'It'll be a squeaky clean friend,' he said. 'I'm a reformed character, my tests are clear, and I'm keeping it that way. Safe sex, and no pick ups.'

That'll be the day, thought Lisa.

Toby reached down from his seat and took an armful of

newspapers off a shelf. 'Best for you to see these right away,' he said brutally. 'Before all your chums are on the phone, cooing with delight.'

'What?'

'The press have got on to the fencing story.'

'Hell.'

'Emilia rang. I said you were in the bathroom.'

'Thank you, Toby. If she rings again, tell her I've gone out for a very long walk, would you?' She picked up the paper on top of Toby's fat pile. The *Sun*. 'Duel of death,' it said in screaming letters. The others were as bad, in their own way.

'Top money man fights friend.'

'Currency supremo in rapier stab horror.'

There was a sarky diary entry in *The Times*, and a reproachful one in the *Telegraph*.

Emilia, who, as Lisa discovered, read some strange papers, was soon back on the phone. 'Toby, I know Lisa's there, and I want to speak to her. At once. This is a most disgraceful business; it's no good her trying to hide from the truth.'

Toby held the receiver aloft so that Lisa could hear the furious quacks. She sighed, and, deciding that she might as well get it over with, picked up her own phone. She listened to the stream of words, the receiver balanced on her shoulder while she held up a transparency to the light. 'Calm down, it's nothing but a storm in a tea cup. As long as Philip and Rory sit tight and say nothing, the whole affair will blow over.'

Of course, Emilia wasn't having any of it. She wasn't going to miss an opportunity like that. Lisa moved the receiver away from her ear, listening to Emilia's moans about seeing the family name besmirched, the *hurt* of her own son being derided in the press.

'Don't read the papers, then.'

More lamentations and barbed remarks. It was, of course, all Lisa's fault.

And later, Alec, lying on the rug drawing what looked like plans for taking over the world, made it clear that he had read the papers and was shocked. Lisa realised she should have told him about what happened. As it was, he thought Philip was seriously stupid.

'How could he do such a thing?'

'Men do.'

'It's daft. He should have more sense. And more self-control.'

Alec was becoming a prig, Lisa decided.

Polly revelled in it, sifting through any papers she could get her hands on and reciting paragraphs of gruesome journalese. She particularly liked it when they mentioned Lisa.

'"Heart-stricken wife visits hospital." Look, what a terrible picture of you. And listen to this: "Philip Maffick's wife Lora" – I think that's supposed to be you, and not a margarine, ha ha – "is planning a holiday with Roy MacLehose, the man who stabbed her husband in the eye. A source close to the family says that he and Mrs Maffick fly out shortly to a secret love hideaway in the Caribbean."'

That was too much for Lisa who snatched the paper away from Polly. 'Go and do your homework.'

'Done it.'

'Then go to bed.'

'So that you can run away with Rory?'

Lisa looked at her daughter in exasperation. Then she saw the alarm in her eyes; she bit back the irritable remark she had been about to make. Calm and indifferent, she thought; Polly needed reassurance. 'I am not going to run away with Rory. Or anyone else. Now, go and find Mrs Juniper, and get her to help you pack.'

'You're sending me away. You hate me.'

'Nonsense, but we're leaving for Heartsease earlier than we'd planned. You and Alec and I are going on ahead.'

'I don't want to go.'

No, thought Lisa, you never want to do anything that anyone wants you to. 'Daddy said he knew you'd understand.'

'I don't believe you.'

'Why don't you go and ring the hospital and talk to Daddy? Then, when he's told you the same as me, you can go and pack.'

Whistling horribly, Polly dragged her feet out of the room.

Rory rang, finally.

He was full of apologies about the papers. So bad for Philip, recuperating. Bad for him personally; his firm disapproved of any spectacular behaviour among its staff.

'Bad for me, too,' said Lisa.

'Bad for you? Oh, you mean that bit about going away to the Caribbean. God, these journalists are crass. No way would I go to the Caribbean at this time of year, full of tourists.'

'That wasn't what I meant, Rory. I'd rather not be known as the woman you and Philip duelled over.'

Rory had gone sulky. 'Not exactly a duel, dear,' he said. 'More a fight in earnest, shall we say. Besides, we weren't fighting over you. It was Claudia. Must go, just shrug it all off, Lisa, in your usual inimitable way.'

Claudia?

Who was Claudia?

CHAPTER 7

Lisa's first port of call in an emergency was Granny Paget. She wasn't actually her grandmother; both Lisa's grandmothers had died before she was born. Granny Paget was her great-aunt on her mother's side, and a gifted clairvoyant. She started in a local way up north, and then, when her husband died and left her his savings, she took off for London. Where she had done extremely well for herself.

Lisa had no gifts of clairvoyance, which annoyed her, because she felt a clairvoyant streak could have come in useful. She suspected that Granny P was longing for a younger member of the family to train up in the profession, but in any case, she said, Lisa was a toff now.

Lisa was sure she had her eye on Polly, though. She used to say that Polly had the gift, and was just like she was at that age. If that was true, Lisa pitied her great-grandmother.

Nonetheless, she kept Polly well away from Granny Paget.

Granny P was tidying out a cupboard in her tiny kitchen. 'I'll just put this lot away,' she said from her perch on a doddery set of kitchen steps. 'You're lucky, I had a cancellation, otherwise I wouldn't be free.'

'Let me do that,' said Lisa.

'All right, love,' said Granny, coming down with nimble ease.

Lisa wobbled precariously on the steps, her head twisted round to talk to Granny P. 'You didn't say anything about a Claudia when I came.'

'Didn't want to upset you. I knew your Philip would be coming in for a nasty injury, that's plenty to think about.'

'Yes, that's all very well, but I need to know who this Claudia is.'

'Never suspected he was after anyone? That he had another woman on the side?'

'He has an old girlfriend that he keeps in touch with. He often goes to see her, takes her out to dinner.'

'Don't you mind?'

'No.'

Titia was no problem. She was older than Lisa, and pleasant, relaxing company in all ways for Philip. She had her own life and job, but kept up with her friends.

'What does this Titia look like?' asked Granny P, gazing at the cards laid out in a perfect line in front of her.

'Plump. Good skin, good teeth. A lovely smile. No pin-up.'

'Then it's not her,' she said with certainty. 'Time to get out the crystal ball.'

This was serious. Granny Paget rarely used the crystal ball. She said she didn't need to.

'But I must today, pet, otherwise I'm not going to get a good look at her.'

Much polishing and huffing and muttering, as she peered and reflected. 'Looks a bit like you,' she pronounced finally. 'Younger, I'd say. Taller, not the petite type. Very slim, though. Witchy eyes. And what a bagful of spiteful old mischief she is. Grasping! Dear oh dear, you are going to have to be very careful with this one.'

'Why?'

'Predator,' she said. 'Written all over her. And allure. The beckoning sort. You know, comes into a room, looks round, gives a man the eye, and it's like he was on a piece of string. Drawn,' she went on dramatically. 'Entangled. Just like that.'

Lisa was unimpressed. Women like that were bogies to scare your girlfriends with. On the other hand, Granny P knew a thing or two, and she could obviously see something in her glass ball. 'Who is she?'

Granny P came down to earth. 'That, dearie, I can't tell you, and you know I can't. Surname, address, those are materialistic details, they don't come through the ether,' she said practically. 'You'll have to do a bit of detective work on your own to find all that out. One thing I will say, though, is that she's going to cross your path quite soon. There's a line of connection there with your hubby, but there's another one, which is to do with you. Through a friend. Through someone who goes back a long way. From the old days in the north, I wouldn't be surprised.'

'A friend?'

'A woman friend, we aren't talking about another man here.'

'And she's to do with this beckoning woman, who's probably after Philip?'

'Yes, someone you know is getting a lot of hassle from this lady, and you're involved. Don't ask me how, because I don't know.'

Lisa sat pensively, looking at the liver spots on Granny P's hands as she skilfully drew the cards together and ran them like water through her fingers. She gave the crystal ball an extra polish with the black velvet cloth in which it lived, and then covered it up and put it back in the cupboard.

'You'll have to go now, I've got an appointment at seven, paying.'

Granny Paget would never take a penny from Lisa.

'Slip out the back way, dear, if you don't want to meet her. And keep in touch from that place in the country you're going to. You're in for a lively time, I can tell you that for nothing. A fax will always find me.'

Lisa bent over and gave her wrinkled cheek a kiss. 'Take care of yourself,' she said.

Granny P gave a raucous laugh. 'Don't you worry about me, you're the one with problems.'

What a cheering thought.

Lisa woke up with a start, and reached out to turn her clock round. Half past three. Grey time.

The hour of the wolf.

She wasn't sure for a moment why she was feeling so grim. A nightmare? She put out her hand to touch Philip's reassuring and solid shape. Philip, who never slept anything but soundly.

Naturally, he wasn't there. He was still in his hospital bed.

Now she remembered.

Claudia.

Why did she feel that Claudia was a threat? Because she knew she was a threat. Because her idiotic husband had fought one of his best friends over her. Moreover, he had lost an eye for her sake. Now, that was no casual affair, it had to be more than a mere passing infatuation.

Because she felt sure that the woman seen in the crystal ball and described by Granny P was Claudia.

Claudia, clearly, meant business.

Lisa wriggled herself up higher on the pillows, and turned the light on. She knew perfectly well it wasn't the time to think. Rationality took a holiday at this time of night, when all the frights and hobgoblins came creeping out of the woodwork.

She was no nearer knowing who Claudia was. Which was bad news; one needed to know the enemy.

She'd dropped into Philip's office on the way home. Millie, his secretary, had collected the cards which came with the flowers and other offerings sent by assorted friends and family.

'I'll just look through them,' Lisa said.

Millie passed a neat pile over to her. They were clipped into bundles.

'These are colleagues, business associates,' she said. 'These are friends, these family.'

Lisa was amused to see that Titia counted as family.

'What are these?'

Millie looked up from her computer screen. 'Odds and sods. Don't knows. I was going to ask Philip about them.'

There it was. Claudia. No message, just the name. That suggested intimacy indeed.

'This one's from our daily,' Lisa said.

'Of course,' said Millie, annoyed with herself.

'This one's an aunt,' she went on, flipping the card with her finger. 'And this one is an old school chum of Philip's. I'll take these, and the other family ones.'

'Ta,' said Millie.

'Claudia?' Lisa said, with utmost casualness. 'I don't recollect a Claudia. No one in his address book?'

'Nope.'

She was indifferent. She wasn't hiding anything. Philip never gave a damn what other people thought of him or what he was up to. If Philip was being this careful, it was bad news.

Lisa took the card along with the rest of her little batch. 'I'll ask Philip tomorrow,' she said.

She wouldn't, of course. Forcing the issue had never been her way. These matters were best handled with subtlety and cunning. She didn't want to force Philip into doing anything stupid.

What was she thinking? That Philip might be serious about this woman, this Claudia?

Too right, that's exactly what was lurking darkly in her thoughts. He'd never shown the slightest sign of being so. But men did, men of his age especially. Philip was fourteen years older than Lisa; fifty next birthday.

Perhaps that was it. Successful man ditches wife, mother of his children, for delightful, adoring bimbo.

Not a hope, Philip. Lisa leant over to turn the light off, and pummelled her hot pillow into a more accommodating shape.

It just wasn't going to happen.

CHAPTER 8

Victor had to duck his head as he went into the Bunch of Grapes in Heartsbane. Wilf, the landlord, was behind the bar, doing a general tidy-up while listening to cricket on the radio.

'Ha,' said Victor.

'Morning,' said Wilf.

'I want to have a word,' said Victor, glancing round the pub as though the walls had ears.

'Nobody listening,' said Wilf. 'What are you having?'

Victor hadn't been planning to have anything except a word, but Wilf wasn't one to let a customer get away.

'I've got some of that Czech beer that Sybil likes.'

'I'll have that,' said Victor. 'As long as it's cold.'

He took a deep draught which left flecks of foam on his well-trimmed beard. 'That's good,' he said. 'Now, Wilf, have you still got that metal detector of yours?'

'Metal detector?' Wilf was being deliberately obtuse. He had discovered all kinds of things with his metal detector, many of which he had no business to keep, let alone to dispose of as profitably as he had.

'Yes. You use it on the beach. Among other places.'

'Maybe.'

'Maybe nothing. I want to borrow it.'

'How long would you be wanting she for?'

'Not long,' said Victor airily. 'Two or three days at most.'

'What you looking for?'

'None of your business.'

'T'ain't that, neither.' Wilf ruminated, making a pretence of deciding. As a matter of honour, because it was always less trouble to do what Victor wanted than to resist him.

'Good chap,' said Victor. 'Bung it in the car.'

39

'I don't know where they instructions are. I know how to use it, so maybe . . .'

'Maybe not,' said Victor. 'I'm sure you can lay your hands on the instructions if you try hard enough.'

Wilf capitulated.

'And you can put in a couple of cases of this beer as well,' said Victor, draining his glass. 'I like it.'

The beer was not well received at Heartsease .

'We have plenty of beer,' said Guy stiffly, as Victor told him about the cases in the boot of his car.

'None of this sort,' said Victor. 'At least, not any that I remember drinking.'

'If you'd mentioned that you wanted this brand, I would have ordered it in the normal way.'

'I didn't know I wanted it until I tried it this morning,' said Victor reasonably. 'Stop making a fuss,' he added, yanking the metal detector out of the rear of the car.

'What's that for?' said Guy suspiciously.

'Never you mind,' said Victor.

'As if I didn't know,' said Guy to Victor's retreating back. He dragged out one of the crates of beer and staggered across the yard.

'What is this?' cried Maria. 'Why are you bringing this into my kitchen? The place for beer is in the cellar.'

'Calm down,' said Guy. 'I shall take it down to the cellar in a minute. There's another box to come in.'

Maria investigated the beer. 'Czech!' she said with contempt. 'Communist beer, what's wrong with a Spanish beer, which is absolutely the best?'

'Not communist any more,' said Guy, heaving the second case on to the table.

'Once a communist, always a communist,' said Maria darkly.

'Crazy thing to do,' said Harry, aiming a skilful shot at the red.

Don chalked the end of his cue. He looked at Harry, surprised. 'Quite a good shot, I thought.'

'Not that.' Harry edged his way round the billiard table, the light over the table throwing his face into shadow. 'Philip. Fighting a duel.'

The billiard room was heavily panelled, with thick rugs laid on the wide floorboards, to hush the sounds of feet and voices; dark crimson velvet curtains added to the muffled and timeless feel of the room. It had always been a favourite place for the Cordovan brothers, although they wished Victor would agree to snooker.

'Snooker? Too many bloody balls. You know where you are with billiards.'

'Very uncharacteristic, when you think about it,' said Don, moving over to the scoreboard and edging the marker along. 'Philip's the most organised man I know. Punctual, a mind with no fuzzy edges, an elegant shoe-box of a life.'

'What, with two children?' said Harry.

Don was amused to see that imminent fatherhood was beginning to alarm his younger brother.

'It would take more than two children to disturb Philip's life.' Or mind, he thought, he was always impressed by the incisiveness of Philip's brain.

'I gathered all children were essentially anarchic and disorganising.'

'I expect he leaves them to Lisa.'

'Isn't she quite high-powered in her own right?'

'Yes, but her business is publishing. Picture books, not figures on screens. Much more inventive and human. Lisa has her life sorted out, I'd say, but not quite along the same lines as Philip. She leaves room for the unexpected. A most delightful woman, I find, although I don't know her that well.'

Harry's run of luck came to a sudden end, and Don crouched over the table, eyes narrowed as he looked at his target. Being shorter than Harry, his reach was less, but his eye was just as good.

Click.

'I think,' said Don, standing back for a moment to reflect, 'that Philip's organised life has been infiltrated by an unruly spirit.'

Clunk.

'A ghost, you mean?' said Harry, interested. 'No, no.'

Click, clunk, clunk.

'Not that kind of spirit. Probably a supremely unpleasant woman who has spotted in Philip what Lisa may have missed. A chink in his armour, a breach in his orderly world. Every man has his weakness, you know.'

Although, Don mused, he wouldn't have expected Philip to be

ensnared by another woman. He was much more the type to set off on a trip up the Congo or across some distant desert on a camel if he was feeling restless.

'Nothing orderly or organised about a duel,' agreed Harry. 'Damn, you've won again.'

'Triumph of experience over youth,' said Don annoyingly.

CHAPTER 9

Even as Fanny turned the key in the lock of the door to her London flat, she knew something was wrong.

She had stayed on in the north after her mother's funeral, where there were all too many depressing tasks to be done. She hated the sadness of sorting through her mother's things. Then letters had to be written, estate agents briefed, the solicitor visited.

'There's the house,' the solicitor said, a whisper of sympathy stirring his unemotional soul as Fanny sat motionless and upright in front of him. Unusual hair, he thought. 'It should sell, if you price it right. I don't think there's anything else of much value; there shouldn't be any problems with probate.'

'No,' said Fanny, concluding that the solicitor knew nothing about the big Harriety canvas hanging in the front room. It didn't look like a typical Harriety; people were always surprised when they knew who had painted it.

'Never knew he could actually paint,' said one visitor. 'Just shows you, doesn't it?'

'Do I need to make an inventory?' asked Fanny.

'I don't think so,' said the solicitor. 'You'll be returning to London?'

'Yes.'

'Good, good. Well, I've got your address, I'll be in touch.' He held out a square hand. 'All the best.'

A thought struck him. 'I'm sorry about your mother. Dying, I mean. A bit of a shock, going off so suddenly.'

'Yes,' said Fanny again, edging towards the door. 'We knew she had a weak heart, though.'

'I see, I see.'

Fanny had packed up the painting, using half a big roll of bubble wrap and all the corner post office's supply of brown

43

paper to wind round a sandwich of canvas and plywood. It had gone off by courier, would arrive in the flat before her. Gerry knew it was coming, they had spoken on the phone.

She had closed the door of her mother's house behind her for the last time, dropped the keys in through the letter box of Grommit and Wendle, Estate Agents, and driven through the silent streets of Getley just as dawn became daylight. She wanted to be back in London in time to have a shower and go to work; she'd taken enough days off.

As she pushed the door open, Fanny automatically looked at the clock which hung above the little table with the phone on it.

Not any more.

No clock, no table.

Only the phone was still there, sitting forlornly on the floor.

Fanny looked at it, uncomprehending. Gerry must be doing some decorating, she thought. That's nice of him, when he's so busy.

'Gerry! I'm back.'

Her voice echoed in the strangest way. Puzzled, Fanny opened the door into the sitting room.

Empty.

Not completely empty. One sad armchair, a saggy affair, which was the last item of their original furniture that she and Gerry had been going to replace. Mind you, its cover had gone. A throw which they had chosen together in a market on their trip to southern India. For a second, the memory flooded back: the colour, the sounds, the smells lingering on the hot dry air.

Fanny put down the bags she was carrying, and flew round the rest of the flat. The kitchen had a few remnants. Tatty crockery and knives and forks, a broken jug; nothing else. The bedroom looked more lived in, since it had a built-in cupboard with a chest of drawers.

Fanny pulled open the drawers. Her things were still here. Her jewellery? The basket in which she kept her bits and pieces was there, but with only half its usual contents. She had bought some good things on her travels with Gerry; they had all gone.

She prowled again from room to room, numb with shock. This time round, she noticed a white envelope propped up above the fireplace.

Gerry's familiar script flowed across the paper.

'*Sorry, Fanny. It wasn't going to work. Rent paid until 26th, then you'll have to leave, as it's been let to someone else. G.*'

Fanny sat down on the floor, feeling sick and dizzy. The words made no sense. She and Gerry had been together for five years. Ever since she came to London as a keen new graduate. They had met at a friend's, immediately clicked, set up house together three months later.

They were a pair. A couple.

They had been going to get married. Have children.

Was that it? Couldn't Gerry face the responsibility, the legal commitment?

No problem. They could carry on, just as they were. She wanted Gerry, not the house outside London, the family.

She must find out where he had gone. She would go upstairs, where a friend lived. She might be in, she kept odd hours. She might know where Gerry was, could offer practical help and advice.

No sympathy, Fanny told herself as she took the stairs two at a time. I will not ask for sympathy.

She could ask as much as she liked. Sympathy wasn't on offer.

Her desperate peal on the bell was finally answered by a complete stranger. He glared at her through tousled hair. 'What the hell do you want?'

A boyfriend, thought Fanny. She made as though to step in.

'You're not coming in here,' he said.

'I want to talk to Claudia.'

'Claudia's gone. No, I don't have her phone number, address or anything else. She doesn't want anything sent on, no messages, no contact. So clear off, will you. I need my kip.'

Bang.

Lisa bumped into Fanny in Gower Street. She rarely went to Gower Street, but she had gone on that particular day to buy a pile of books from Dillons. Books for herself, books for Alec and Polly – although she was sure they'd be all wrong – a new book on Arabian horses as a present for Philip, some strange picture books to amuse Toby while they were away, and a sumptuous book on herbs for Hester.

Pleased with her morning's work, she was looking round for a likely place to pause for coffee when she spotted a bedraggled figure, standing at a bus stop, gazing into space.

'Fanny, my dear, what are you doing?'

She'd been crying; Lisa had never seen such a blotchy face.

'Your mother?' she enquired, thinking of delayed shock.

Fanny shook her head, unable to speak through her tears.

'You're making an exhibition of yourself,' Lisa said. 'Come along.'

She pushed her, unprotesting, into the pub on the corner, and ordered a coffee for herself and a double brandy for Fanny.

'No, I don't drink,' she said between sobs.

'Yes, you do. Medicinal.'

It took the whole of the glass of brandy and many tissues to produce any kind of coherence.

Lisa listened in silence. She might have problems with Philip; no, she *had* got problems with Philip, but she was on the warpath, and she certainly hadn't had the series of blows which poor Fanny had.

'Right,' she said. 'You're coming home with me.'

Tears bored Lisa, but Mrs Juniper could cope. A grim smile crossed her thin face when Lisa murmured that Fanny had been ditched by her boyfriend. Mrs Juniper thought men a worthless breed.

Lisa wondered about Mr Juniper, and indeed once ventured a question about the mysterious husband whom she had never met, but Mrs Juniper knew how to keep herself to herself. 'Never ask,' she said.

Crashing noises were audible along the passage outside the sitting-room. Lisa waited for Polly to burst through the door, which she duly did.

'Mummy, there's a terrible woman with Mrs Juniper, moaning and weeping. Floods and floods of tears. Who is she? Can't you get rid of her?'

The warmth of the young towards those in trouble.

'Darling, that's Fanny. She's an old friend, her mother was my godmother.'

'The one who died? Is that why she's bawling?'

'Partly. But also, her boyfriend walked out on her, taking, one gathers, everything with him. And then when she rang her office, she found she'd been given the push.'

By this time, Polly was entranced. 'Sacked? Didn't she know it was coming?'

'Not a word.'

'Oh, well, I suppose she's got something to howl about then, but I wish she'd do it more quietly. I can't hear myself think. And what about my lunch?'

'Get yourself something from the kitchen, darling. I've a phone call to make.'

Polly's eyes lit up. 'Anything I like? Old Jay was planning an omelette.'

'Anything you like, and don't call Mrs Juniper old Jay.'

Another crash of the door and Polly was gone. What greed did for a child. Now, Lisa said to herself, what did Fanny say was the name of that company? Parcel Star. Crazy, entrusting what sounded like a valuable painting to some courier service like that. It probably wasn't even insured.

Toby was very helpful, ringing up the company, throwing his weight around.

'She's out of luck,' he said, putting the phone down. 'Duly delivered, signed for by one G. Rathbone.'

'Ah. That must be Gerry.'

'A Harriety, did you say?' His face took on a calculating look. 'Worth a lot of money, those are.'

'Fanny says not. She says her mum had it valued a few years ago. It's worth something, but not that much, because it isn't typical.'

'That was then. Now those early Harrietys are very much flavour of the month. Your little friend had better get it back.'

'I don't think my little friend is capable of doing anything just at the moment, but we'll work on her when she's calmed down.'

'What a bastard this Gerry sounds.'

'He's in the hands of a grasping woman, by the sound of it. A friend of Fanny's.'

'Oh, great.'

'Called Claudia.'

Not a flicker on Toby's face. Obviously the name didn't have any associations for him.

'It's the second Claudia I've come across in two days.'

'Then there's bound to be a third. Unless your and Fanny's Claudia are one and the same.'

'Not very likely.'

Emilia was sitting bolt upright on Lisa's sofa, looking twitchy.

'What are you going to do with that person?' she said to Lisa. 'Philip's coming out of hospital tomorrow. He'll hardly want a stranger in the house.'

'Fanny isn't "that person". Or a stranger. Fanny is my godmother's daughter.'

Emilia gave an elegant snort. 'Hardly a strong connection.'

'Her mother was very kind to me. Fanny's in trouble, I'm not abandoning her.'

'She's penniless, I suppose.'

Toby slid into the room, took in the situation at a glance and, oozing charm, offered to top up Emilia's drink.

Emilia was putty in Toby's hands. Lisa wasn't sure why, since he was more or less everything she most disliked. At first, she thought he was some kind of gigolo, installed by Lisa so that she could deceive Philip under his – and her – very nose. When she realised it wasn't very likely, she mellowed. Now she regarded Toby as a kind of resident eunuch. She had no idea about his little friends, and he was always very discreet when with her.

Lisa could see him pouring out a much stiffer gin than Emilia would approve of. From Toby, she would accept it without a murmur.

'More wine, Lisa?'

'Thank you, Toby. Pour yourself a drink and come and sit down. I was just going to tell Emilia that you're going to look after Fanny for me.'

Emilia's disapproving look reappeared. 'You'll hardly trust her alone in the house,' she said. 'If she's hard up . . .'

Emilia pictured her scuttling off with bagsful of silver spoons and probably the grandfather clock under her arm.

'Not alone,' said Toby. 'I will be here. Though I must say, she doesn't look the criminal type.'

'She comes from the north,' said Emilia.

'Fanny has plenty of money.'

'Where from?'

'Her mother has just died, which is another reason for her to be so upset. She will have money from the house.'

'What kind of house?'

'In the north.' Not what Emilia meant by house, Lisa knew. But it'd be enough to tide Fanny over.

'And to buy her some more clothes?' Toby asked hopefully.

48

'What she's got is dire. And that hair! I thought I'd get Robert round.'

Robert cut Emilia's hair, and she doted on him. 'I hardly think Robert would want to cut just anybody's hair.'

'He adores a challenge,' said Toby with infinite tact.

'I still think you're making trouble for yourself, Lisa, and probably for everyone else as well. Lame dogs are never worth the effort.'

Fanny was not a lame dog. Underneath the tears and the baggy clothes and the lovelorn wetness Lisa sensed a spirit as original and interesting as her mother's.

'Tragic, this guy walking out like that.'

'It happens.'

'Living in sin leaves you very vulnerable to that kind of treatment,' said Emilia firmly.

Lisa reflected grimly that it wasn't only the sinful ones who were vulnerable. Fanny had lost her Gerry to one Claudia, and Lisa had the shadow of another Claudia hanging over her. She liked to think that Philip was too settled, and had too much sense, but that was hooey. He could fall for a dazzler just like Gerry had.

'It's dishonest,' said Toby. Unusual for him to take a moral line, since his ideas on right and wrong tended to be elastic. 'I mean, poor Fanny, this twerp's taken a lot of stuff which belongs to her.'

'Then she must get it back,' said Emilia. 'What kind of things?'

'Everything. Furniture, linen, silver, china, some of her jewellery.'

Emilia sniffed. 'I don't imagine she has much valuable jewellery.'

'No, but what she had, she probably wanted to keep,' said Toby mildly.

'And pictures,' Lisa went on. 'Including a Harriety.'

That made Emilia sit up.

'A Harriety? Hardly very likely.'

'Her mother was a friend of Harriety. They worked together in Getley, years ago. He gave her the picture when he left the north and came to London.'

'Then she must take all possible steps to get it back. I shall advise her to contact a good lawyer at once.'

'She must have a solicitor in Getley. Dealing with her mother's affairs, probate and so on.'

Emilia cast a look of loathing in Lisa's direction. How she hated any mention of Getley.

'A northern firm? No use at all. She needs a London man. I will recommend her to someone who will handle this kind of sordid affair. It's most unfortunate, Lisa, that you've got yourself mixed up in this. Other people's domestic troubles are much better avoided. They're often so harrowing.'

CHAPTER 10

Hester picked up a shallow basket from the scullery and walked down the stone path to the vegetable garden. She was going to pull up some leeks for Maria, and pick some herbs for her pot pourri.

There was someone in the old walled vegetable garden, which was one of the sights of Heartsease. Victor? In the vegetable garden? He never set foot in the vegetable garden. What was he up to?

'Victor, what on earth are you doing?'

Victor was concentrating, and didn't look up.

'Turn that machine off. And whatever it is you're planning, you're not doing it in my vegetable garden. You're squashing the shallots.'

Victor looked up. 'Shallots! What do shallots matter?'

'If you want to play historical finds, Victor, please go and do it somewhere else.'

Hester never raised her voice, but she was none the less formidable, and Victor knew when to retreat.

'Grumble, grumble,' said Harry, as a furious Victor stormed off towards the orchard. 'What's he got hold of now?'

'A metal detector, I fancy,' said Hester. 'I believe Wilf has one, I expect he's borrowed it. Now you're here, Harry, you can help me with the leeks.'

'Can't stop,' said Harry. 'Only popped in to say that Zoë's had a scan this morning, and all's well.'

'Good,' said Hester. 'If it's a boy, you can call it Julius.'

Harry stared at her for a moment, and then let out a crack of laughter. 'Oh, excellent, Hester. I'll pass that on to Zoë, does her good to laugh.' He became serious. 'However, they predict a girl, and there's no way I'm calling any daughter of mine Julia.'

'Volumnia would be nice. A good Roman name.'

*

'Pa's turned into a giant mole, I see,' said Don. He had abandoned his vines for a while to have tea at the Hall. 'Catch up on the news,' he said, pouring himself a cup of Lapsang. 'I came over by King's Meadow, you can see him digging away. The neighbours will talk; they'll think he's up to something which is against the planning regs.'

'That would be nothing new,' said Hester.

'Has he found anything?' Don dunked a piece of gingercake in his cup.

'Lots.' Hester was philosophical about her brother and his ways. 'A little hoard of old coppers – from a child's money box, at a guess. Any number of rusty old nails, hasps, bits of garden tools. A battered measuring cup. Half a galvanised tin bath. A stirrup. A colander with a dent in it – I recognise that; Esme hurled it into the bushes last summer.'

'Why?'

'She thought there was a prowler.'

'Of course,' said Don. 'I remember that. It was Jarvis, having a quiet pee.'

'I wish he'd use the outside lavatory,' said Hester with a sigh.

'You know perfectly well why he won't,' said Don. 'He thinks it's haunted. And talking of haunted, when are the guests arriving? If Victor's serious, and you're putting them in the tower?'

'I am,' said Hester. 'I don't think the ghost will bother Lisa,' she added.

'Might give the invalid a fright,' said Don, inspecting the table for further goodies. 'You're right about Lisa, though. More than a match for any ghost.'

'It's a family-minded ghost, in any case,' said Hester comfortably. 'It would be most unlikely to bother visitors.'

Victor came forcefully into the room, rubbing his large and dirty hands together. 'Ah, tea. Just what I need. Gives you a thirst, all this outdoor activity.'

'I've told you, Victor, there's plenty of outside work on the farm and in the vegetable garden.'

'You have an earthy soul, Hester,' her brother said.

'You have earthy hands,' said Hester. 'Go and wash them.' She snatched a plate of cake out of his reach. 'Right away.'

'Nag, nag,' muttered Victor, heading for the cloakroom.

He was back in no time, perfectly cheerful and ready to

consume large quantities of food and several cups of tea. He was dying to ask Don if he knew what was happening over at the site of the Roman kiln discovery, but he didn't want to bring up the subject.

Don took pity on him. 'The archaeologist has done a lot of staking out and photo-taking,' he obligingly told his father.

'Huh,' said Victor, trying not to sound interested. 'Says it's nothing, I dare say.'

'No, no, he thinks it's a tremendous find.'

Victor glowered, and gulped down the rest of his tea. 'Give me another piece of that sponge, Hester; I'll take it with me, got to get back to work.'

'To your study?' asked Hester. 'Many messages there for you, so Guy said.'

'They can wait. I've got more important things on my hands just at the moment, I've started in the orchard now. I'm getting close, I can tell, because I have this prickling sensation in my spine.'

'It's all the bending over,' said Hester helpfully. 'I've got some cream you can rub in.'

'I will ignore that remark. I am very fit, and my tingling spine is only to do with emanations from the past. We aren't dealing with mundane matters here, you know.'

'You felt you were about to make the big find yesterday,' observed Hester.

Victor was offended. 'Rome wasn't built in a day,' he said.

Guy limped into the large kitchen at Heartsease.

'What have you done to yourself?' asked Maria, casting a heavy lump of dough on to a big board on the long refectory table with a satisfying thump.

'Been attacked by what looks like a man trap,' said Guy bitterly, examining his shin.

Maria made one of her expressive Spanish noises. 'Man traps would not surprise me at all. Where is this?'

'Outside the back door,' said Guy. 'Nasty, rusty thing, with spikes.'

'Victor has put it there,' said Maria. 'Hester was saying there are metal pieces everywhere, in the garden, in the yard, even in the hall. Victor finds them, and then, because they are not Roman, he leaves them. There, where he is.'

'You can't expect Victor to tidy up after himself,' said Guy reprovingly.

'And why not?' Maria attacked the dough with her fists. 'You have to, and I cannot leave the kitchen untidy for someone else to clear it up.'

'Victor's a busy man.'

'Busy, yes, digging holes in the garden into which we will all fall.'

Hester came into the kitchen holding a dingy-looking, mis-shapen little bowl. Her face gave nothing away as she handed it to Guy. 'Victor left this on the hall table. He says, would you polish it up for him? He believes it's silver.'

Guy took it with fastidious fingers and a look of distaste on his beautiful face. 'I think not,' he said. 'But I'll put it in to soak.'

Hester sighed. 'I hope Victor gets over this excavating frenzy by the time the Mafficks come, otherwise they aren't going to see much of him.' She sat down on one of the benches that ran along-side the big table. 'Now, Maria, all these extra people. Will you need any extra help?'

Maria cut her dough with a large and sharp Sabatier knife.

'I will manage, because I have to.' She took a quick, dark glance at Hester. 'Besides,' she said, relenting, 'is not so very much. Now Harry is not here, much, and Zoë cooks for him, and Julia is away.'

'We'll see how it goes,' said Hester. 'Oh, thank you, Guy. Just what I need, hot coffee. It's chilly today.'

'Chilly!' said Maria with scorn. 'Not chilly. Extremely cold, with wind blowing from Russia.'

'The forecast says rain,' said Guy helpfully. 'The fine spell has definitely finished, and we're going to have rain and wind.'

'Heavy rain?' asked Hester hopefully.

'Disorganised downpours, it said on the radio just now.'

'He'll never go on digging in the wet,' said Hester.

'Perhaps this would be a good time to sort out the downstairs cloakroom,' said Guy. 'All those macs and so on. They could do with a look over; they may need reproofing.'

'Thank you, Guy,' said Hester. 'I think that's an excellent idea. Send them to that place in Heartsbury to be done; they take forever there.'

Full of tea, Don thought he would take the scenic route back to his house and vineyard and see just what his father was up to. He went along the stone-floored passageway to the back door, and out across the stableyard towards the orchard.

He found Victor having a conversation with a pig.

White and black Gloucester Old Spots roamed freely in the orchard at Heartsease, eating windfalls in season, and being fed by the kitchen the rest of the year. Victor was very fond of his pigs, but he hadn't reckoned with their curiosity as he came briskly into the orchard to get on with sinking a few more trenches. The pigs all longed to know what the metal detector was, and came lumbering up to investigate both trenches and finds.

Don choked back his laughter as Victor tried to reason with the pigs. Poor Pa, he thought, he could do without the porky help. As he watched, another pig trundled up behind Victor. In its enthusiasm to be a part of the discovery, it gave him a good nudge, sending him flying into the trench. Now it was looking at Victor with its wicked little eyes.

Victor had a strong suspicion that if he tried to get out of the trench, the pig would give him another shove, and he'd be back where he started.

'Bloody pigs,' he bellowed.

'Did you call, Pa?'

'Harry? Come and help.'

'It's not Harry, it's me,' said Don. 'Good heavens, that pig seems very fond of you.'

The pig had lowered its head into the trench, and was leering into Victor's face. Don advanced in a menacing way, and biffed it on the rump. It gave him an offended look and trotted away.

Don stretched out a hand to help Victor haul himself out. 'Drains?' he said with interest. 'I didn't know you were planning anything this year.'

'It is nothing to do with drainage,' said Victor, dusting himself down. 'This is one of my archaeological trenches.'

'Pa, you aren't serious? I had no idea you were digging so deep. Or in so many places,' he added, looking round at the piles of earth. 'All this because of a Roman kiln?'

'A minor find,' said Victor. 'Of no importance. Now, I am convinced that the Romans built on this spot. Right here, at Heartsease. Look at the superb setting. South-facing, on a hillside, the sea over there, the river below. Those Romans were sensible chaps. They didn't go round with their heads in the clouds like those Greeks. No, no. They were practical. They wouldn't have passed up the chance of a site like this, now would they?'

Don look at his father with exasperated affection. 'It is a good spot,' he said noncommittally.

'There you are. That paltry kiln they found was clearly built to make things for the villa here. Tiles and so forth. Cooking pots.'

'We often turn up scraps of Roman pots at the vineyard.'

'Exactly.' Victor was getting into his stride. 'So, in the interests of science, I'm going to find this villa.'

'Um, where? Here in the orchard?'

'Possibly, possibly. I'm feeling my way into the Roman mind. I have a real affinity with these long-ago residents. That's why I'm so sure they had a house here. And a farm, they'd have to grow their own food. I expect to find a villa. A *big* villa, because I see the family living here as being important. Kitchens, bath houses, traces of the garden. And mosaics. They must have had mosaic floors.'

'I think it's going to rain,' said Don, looking up at a lowering blue-black sky. 'Thunder, too, I fear. I think we'd better make for the house.'

CHAPTER 11

'We'll have to leave the chair,' said Toby.

It made Fanny's flat look so desolate, that solitary, tatty armchair with its sagging springs. Lisa decided they couldn't just leave it there, as Toby had suggested. 'The incoming tenants would get on to Fanny and make a fuss about having to dispose of it. People always do.'

'Okay. Then we'll heave it downstairs, and leave it outside.'

'That's a bit anti-social.'

'Not at all. If anyone asks, we'll say we've arranged for the council to come and take it away. My bet is, we won't need to. By the time we've locked up this place, it'll be gone.'

It was worth a try. But first of all, they had to pack Fanny's belongings. She couldn't bear the thought of going back there to collect her things. Mrs Juniper had vetoed the suggestion at once.

'You can't ask it of her. Not in her state.'

'Will she start crying again if we make her?'

'Undoubtedly,' said Toby. 'Don't risk it. You and I will go, Lisa. It can't be much, we can be over there and back in a trice.'

'Just tip her things into the suitcases,' said Mrs Juniper. 'I'll sort everything out for her.'

She loved sorting things out.

Toby was right; it didn't take long, although he kept on stopping to hold up some dingy and shapeless garment with exclamations of shock and horror.

'This has to change,' he said. 'No tears, a proper hairdo, and lots of new clothes, that's what Fanny needs.'

The armchair turned out to be a lot heavier than it looked with an awkward malevolence about it.

'The perversity of inanimate objects,' said Toby, as the armchair hit his knee for the third time.

'Toby,' said Lisa, letting her end down with a thump, 'I have a

57

feeling of being watched.' She peered over the banisters into the stairwell. There was a young man down there, looking up at them and their efforts with some alarm. He was the most astonishingly good-looking man, with Byronic curls and smouldering eyes.

'Wow,' said Toby, abandoning his hold on the chair and joining Lisa at the banisters.

'You shouldn't be doing that,' the young man said to Lisa, leaping up the stairs two or three steps at a time. 'Here, let me.'

He was deceived by her lack of inches, or perhaps, in the gloom, he thought she was a little old lady; what a dispiriting thought, Lisa said to herself. However, they were now on the pavement, and the young man approved of Toby's plan.

'Numerous grasping eyes fixed on us right now, I should say. Ready to leap out and grab the armchair.'

'It seems a pleasant area,' Lisa said, looking around. 'Do people here really want a battered old armchair?'

'Something for nothing,' he said. He held out a hand and clasped hers in a firm grasp. A good handshake, and a cool, dry hand. Lisa approved; she hated people with sweaty palms and limp hands.

'George Sermion.'

'Hey,' said Toby. 'The poet?'

George looked mildly surprised, but admitted to being a poet. A published poet, too. Lisa had heard of him.

'Do you live here?' asked Toby.

The poet's face darkened. 'No, I'm visiting a friend,' he said shortly.

'Which floor?'

'Fourth.'

Toby didn't like that. 'The rude guy?'

'No,' said George with intensity. 'A woman lives there. Claudia.'

'Ah,' said Toby. 'There's a problem there. She's gone.'

'Gone?' George's voice was anguished. 'Gone where?'

'Run off with the man from the flat below,' said Toby.

George was stunned. 'With Gerry? She can't have.' He turned to Lisa as though wanting to hear a denial. 'Gerry's a friend of mine,' he said. 'From way back, we were at school together. He told me about the flat, when Claudia broke up with her husband and needed a place of her own. He wouldn't do this to me.'

It was quite clear that Claudia was more than just a friend of George's. Toby put Lisa right on this.

'Is that the Claudia you wrote all those love poems to?'

George nodded.

'Ah,' said Toby. 'Well, she's gone. We're here to pick up Fanny's clothes. Do you know Fanny?'

George nodded, his face stricken.

'The pair of them have stripped the flat clean,' Lisa said. 'Taken most of Fanny's goods and chattels, there are only a few clothes of hers left.'

'That's Gerry's doing,' said the poet at once. 'Claudia has a beautiful nature. She wouldn't take Fanny's things.'

Lisa thought George was an innocent abroad in a wicked world. And she didn't at all like the sound of this Claudia.

George plunged towards the entrance. 'I have to speak to this man in the flat. He must know where Claudia is.'

Toby, although still entranced by George's dramatic good looks, was fast realising that this passion for Claudia was indicative of a mainline heterosexual. 'Fanny didn't get anything out of him,' he said with a shrug. 'But you can try.'

'If he does tell you,' Lisa said, 'could you give me a ring? You can speak to Toby if I'm not there, I'm off to the country shortly. Fanny is staying with us for the time being.' She handed him a card. On an afterthought, she looked up the Cordovan number in her little red book and scribbled it on the bottom of the card. 'That's where I'll be staying,' she said, passing it to him.

He looked at it with unseeing eyes, and then stuffed it into his pocket.

'Thanks for your help,' Toby called after him. 'With the armchair.'

Lisa spotted a cruising taxi and put up a hand. 'I don't think we'll hear anything more from him,' she said, as they sank back into the seat.

'Mad, that Claudia,' said Toby. 'Of course, I don't know what Gerry's like, but I doubt if he's in the same league as George there. Phew, fancy casting that aside.'

Lisa agreed with him. 'And think of the loss to literature.'

'Bother literature,' said Toby.

There had been a change of plan.

Philip had come home. In considerable pain, by the look of him. What the doctors called uncomfortable. Their own doctor popped in to see him, and read him the riot act. Would Philip pay any attention?

Lisa doubted it. 'I'll arrange for a nurse to come in every day at Heartsease, to see to the dressings,' the doctor said as he left. 'Try to keep him as quiet as possible for as long as possible.' He grinned. 'Some hope,' he said, turning his collar up to dive out into the rain.

Then Polly came in, mouth turned down, spoiling for a fight. She demanded to see Philip's wound. She had decided she wanted to be a doctor, so she had to get used to gruesome sights.

'No,' said Lisa, and had to eject her forcibly, as she flung herself into a five-star tantrum.

When Philip heard Lisa was planning to let Mrs Juniper go off for three weeks, he threw a tantrum as well. Lisa pointed out that she was entitled to her holiday; Philip said she could take her holiday at some other, more convenient time.

Lisa went on with her plans.

Philip was driven down to Heartsease by Toby. This was because it wasn't good for him in his present state to be driven by Lisa. Clenched teeth and a foot hovering over an imaginary brake pedal didn't make for easy driving for either of them. With Toby, he could go to sleep. Toby loved driving and was very good at it.

Alec sat in the front of Lisa's car with his mother. Polly sulked in the back. As usual when Polly was behaving badly, Alec was at his best and most grown up. He wanted to know more about the Cordovan family; he hadn't been with his parents when they last went to Heartsease. Lisa told him about jovial, dominating Victor. 'You'll know him at once, he's a big, dark man, with a very smart beard and a booming voice. His wife, Julia, is in Sweden at the moment.'

Polly, who was listening hard, piped up from the back seat. 'Is she his wife? I mean, I thought she was, and they split up and he married someone else, and then Julia came back.'

'Polly, how do you know these things?'

'I listen,' said Polly smugly.

'Yes, Julia is the first of Victor's three wives, but they're together again now.'

'He has lots of girlfriends,' said Polly. 'So I've heard.'

Alec got very stiff and proud. 'You should be ashamed of yourself, saying things like that.'

What a useless thing to say. Polly was never ashamed, and Alec normally had the insouciant acceptance of adults' peccadilloes natural to his generation.

Lisa thought it best to ignore their remarks. 'Victor has several brothers and sisters. Hester lives at Heartsease and looks after everybody. She isn't married.'

'Perhaps she's got a boyfriend,' said Polly cheekily. Alec turned and gave her a quelling look.

'There's another sister, Prim, who lives in a nearby house. She looks after the farm and so on. Loves growing things. That's the older generation. Then there are Victor's children. Harry lives in the lodge. He's the youngest, he's in communications; very successful, I gather. He got married about a year ago, to someone I've never met, called Zoë. He met her at a ball and they fell in love, just like that.'

Polly hadn't reached the age where Romance held any attraction. She wasn't impressed by this tale of that rarest of things, a *coup de foudre*.

'Zoë is expecting a baby,' Lisa went on.

Polly didn't approve of babies at all, so she made sick noises in the back of the car, until Alec leant over and thumped her and they started to quarrel in earnest. Lisa felt like stopping the car and throwing them both out. Then she had a brainwave, and produced two bags of crisps, each of their favourite brand, which Mrs Juniper had so thoughtfully provided. They fell instantly into peaceful crunchings.

'Who else? Oh, Don, of course. I don't know him all that well. He has a vineyard there, flourishing, they say. He's not like his father, Victor, at all, being slightly rotund, and I believe Philip said he's going bald. But he has a wicked sense of humour, from what I remember, and a kindly nature. He enjoys life.'

'Toby said he likes the ladies,' remarked Polly, spitting out crisp crumbs as she spoke.

Alec loftily told Polly that personal comments were childish, and if she behaved like a seven year old, she'd be treated like one. A terrible threat, which made Polly subside in a fuming heap.

'Are we ever going to get there?' asked Alec.

'It's not far now.'

They were driving in an enchanted world. The motorway and the drone of traffic heading down to the more popular and populous parts of the West Country were behind them. They climbed steeply now, driving through endless green tunnels, with the sun dappling through the leaves.

They came suddenly to the open landscape at the top of the hill, and Alec and Polly let out a cry of delight as they saw the distant, gleaming line of the sea. Then they were back in the green shade again, driving through woods and past trim fields. The sun shone dramatically at the edge of a midnight blue cloud, threatening thunder. They drove through villages with names that made the children laugh: Sniggle and Snitch and Utter Oath, and came out into a darkening landscape with rain sweeping over the hills.

'I tell you what,' shouted Polly, her head hanging out of the window like a dog. 'I think we've gone through a space warp and come out in a different world.'

'Talking of different worlds,' said Alec, as Lisa made her cautious way up the twisting drive, 'I think there's someone there who's just landed.'

She slowed down to a snail's pace in order to take a closer look, and recognised Victor.

'Hello, Victor. What are you doing? And why are you wearing a bin bag?'

'Excavations,' said Victor. Despite the bin bag draped around his shoulders, he was very wet. He loomed in at the passenger window, giving Alec a nasty fright.

'Hop out and get in the back,' he said. 'Hello, Lisa. I'm glad to see you. You can take me up to the house.'

There was no arguing with Victor, and in less than a minute Alec was installed in the back and Victor was pushing his seat back. 'Pokey car,' he commented. 'Where's Philip?'

'Coming separately.'

'Sensible chap, I couldn't abide travelling with my youngsters, they fought every inch of the journey.'

'Why are you wearing that bin bag?' asked Alec. There was no point in shushing him. If Alec wanted the answer to a question, he'd go on until he got it.

Victor didn't seem to mind. 'Fools have removed my mac and Barbours, sent them off for cleaning, what a waste of time. Just when I need to be outdoors, digging up the Romans.'

Alec liked the sound of that. 'Romans? Here?'

'Yes, indeed,' said Victor, pleased with the enthusiasm in Alec's voice. 'I haven't found the exact spot yet, but I will.'

'I'll help,' said Alec.

'I hate the Romans,' said Polly at once. 'We did them at school. They're boring.'

Lisa looked out of the window at the countryside they had driven through two hours before. Now it was grey, with billows of rain sweeping across.

She turned back to her unpacking, thinking what an unusual room it was. She was in a circular tower room with a stone spiral staircase wrapped round outside one of the walls. If she went down two steps she came to a bathroom, and another half-turn and a door brought her to the landing where Polly and Alec were installed.

Going the other way, the staircase led up to the King's chamber – best avoided, Hester had said, on the grounds of general historical mustiness and gloom. Lisa found it hard to believe that any room in a house with Hester in charge would be like that, but she assured her it was.

'Bars on the window. We've never been sure whether they were put there to keep the king's enemies out, or the king in. It makes for a melancholy atmosphere. And there are depressing calico covers, to keep the hangings in good order.'

'Don't you ever use the room?'

'When we're very full. Like for Aimée's ball last year, when Gray stayed in it.'

Gray was another of Victor's many brothers.

'He wouldn't notice how gloomy it was.'

'No, he likes the gloom.' Hester cast a final, expert glance around the room, before asking Lisa if she needed anything else, and then flitting away. She had already given her the run of the library, where she could leave everything out while she was working. 'Nobody will touch it. Guy cleans that room himself, and you know how scrupulous he is.'

'The lovely Guy,' Lisa said. And then laughed, thinking of the effect he would have on Toby. She didn't laugh for long. Where was Toby? More to the point, where was Philip? It was a long journey for someone so recently wounded and out of hospital. Even if Philip had got the constitution of an ox, an eye was an eye.

She was surprised to find herself worrying about Philip; it wasn't something she often did. She shook herself, and opened the window so that she could lean out of the window and breathe in the damp air, so full of the country and the smell of the sea that it was almost tangible.

She heard a car coming up the drive. They were here, and her concern evaporated. Only to resurface as she saw Philip getting slowly out of the car. He was leaning first on Toby, and then, as their host surged out of the house, he was supported by Victor's powerful grasp.

Lisa felt a flash of anger. Philip was a man who rarely showed any weakness. He was strong physically and mentally; she'd never seen him like this, not in fifteen years of being married to him. Colds and a rare attack of flu had sent him to bed on infrequent occasions, but never for long, and he was always back in his stride in less time than was reasonable. He was a younger man than Victor, and yet now he looked older and even dependent on those about him.

He's not going to lie around, Lisa decided, whatever their doctor had advised. That would be disastrous. She told herself to warn Hester. She wasn't going to let him be waited on hand and foot, it would make him fret.

He looked now like a man who was fretting. Was he fretting because he was shaken up by the journey? Because he felt helpless? Or were there other things on his mind?

Claudia, for instance.

CHAPTER 12

Toby was on the phone; Fanny could hear him from the other side of the door.

'No, Rudi, I've got things to do this evening. No, I'm not going out with anyone else, not in the way you mean. I'm going out with a young lady.'

Fanny hovered.

Toby removed the earpiece to a safer distance, flicked his fingers at Fanny and picked up a colour proof from his desk for closer scrutiny. 'No, quite the wrong end of the stick; I'm afraid you've got a very vulgar mind. I'm going shopping . . . Late night, remember? Well, if you insist, come over at about nine. We'll be back by then, I can throw a few bits and pieces together from the freezer.'

Fanny knew why Toby was shutting his eyes in that pained gesture. She was right; Toby was still unable to believe the long, thick plait of dank hair which dangled over her shoulder. Fanny was well aware she wasn't looking her best in jeans of a dispiriting cut and hue, but she didn't care. Her face was bare of make-up, and her eyes looked tired and full of unshed tears.

Toby made tsk-tsking noises. 'What a sight, dear oh dear. Now, run along, leave me in peace to finish these proofs, or Lisa will be after my blood.'

Fanny came a few steps into the room. 'Do you always work here?'

'Yes, duckie, I do. Lisa sits at that big desk over there, and I slum it here.'

'What do you do?'

Toby sighed. 'I can't explain it all to you now, sweetie, or I'll never be done. Gift books, that's our line. Speciality books, pop ups, packs, cut outs. All very classy.'

Fanny wandered over to a table where a book lay open,

revealing a 3D scene of Olympus with the gods at table. A shaft of light was directed to the corner of the page; when Fanny turned over, human figures were fighting in the dust and grime of Troy.

'It's incredible,' she cried, fascinated. 'The detail! Look at this chariot, and the weapons lying on the ground!'

'One of our best,' said Toby, his mind on colours.

'Who writes them, or devises them or whatever you do?'

'The ideas are nearly always Lisa's. Except for a few which come in from authors. People we know, we don't accept work from just anyone.'

'Of course, they must cost a lot.'

'They do.'

'Wouldn't it be better to do simple books, which could reach a wider audience, and which more people could afford?' said Fanny, her caring habits getting the better of her.

Toby raised his eyes to heaven. 'That's not the point, actually. Any child is going to be thrilled by our books in a way that they aren't by flat artwork. Which has its place, naturally. So do books which are all text. You want to live the Trojan war, you have to read Homer. But how many do? No, we aim for a bit of magic. Very pretty, very profitable, and very good fun to do. When it goes right,' he added, viciously encircling a chunk of artwork.

'I'd better leave you in peace,' said Fanny, with a last, wistful look at the open book.

'Take it,' said Toby, getting up from his chair. 'And here are some more. Go and enjoy yourself. Then Robert is coming to do your hair this afternoon.' He raised a languid hand. 'No arguments, please. It's a present from Lisa.'

'I don't go to the hairdresser,' said Fanny, rather drearily. 'I just wear it naturally.'

'Yes, one can tell,' said Toby. 'Three o'clock, he'll be here. So run along and amuse yourself until then. I'll finish work early today; wouldn't Lisa be angry if she knew, but she won't. And I'm taking you shopping.'

'Thanks, Toby.' Fanny was determined not to give in, even though it was an effort to stand up to Toby's steamroller tactics. 'I'd rather not.'

'About half past four,' said Toby, back in his proofs.

Robert unwound Fanny's plait with deft, vigorous hands. Her hair hung in a loosened twist, reaching to below her waist. Robert weighed a chunk of it in his hands, looking at it with a very doubtful expression. 'When was it last cut?'

'About three months ago,' said Fanny. 'Just a trim.'

'Who did it?'

'Oh, I did.'

Robert dropped the hair and jumped back as though it carried an electric charge. 'What?'

'Yes, I always do it. It's long enough for me to pull it round, and then I just tidy it up.'

'Tidy . . . Just so. And you like it long?'

'I've worn it long for years and years,' said Fanny with simple pride.

'Why?'

Fanny stared at Robert's reflection, a puzzled expression on her face. 'Because I like it long.'

'It's hot, it must take hours to wash and dry, it's in terrible condition, it doesn't suit you . . . and you like it?' His eyes narrowed. 'I think not. I think the boyfriend likes it, huh? Undoing it and wrapping it round him? Very Eve, very basic.'

Fanny flushed. 'Yes, he likes – liked – my hair long.'

'And his hair? Did he wear that to please you? If you'd wanted him to be a Samson, with hair down to his bottom, would he have done that for you?'

Fanny laughed. 'Of course not.'

'But it's okay for you to encumber yourself with it?' Robert shrugged. 'Me, I wear my hair to please myself. And all my most attractive clients wear their hair to please themselves.'

'I told you, I like it long.'

Robert sniffed. 'Then you're blind. Look, have a really good look. Is this appealing? Shining, healthy, easy to wash and dry? Does it suit your face?' He grasped her jaw and held her face still. 'No, no, you must look. Properly, not turn away.'

Fanny looked, and felt more depressed than ever. No wonder Gerry had upped and offed. How long was it since she'd really looked at herself, seen what he looked at every day? Not to mention all the people in the office.

Why did she look like this? Gerry had encouraged her, told her how much he hated women with make-up, fussy clothes, short hair . . .

Fanny wrenched her head away from Robert. 'Cut it off,' she

said. 'All this,' and she gestured with her hands. 'I want it short. And not dowdy.'

Robert was shocked. 'Dowdy? I've never, ever done a dowdy cut in my whole life.' He held a hank of hair between his fingers and gave it a ferocious but expert snip. 'Dowdy, indeed!'

Toby rang Lisa later that evening, full of mirth and merriment. He told her about taking Fanny shopping, and how she had made a dive for all the sludgiest and most depressing colours. 'Shockingly unsuitable, she needs autumnal shades with that hair. And, I must say, Lisa, Robert's done her proud. She told him to cut it off, just like that!'

Lisa was surprised to hear that.

'I can't tell you the improvement, although I think she regrets it now. I told her, I would have been very unhappy about being out with her the way it was before, anybody could have seen us; the shame. Anyway, Rudi turned up, hours before he was supposed to, the naughty boy, he doesn't trust me at all. So between us, we dragged Fanny off the drears and headed her in the right direction. I hope she's all right for funds, by the way, because we did make her spend a lot. Honestly, Lisa, her underwear.'

'How did her underwear come into it?'

Lisa didn't need to ask; she knew Toby had no shame. Of course, they hadn't let the poor girl go into the fitting room by herself.

'It's the attention to detail,' explained Toby. 'And there it was, practical, one might say, and clean, I will admit, but totally unalluring. So we whipped her off to lingerie and had a wonderful time.'

'Did Rudi buy a bra?'

Peals of laughter from Toby. 'No, but he was terribly tempted by some of the silk undies, quite blissful.'

'Tell Fanny not to worry about the cost,' Lisa said.

'Darling, don't get too involved with this little Fanny, will you.'

'She isn't little, and her mother was very kind to me when I was a girl, so I owe her. Now, Toby, back to our sheep. How's business?'

They talked about books and projects and printers, and then a thought occurred to Lisa.

'Never mind that, Toby. Now listen, can you do something for me?'

Toby was just the person to track down Fanny's painting. She had asked him to get a good description of the Harriety from Fanny, and then to ring round a few picture dealers, to see if her ex and his floozie were hawking it round. Lisa felt almost vengeful about that picture. It meant a lot to Fanny, for one thing, since it was her mother's. And besides, it could be worth quite a lot of money. Why should that worthless pair get the benefit? Thieves, she thought.

Toby rang back quite early the next day.

'Bullseye; it's at Lorder's. The third one I tried. Mind you, it took some doing to wring a description out of Fanny, she thinks Gerry's going to get into trouble over it.'

'Too right,' said Lisa. 'He's a thief. I can't understand Fanny being so wet about this. Her mother gave me a lot of sound advice about Life when I was young. How come she didn't set her daughter off on the right track? She should be screaming for Gerry's blood, not whining about him getting into trouble. Trouble! I'll give him trouble.'

'Do you want me to do anything more about this?'

'No. Oliver works at Lorder's. I'll take it up with him.'

Oliver was inclined to be sniffy.

'We can't discuss ownership of a picture which may or may not have been brought to us to be put up for sale. It isn't your picture, in any case.'

'Listen, Oliver, that picture was stolen. Its owner is staying in my house at the moment. She has not sent it for sale.'

'Lisa, the owner brought it in.'

'Hooey.'

'She told me all about the picture, how it had belonged to her mother, who'd died and left it to her. She wants to sell it privately.'

'Privately?'

'Oh, come on, Lisa. I don't expect she's let on that this very valuable picture is part of her mother's estate.'

'Describe this person.'

'Lisa, I'm extremely busy . . . Oh, very well. Not unlike you, since you ask, only taller. And thinner,' he added spitefully. 'Brownish hair, huge dark eyes. Compelling personality. Bit of a turn-on, actually. Made one or two people sit up around here.'

'From what I know about the men who work in your department, I find that hard to believe.'

'Who said anything about men?'

'Oliver, pay attention. The owner of that picture is one Fanny Jenson. About five nine, reddy-brown hair, light eyes. And she hasn't seen the painting since she sent it off to London to await her return.'

'I can't take your word for this.'

'You'd better. I can tell from your voice that you've got a customer lined up for this picture, haven't you? Nice, easy sale; fat commission.'

'Lisa!'

'Forget it. You know you can't do it, it isn't worth the risk. And why should I lie to you?'

'There is that.'

'You just put that painting on ice, Oliver. It's as safe with you as it is anywhere.'

Oliver's voice rose to a wail. 'And what happens when this woman rings me up about what she says is her picture?'

'Stall, Oliver. Stall.'

CHAPTER 13

Victor had risen early that morning. He stood bellowing beneath Alec's window, waking everyone in the tower, until Alec slipped out of the door to join him.

'Early start,' said Victor. 'Plenty to do.'

The real reason for the early start was Victor's audacious plan to sink a trench across the velvet smoothness of the sunken garden. Victor thought it best to begin work before anyone was about. Such as Hester or Jarvis.

Alec bounded down the stone steps to the lower level, sniffing the clear morning air. 'How do you make hedges grow like that?' he asked.

The yew hedges at Heartsease were spectacular. Some twelve feet high, they were trimmed in an undulating form. They grew all round the rectangle of the sunken garden, with ten feet of rolling sward in front of them before you came to the banks which sloped steeply down into the lower part of the garden.

'They look as though you could climb them,' said Alec approvingly.

'Prickly,' said Victor. He thrust his spade forcibly into the ground and called Alec over to look at the carp in the central pond.

'Must be noisy down there, with the fountain going,' said Alec, leaning over the stone balustrade.

'They're used to it,' said Victor. 'Look, he's a big fellow.'

The fish, gleaming pink and golden and black, came crowding to the side, hoping for food. 'Later,' said Victor, who had been severely reprimanded for overfeeding the fish.

'I'm not allowed to have anything to do with them,' he told Alec. 'My fish, in my garden, and they won't let me near them.'

'Fish can be temperamental,' said Alec cautiously.

'Lot of fusspots,' said Victor. 'Now, we need to mark out this trench.'

On the previous day, they had dug a small experimental hole in a discreet corner, and that was where Alec had found the tessera. Victor had staked out a line from this point; that was where they were going to dig.

Alec was much impressed by Victor's expertise, not dreaming that the line was entirely random.

'Is it something special?' Hester had asked doubtfully when Victor had triumphantly waved the tiny square under her nose. 'It looks like a bit of old pot.'

'No, no,' said Victor. 'No question about it. It's been cut into that little square shape deliberately, anybody can tell that. It's part of a mosaic, and I know just what it's going to look like. It'll be about twelve foot square, dolphins round the edge – they went in for dolphins, you know. Jupiter in the middle, scenes around him. Leaves, flowers and so forth, for decoration.'

Hester gave him a doubtful look. 'You always were inventive, Victor.'

'Should have thought of this in the first place,' said Victor, settling down to some powerful digging. 'Lower level, unnaturally flat, when you come to think of it. Wonderful position, just the kind of place the Romans would go for.'

He paused in his badgerlike efforts, and instructed Alec to retrieve the wheelbarrow from the bushes where he had thoughtfully hidden it the night before. 'I'll shovel, you make a pile with the earth over there.'

Victor liked company when he was working, and he liked to talk. 'I've got a lot of time for the Romans. Pretty rough bunch, but practical, you know. Bridges and arches and roads and so on.'

'They didn't think about money,' said Alec, heaving the barrow up by its handles. He trundled it over to the spot indicated by Victor and wheeled it back.

Victor leant on his spade, alarmed by this heresy. 'What do you mean, they didn't think about money? Astonishingly rich, some of those Roman types.'

'You had to be rich to buy clients and get power,' agreed Alec. 'But our Latin teacher told us that most people couldn't ever be rich and they didn't mind, as long as they could have enough food. I mean, they didn't want money in the bank like people do today. And savings and mortgages and things. What they had, they spent. The Romans didn't like people who worried about money. They thought that was being a miser, which was unRoman.'

Victor didn't like the sound of this. 'I tell you what,' he said. 'You've got an old-fashioned socialist teaching you classics by the sound of it. What school are you at?'

'Hendreds,' said Alec.

'Never heard of it,' said Victor. 'Day school?'

'Yes.'

'Good, good,' said Victor. 'Much better. I always tell people that. Youngsters are much better off at schools where you can keep an eye on them. Then when they come home after school you can find out straight away what rubbish the teachers have been filling their heads with. Like this Latin master of yours. I'll tell Philip to watch out for him.'

'Her,' said Alec. 'Mrs Browning.'

'Her! Worse and worse.'

'Did all your children go to day school?'

'My children?' said Victor digging furiously and hurling the soil about in earthy clumps. 'My lot went all over the place, always getting chucked out and running away and so on. Hopeless!'

They dug and shovelled and wheeled, while Victor shared his views on this and that. Then he looked up, hot and perspiring, as Hester appeared at the top of the steps. He waved in a hopeful fashion as she bore down on them.

'Victor, not the sunken garden, surely.'

Victor, who had geared himself up for a fight, was taken aback by Hester's mildness.

'Ho,' he said at last, while Alec fiddled with the rubber handles of the wheelbarrow and waited to see what would happen.

Hester turned her attention to Alec. 'Have you had breakfast?'

He shook his head.

'Then you must be hungry,' she said with concern. 'Victor, what are you thinking of, letting Alec come out here and work like this without any food inside him?'

'It's okay, really,' said Alec.

'He wanted to help,' said Victor, aggrieved. 'I don't know why it is, but the smallest thing I want to do, and you're all ranged against me, complaining.'

'If you're planning to dig a trench here, on Jarvis's precious lawn, then it's no wonder we complain. Jarvis loves this lawn. Jarvis will probably hand in his notice.'

'Not him,' said Victor.

'At least let him come and take the turf off properly,' urged Hester, who could see her brother settling down for a spot of Cordovan obstinacy. 'Then he can put it back when you've finished.'

Victor exploded. 'Finished? Good God, Hester, we'll have to have the whole lawn up, when I find this mosaic floor. It means the villa will stretch, oh, under the pond, right over there.' He flung his arm out in an extravagant gesture.

'I hope you aren't suggesting that you're going to tunnel under the conservatories,' said Hester.

Victor looked startled; his sweep had been meant in a general way, and not intended to take in the miniature version of the Palm House at Kew which a Victorian occupant had built behind the main house. But he wasn't going to give in. 'If it's necessary,' he said airily. 'In the interests of science . . .'

'That's enough of science,' said Hester, who had things to do. 'Come in and have your breakfast.'

CHAPTER 14

Alec rattled his fingers on Lisa's shoulder, making her jump. 'Are you going up to Dad? Can I come and show him my finds?'

Lisa wished, not for the first time, that Alec would pick up his feet. Slop, slop as she followed him up the stairs, to find Philip sitting on the edge of the bed, swearing and muttering as he pulled on his trousers.

'No,' he said through gritted teeth. 'Don't try to help me, I don't need help, I'm going to do it myself. I can't see straight, that's the problem.'

Of course it was. It was going to take some getting used to, one eye. And the other one wasn't working too well, yet. The doctors had warned Lisa about that; it had been bruised during the fight and the operation.

'Victor popped in,' he said.

That accounted for it. Five minutes of Victor was exhausting even when you were fit.

Alec plonked himself down on the end of the bed.

'Don't *do* that,' said Philip.

'Sorry,' said Alec, a shuttered look coming over his face.

'It's time to take your tablets,' Lisa said, putting a glass of water down beside Philip.

'I don't need to be reminded,' said Philip. 'And I don't want the bloody things, in any case.'

Lisa refrained from pointing out that Philip knew as well as she did that he had to have them, he couldn't risk an infected wound. He would take them when she'd gone.

Alec lounged against the tallboy in the corner of the room, and Lisa could see Philip eyeing him crossly. How Alec did irritate him.

'Do stand up straight,' he said.

'I'll go,' said Alec, and slunk off through the door.

Slop, slop, slop down the stairs.

Wait for it . . . bang!

'Bloody boy,' said Philip. 'Why does he have to make such a noise? Why can't he shut the door quietly?'

'It's his age,' Lisa said. 'And you weren't very kind,' she added, perching herself on the fender.

'What did he want?'

'To show you what he's dug up in the garden. He's been helping Victor on his great Roman quest.'

'Victor says they've found a mosaic.'

'That's what Alec wanted to show you. Mind you, I don't think a single tessera, which is their haul so far, exactly constitutes a mosaic.'

'I told Victor to tell him to buzz off if he's a nuisance, which of course he is.'

'They seem to get on all right.'

'That's what Victor said. Loud in his praise.'

'Alec's okay.'

Philip wasn't having any of that. He was fed up with being convalescent. He couldn't read, of course, but then he wasn't much of a reader at the best of times. He was infuriated by the radio. 'It never has anything on worth listening to. Cricket, droning on hour after hour. News! They may call it news, but it's simply a collection of gloomy stories about distant parts of the world, endless interviews with pin-witted politicians, and food scares.'

'Tune to a different programme,' Lisa said.

Philip took no notice. 'If I go on listening to that nonsense a day longer, I'll be anorexic,' he said, drawing on a sock with agonising care and slowness.

There was no point in Lisa suggesting music, Philip was too restless to lie back and listen to music. He liked music, but only if he was there in person; live or nothing. Music had to be physical for Philip, he wouldn't listen to sounds drifting through the air from nowhere.

Lisa offered to play cards with him.

'No, you always cheat, so you always win, and I've never worked out how you do it.'

She had told him, more than once, that it was telepathy. Philip was a scientist by training and he held that there was no evidence whatsoever for telepathy. Ergo, it didn't happen. So Lisa went on winning at cards.

If she could use telepathy for cards, why couldn't she pick up what was going on in his little mind re the duel and this Claudia, she wondered. Presumably it was buried deep beneath the tangle of thoughts that people like her could pick up. Bad news, that.

'Where are you going?'

'I'm going to look at the bloody horses.'

Yes, he would. His passion for horses was even stronger than his passion for the hurly burly of currencies and economies.

'I'll have to help you down the stairs. Steps are going to be difficult.'

'I suppose so. I'm not ill, you know.'

'Nobody said you were. Simply injured, and recovering.'

What tact. His taut, sinewy face might be half-bandaged, but she could see he hurt. His temples and brow had beads of sweat; Philip's hair grew back off his forehead in a forceful way. His hair was still dark, but there were threads of grey here and there. More now, probably. He was still a very striking man, thought Lisa, looking at him with silent affection. She wished she knew just what he was up to.

She didn't help him down the stairs. Cross Polly heard their door open, and was there.

'Come on, Dad, I'll hold your hand,' she said, giving Lisa a defiant look.

In fact she had to hold both his hands, and she went down the stairs backwards, facing him. Very slowly and carefully. Polly had power over her father, and so he let her help him.

As they came out of the curved door at the foot of the tower, in slow procession, Don appeared. He was wearing a pink silk shirt tucked into khaki trousers, and looked very cool and merry. He was quick on the uptake, taking in the situation at a glance, and in no time was guiding Philip across the yard and out towards the stables.

'Don't stay,' said Philip, once he was propped against the mounting block in the stableyard. 'I don't need you to hover about, and I know you don't want to look at horses. I'll sit here for a while, talk to James's man. Then Polly will give me a hand over to the paddocks, won't you, Pol?'

She nodded vigorously, willing her mother to go so that she could have her father to herself. Lisa found that touching, but why was Philip so anxious to avoid her? Normally he liked to have her around, at his beck and call. She'd never been enthusiastic about it, though, so perhaps he'd given up.

Perhaps.

Don was having a word with a person who looked just like a gypsy or possibly a poacher, but who turned out to be James's head groom, one Geraghty. 'He'll look after Philip,' said Don. 'Now, if we head for the kitchen, Maria is likely to be making coffee. Or if not, I can.'

CHAPTER 15

Lisa had forgotten the kitchens at Heartsease. She looked round with pleasure, taking in the relics of past ages, which existed side by side with all kinds of modern conveniences. A perfect combination of charm and practicality.

She said this to Maria and was given a very dark eye. Maria threw her hands up to heaven, and described in some detail how difficult it was to work in such a place. 'It is primitive,' she said dramatically. 'Great stone flags on the floor.'

Quite sensible, Lisa would have thought. Hard-wearing, too.

'Hard-wearing, yes, they wear my feet out. And you cannot ever, ever, get them clean. And when it rains, which in this benighted country is all too often, then they go dark, and are damp. It is uncivilised. Now, here is coffee.'

Don sat at the long refectory table and sipped his black brew.

'You're looking in very good form, Don,' Lisa commented, sliding herself along the bench opposite him.

'Why not? It's summer, the grapes are ripening, we have delightful company staying up here at the house.'

What a charmer Don was, Lisa thought, as she watched him drink his coffee and flirt with Maria. He overflowed with vitality. He wasn't tall, svelte, muscular or handsome. Going bald, tanned, big nose, love jugs lurking under that classy shirt, endless delight in everything life-enhancing: wine, song, poetry . . . and love-making, Lisa had heard. His company took you out of yourself.

Although he had a mad side, so Hester had told Lisa years ago when she first met the Cordovans,. She said he went over the edge, from time to time. Uncontrollable. Wild, in fact.

It seemed unlikely to Lisa.

'I will escort you to the library,' said Don, when Lisa, reluctantly, refused more coffee and announced that she had work to do.

Lisa had installed herself and her papers at a table in the library next to a deep window embrasure. The stone mullions glowed in the sunlight flickering briefly through gaps in racing clouds, and looking out along a grassy terrace she could see the stone urns, full of tumbling purple flowers, which marked the steps leading down to the sunken garden.

Don looked out of the window, his attention caught by the figures of Alec and Victor.

It seemed an odd friendship to Lisa. Alec was so wary of Philip that she was surprised he seemed so at ease with Victor. He was every bit as forceful as Philip in his own way. She had to admit, though, that Victor had the better temper, and of course, he wasn't Alec's father. And Victor was too large minded and generally agreeable to find fault all the time, as Philip seemed to more and more as Alec got older.

Lisa couldn't see either of them, but she could see showers of earth flying into the air. She could also hear, just, the rumble of Victor's voice – how that man loved to talk – and the higher and slightly croaky strains of Alec's voice, when he could get a word in edgeways. Much of the time they seemed to be speaking simultaneously.

'Lost in thought?' enquired Don, hitching himself up on to a nearby table.

'Only wondering about those two out there.'

Don laughed. 'An odd pair.'

'Will they find anything, do you suppose?'

'Possibly. If they do, Pa will be triumphant and impossible, and no doubt very horrid to our neighbours. If they don't, Hester will nag him to fill up all his holes, and he'll be in a terrible temper.'

'Will he fill in the holes?'

'No way. Jarvis will have to do it. If he doesn't quit first.'

'Philip's here for a quiet and restful recuperation,' Lisa said. Her face showed her amusement.

Don smiled, his eyes creasing up in a most attractive way, Lisa noticed. 'Nonsense. You've brought him here to get him out of the way. Although I do think that Philip isn't looking too pleased with life. Is he very pissed off about losing the eye?'

'He might be, but I don't believe it's that,' Lisa said. 'I've never known him to be like this.'

'Business okay?'

'No problems.'

'A few weeks at Heartsease will liven him up,' said Don confidently. 'Never a dull moment here, you know.'

Lisa's opinion was that dullness in the country might be what Philip needed to keep him out of any further mischief.

'Are the press still on his tail?' asked Don.

'I don't think so. They pestered for a bit, but everyone kept their mouths shut, thankfully. Then that Newcastle footballer got arrested in the Ukraine for molesting a gymnast. A much livelier story. No one except Philip's secretary and partner at his office know where he is, and they won't be telling. My Toby knows, but he hates the press. So we should be left alone.'

'The locals will talk,' said Don. 'A one-eyed man? They'll love it. But that'll just be gossip at the Bunch of Grapes, it won't go any further. Lucky for you that the archaeologist has left, there were quite a few newspaper and TV people down here a few days ago.'

'These things usually blow over very quickly.'

'Yes,' said Don, watching her. 'So, let's have the truth, Lisa. We've known each other a long time, even if we've never been close. Spit it out, what's Philip been up to? Why have you brought him here?'

'Victor invited Philip, and us, and Philip accepted. Nothing to do with me.'

'If you hadn't wanted to come, you would have persuaded Philip to go elsewhere.'

'I'm not sure about that. Philip isn't exactly malleable at the moment.'

A raised eyebrow at that. 'Malleable? Is Philip ever malleable?'

'Mmm. Where he goes when he's not working isn't important enough for him to make a fuss about it. Usually. In this case it doesn't matter, because I think it's an excellent place for him to be.'

'So, if it isn't rest he needs, why are you here?'

'He does need rest.'

'Ah, but Heartsease isn't the place for that, admit. In some harpy's clutches, is he?'

Lisa gave Don a very sharp look and he lifted his hand in a calming way. 'I haven't heard any gossip; well, only a smattering. About how he lost his eye.'

'Yes?'

'There are rumours.'

'That's all they are, as far as I know.'

'And if they aren't, then here is a good place for him, under your watchful eye.'

'Not many strangers around here,' was all Lisa said.

'No, and very visible when there are any. Going to flush this harpy out, are you?'

'If there is a harpy.'

'I think you can take the harpy as read,' said Don.

The sun had vanished behind a ferocious-looking cloud. A huge drop of rain landed on a stone outside with a splat, followed by a dappling of others. It turned into a veritable downpour, bringing Victor and Alec, spades in hand, hurtling into the house. A streak of lighting jagged across the sky, followed by a crack of thunder, and another and another.

'Better put the lights on,' said Don.

'Never mind the lights. What about Philip?'

'There's a shelter out there by the paddocks. Would you like me to take a large brolly and go to bring him back to the house?'

'Will this last long?' she asked, looking doubtfully up into the black heavens.

'Hours, I should think,' he said cheerfully.

Two minutes later, Lisa watched him and Victor battling through the weather on a rescue mission. Victor was wet and magnificent, the rain streaming over his face and beard, and his soaked shirt clinging to his chest and back. Don was holding a rebellious wine-red golfing umbrella in an iron grasp. He looked a small man against his father, and yet, somehow, just as powerful.

What a pair.

In fact, Lisa said to herself, thinking of the rest of them, what a family.

CHAPTER 16

Once Philip was back, not at all pleased, but cajoled into a better mood and on to a sofa by Hester, Lisa's mind returned to harpies.

She decided to go and phone Titia. Titia was not a harpy. On the contrary, Titia was a civilised and kind person. She was also one of Philip's oldest friends. Lisa cheerfully admitted that Titia could read Philip like a book.

'I'm glad you rang,' she said in her rather deep voice. 'How is Philip?'

Lisa told her, and then asked how she had found Philip recently. Strange?

There was a silence. So long a silence that Lisa began to think she had been cut off, and was about to give the phone a good shake.

'Lisa, recently doesn't come into it. I haven't seen Philip for weeks. Months, in fact.'

This was truly startling news. 'Months? I thought he popped over to see you every two or three weeks.'

'Not since before Easter.'

Titia was a churchgoer of the Anglo Catholic persuasion, and she measured her year from festival to festival. Since Lisa was a pagan, she had to think hard to remember when Easter was this year.

She finally got there. 'Late March.'

'Yes, it must have been the middle of March that he came.'

'He said he was going to see you.' What a fool, never to question those regular visits to Titia.

'Well, he didn't.' Titia was never one to beat around the bush.

'What was he like last time you did see him?'

Another silence.

'Titia, please.'

'Lisa, I'm thinking. Look, his mood was strange. He was, how can I put it . . . *distrait*? I thought it was work, you know how absorbed he is, when there's a big coup coming, or the markets have plunged and currencies are rattling up and down.'

'Yes,' Lisa said. She had always known that Titia offered Philip a companionship which he needed. Comfort, and a kind of mumsy softness that he didn't get with her. She, Lisa, was not at all mumsy, but with a father like Emilia, she felt that Philip needed some of the cosy closeness he had never had as a child. She didn't grudge him his hours with Titia. It kept him on the straight and narrow.

Or had done.

'He said nothing?'

'Not a word. A barely affectionate goodbye. I wondered if I'd offended him, said something out of place, but then, looking back on the evening, I realised that he was in that mood when he arrived. Frankly, I don't know why he came.'

'I think there's someone else,' Lisa said.

'I'm afraid you're almost certainly right,' said Titia with a sigh. 'And, judging by the way he was, and by the fact I haven't seen him since, I suspect she isn't doing him a lot of good.'

'Apart from costing him an eye.'

'That was it, was it? Can't you wring any details out of Rory?'

'I've tried.'

'I'll see what I can find out,' said Titia, after another pause. 'We don't move in the same circles, but I can get in touch with one or two of my more gossipy friends.'

'Discreetly.'

'Trust me for that.'

Lisa did. They trusted each other, and they both cared for Philip in their own ways. Lisa knew that Titia had a new man in her life. Was Philip cross about that?

Clearly Titia didn't think so. Philip would have staged a cutting scene; he trampled on his enemies, men or women. A visible lover would have pushed Titia straight into the enemy camp.

What had Philip been up to?

CHAPTER 17

Having started, the rain wasn't going to stop in a hurry. The thunder growled on, interspersed with brilliant flashes and streaks of lightning. Eventually the rain slackened, the thunder became fainter and the sky brightened. Then, with another flash of lightning, the clouds hurtled together once more in great black eddies, the thunder reverberated around the skies, and the heavens opened again.

Don had left, splashing his way back to his home and his vineyards, not at all happy. 'Rain is fine, but not buckets of the stuff,' he said. 'Just as long as it doesn't hail, that's all.'

Victor rumbled and roared with vexation. 'Just like having our own thunderstorm indoors,' said Hester. He finally gave up glaring at the rain lashing against the windows and carried Alec off for a game of billiards.

'I don't play billiards,' said Alec. 'Snooker's my thing.'

'Here at Heartsease,' said Victor, 'we play billiards.'

Philip, more tired than he would admit, had retreated to his room for a rest. 'At least that bloody nurse will probably leave me alone for a day,' he said as he went off, brushing aside Polly and Hester's offers of help. 'I'm not ill, I'm not an invalid, I can manage perfectly well.'

Polly frowned, to hide the tears that had sprung into her eyes. Polly had odd eyes. One was blue-grey, the other grey-brown. They were disturbing eyes, which Lisa thought might be a great attraction when she was older. But she didn't like being ignored by Philip.

Hester alone was unperturbed, as the storm crashed about Heartsease. 'Polly,' she said. 'Let's go and do some baking.'

'Baking?'

If Hester suggested gingerbread men or some such childish goody, Lisa knew that Polly would resist.

Hester had too much sense. 'Dark, rich chocolate cake. For tea. Victor loves chocolate cake.'

'So does Daddy,' said Polly, her face brightening.

Jarvis was skulking in the kitchen, imbibing many cups of tea, and expressing his negative views on householders who came out of their studies and started burrowing about in the ground.

'The pigs are upset, my lawn will never be the same again, my tools are all in disorder.'

'Listen,' said Maria, jabbing Jarvis in the chest with a large wooden spoon. 'Victor is your boss, right? He pays your wages. The work here is good work, and he's a good employer. So be grateful that you have your feet under his table, and are drinking his tea.'

'You wouldn't say that if he came into your kitchen and started excavating.'

Maria looked at him with scorn. 'Excavate? In a kitchen? Now, you say Victor is mad, and I tell you that it is you who are mad.'

Polly stood at the door, eyes round. She looked up at Hester. 'Do you think Victor might? If he thought there were Romans under here? Dig it all up, I mean.'

Maria's expression grew even darker. 'There are no Romans in my kitchen. No, and no and no. I have nothing to do with these Romans. Romans are for Italy. Victor would not dare.'

'He might dare,' said Hester placidly, 'but if he did, he wouldn't get anything to eat, and that would never do. Calm down, Maria, Victor is quite happy digging his pits in the gardens. Jarvis, I know you can't do anything outside with this weather, but there's plenty to do in the conservatories.'

Jarvis sniffed. 'I was going to do that on Friday.'

'Do it today, instead.'

Jarvis grumbled off, pointing out that his whole week's schedule had been knocked out, what with trenches in the orchard, holes in the lawn. 'Holes in Victor's head,' he muttered, as he battled across the courtyard outside the kitchen.

Maria was loud with enthusiasm at Polly's offer to help with baking, and whisked mixers, flour and other ingredients out of larders and fridges with extraordinary rapidity.

86

'Goodness,' said Polly, as she carefully tied a blue and white apron round herself at Maria's command. 'You do everything so fast.'

'You have to move fast in this household,' said Guy, coming in with a tray of vases. 'I'll just put these in to wash, and then I'll make some tea for your father. The nurse said he's to have plenty of liquid. It'll just be ready when he comes off the phone.'

'Is he on the phone?' said Polly, measuring out a pyramid of flour. 'How do you know?'

'The light for that extension is on in Victor's study. Your mother's in the library, isn't she? So it has to be him. Talking to his office, I expect, all those deals and so on.'

'He isn't allowed to talk to his office,' said Polly, licking a finger. 'Not while he's down here and convalescing. Mummy won't let him.'

'A friend, then.'

'Excellent cake,' said Victor, scattering crumbs as he spoke. 'Excellent.'

'I made it,' said Polly with pride.

'Bet you didn't,' said Alec. 'Bet Maria made it.'

'She did not. Why do you always have to think . . .'

'That's enough.' Lisa's voice rang out from the door. 'Victor, Don wants you outside. He says the pump's backed up in the pond, and the fish need rescuing.'

'Oh, bugger,' said Victor, cramming the rest of his cake into his mouth and striding to the door. 'Alec, get Maria to give you some buckets. Polly, you go and tell Guy to top up the tank in the stables. Hester, where's Jarvis?'

'Lurking in the conservatory,' said Hester. 'I'll get him.'

Lisa followed Victor out of the room. 'Does this often happen?'

'The rain must have swept some gravel into the pond. It's an old pump, and a bit erratic. If a piece of gravel gets into the propeller affair inside the fountain, it jams it. The pond will have to be drained, so that Jarvis can fix the pump. What a bloody nuisance, just as the rain's easing off. I want to get back to my digging.'

Victor seized a large long-handled net from the cloakroom and sailed off to his fishy duties, followed by an enchanted Polly and Alec, and a still grumbling Jarvis. Lisa caught up with Don.

'I told you, never a dull moment.'

'No, who knows what's going to happen next?'

CHAPTER 18

Victor was in glowing form at dinner. He had beaten Alec soundly at billiards, imparting much useful advice. He hadn't noticed that by the time they came to the end of their game, Alec was already much more skilful than he had been at the beginning.

Alec was planning some solitary practice. He, too, liked to win.

But for the moment, Victor was content. 'Come and sit beside me, on my right, young Polly,' he said. 'Your mother won't mind for once.' He glanced along the table. 'Too many men,' he announced. 'Unbalanced.'

Harry had joined them for dinner, leaving Zoë large and happy in bed with a fat book, the radio and the bananas she ate all day long. 'You go and eat at the Hall,' she said. 'I don't want any supper, and I'd much rather not have to cook for you.'

Don had stayed on, and as Victor observed, that made for only one wife between them. 'Plus young Polly and Hester, of course, but they don't count.'

Hester took no notice of Victor's tactless remark, she was too used to him to be bothered. Polly went pink, and an inquisitorial look came into Alec's eyes.

'Haven't you got three wives?' he asked.

'Shut up, Alec,' said Philip furiously.

'What? Three wives? Oh, very good. That would fill the table up all right, but I'll tell you what,' he went on, leaning conspiratorially towards Alec, 'the sparks would be flying. None of them could stand the others.'

He sat back in his seat with a satisfied grunt. 'What do you think of that?'

Polly was looking at him with a very severe expression. 'You can't have three wives. It isn't allowed. Or are you a Muslim?'

Now Victor was affronted. 'A what? A Muslim? A Mohammedan? Philip, how dare your daughter say things like that?'

'Stop it, Polly,' said Philip wearily.

Polly wasn't finished. 'Alec said you had three wives. Well, how?'

'He got divorced, stupid,' hissed Alec.

'Then he's got one wife and two ex-wives,' said Polly triumphantly.

'No, no,' said Victor. 'Three ex-wives. I divorced them all.'

'What about Julia?' said Alec, who remembered Julia from an earlier visit. 'Have you divorced her as well? Is that why she isn't here?'

'Nosy lot, your two,' said Victor to Lisa, who had caught Don's eye and was trying not to laugh.

'That's enough, Alec, Polly,' said Lisa.

'More than enough,' said Philip. 'What manners. If that's all they can do with you at that school of yours, Alec, then . . .'

Victor intervened. 'No, no, he's confused, course he is. Mind you, he'll find out for himself soon enough about wives and ex-wives and the whole caboodle. I'll explain. Now listen,' he said magisterially. 'Julia was my first wife. I then married two others. And divorced them. Now Julia's back here again. Not physically at this moment, no, because she's gone to a conference in Sweden. But usually. Now, is that clear?'

'But did you divorce Julia?' said Polly, not giving up. 'Because you must have done, to marry the other two. So you can't be married to her unless you did it again.'

'Pudding, Guy,' said Victor in a loud voice.

Victor unearthed a large and powerful torch, and dragged Alec off to investigate the damage to their earthworks. 'We need to make plans for the morning,' said Victor.

'If it ever stops raining,' said Alec.

Harry went back to the lodge to watch a late-night film with an insomniac Zoë. 'Very exhausting, this,' he said, waving the remote control. 'What do you want to watch?'

'Anything, as long as it's funny.'

'I hope that once the baby's put in an appearance, you're going to revert to sleeping at night and being awake in the day.'

'Let's hope the baby isn't a nightbird,' said Zoë.

'She'd better not be. Otherwise, kiddo,' said Harry, patting Zoë's tummy, 'it's the Valium for you.'

Hester drifted off for a spot of domesticity, and Polly went away to read to Philip. He was feeling very weak by the end of dinner, and wasn't at all reluctant to get to his bed, despite denying any trace of tiredness.

'It's just so that you can get some reading practice, Pol,' he said, as he sank gratefully back into his pillows. 'And none of your children's books, they scare me witless. Get that book on horse-breeding, it's over there by the window. Just the thing at the end of the day.'

'Have a cognac before you retire, Lisa,' said Don. 'We'll sit in state in the great hall and pretend we're living in olden-times.'

Lisa was suspicious. 'Why?'

'There were some good things about the old days,' said Don in his blandest voice.

'Plague, boils and lousy sanitation.'

'And soldiers swarming through the house, the clash of swords . . .' Don switched on the wall lights, which sent eerie shadows up into the beamed darkness above them.

'I can do without the clash of swords, thank you,' said Lisa.

Guy walked silently across the stone floor, carrying the cognac and two glasses.

'Still raining?' asked Don, relieving him of his load.

'Beautiful, your Guy,' said Lisa, as she watched his elegant progress from the hall.

Don handed Lisa a cognac and installed himself in a big oak chair, holding up his glass to the light to admire its colour. 'Ah, you like beautiful boys, do you?' He shook his head. 'You're getting to a dangerous age, Lisa.'

'What's dangerous about it?'

'The age when husbands pall, and young men seem more delightful than they ever did when you were young yourself.'

'No point hankering after Guy, is there?' said Lisa. 'And what do you know of husbands palling? You've never been married, you can only speak as an observer.'

'True, but a concerned observer. And also as a long-time beneficiary of wives' disillusionment with their husbands.'

'From what I hear, Don, you don't hang around waiting for disillusionment to set in.'

'Some women manage husbands and lovers in a very satisfying way.'

'It's not as easy as you think,' said Lisa, enjoying the warm glow of the cognac as it trickled down her throat. 'You think you're managing, and then you have to ask, are you? Or is the other person managing you.'

'And you don't like being managed.'

'No.'

'Or out-manoeuvred.'

Lisa looked at him sharply, but his face gave nothing away.

'I shall make sure I'm not out-manoeuvred.'

'No, I would imagine anyone who is going to try and get the better of you is going to be a very lively proposition,' said Don. 'I long to meet her. Now, drink up, and then you can have another glass before you return. A loving wife, at the side of her wounded husband.'

Lisa gave Don a very speaking look.

'Sweet dreams,' he said, raising his glass to her.

Philip had turned all the lights out, and he lay across the bed, tossing in an uneasy sleep. Lisa pushed him over and climbed into bed beside him.

And I wonder what your dreams are about, she said to herself, as she buffeted her pillows into shape and lay back, her eyes open in the darkness.

CHAPTER 19

Victor was out early, Alec at his side, to repair the damage to his diggings.

The rain and wind had blown themselves out overnight, leaving a fresh landscape with a faint mist rising from the meadows. The sun was just breaking through, bringing the promise of a fine summer's day.

'It's a mess,' said Alec, staring down at the dark, damp earth. 'And the water from the pond's swept a lot of the bank we made away. I didn't see that last night.'

'We'll soon tidy that up,' said Victor. 'Hop in, and have a scrabble round, you've got wellingtons on, they'll keep your feet dry.'

Alec eased himself down into the trench, feeling very frog-like. He had a horrid feeling that the inky earth might be a quagmire; at any moment it might suck him under with a series of terrible slurps and gulps.

It didn't.

'Hey, Victor,' he said. 'I think we've hit a stone or something.' He reached out for his spade and jabbed around in the oozing ground under his feet. There was a dull thonk. 'There, do you see?'

Victor let out a yell which the peaceful late-breakfasters in the house could hear quite clearly.

'This is it,' he bellowed. 'We've found it!'

Thirty seconds later, he erupted through the door of the house, leaving large and dirty footprints as he went.

'Victor,' said Hester. 'Outside, please, with all that mud.'

Victor was rarely rude to Hester, but he was too excited to control himself. 'Mud? Now is not the time to go on about mud. You have a petty mind, Hester. This is the time to turn your mind to a wider horizon. To contemplate the sweep of the past, to see with a greater vision.'

'And what exactly is it that I'm supposed to see?' asked Hester, looking at the dirty artefact held triumphantly in Victor's large hand.

'This,' said Victor, waving it about. 'This. Evidence of Roman occupation at this very spot. Just as I always said.'

'It looks like a piece of drainpipe,' observed Polly through a mouthful of toast.

'It *is* a piece of drainpipe,' said Victor. '*Roman* drainpipe.'

'Nonsense, Victor,' said Hester. 'It's Victorian, you can see it is.'

Victor glowered. 'It is not Victorian. Do you think I don't know the difference between something a hundred years old and something with the patina of nearly two millennia on it?'

'I doubt it,' said Philip. 'Needs an expert to make anything of this.'

'Then we'll find an expert. Hester, are you on speaking terms with Heartwell House? Where they found the kiln?'

'I am on good terms with all our neighbours,' said Hester.

'More fool you. Ring him up, then, find out if that Cambridge johnny is still here.'

Don stood in the doorway, surveying the scene with considerable amusement. 'Made a find, Pa?' he said. 'If you mean Buonamici, I think he's gone.'

'Ring up, Hester, find out.'

With a sigh, Hester gave in to the inevitable. She looked up the number in the leather book which lived on the old oak chest beside the phone. Her movements were calm and precise, as always.

'Get a move on,' said Victor.

Hester laid the address book down by the phone. 'Victor, that is enough,' she said. 'And I am not going to make a phone call to anyone with you breathing down the back of my neck.'

Philip guided Victor back into the morning room, where he thundered up and down, too excited to drink the coffee which Polly poured out for him.

'Ha, this will make them all sit up. Ha, who said there weren't Romans here? I knew it. You see, I was right.'

'You don't know yet,' said Polly. 'And where's Alec?'

'Digging,' said Victor. 'Looking for more. And he'll find them, just you wait and see. There'll be heaps of things. Mosaics, of course. Statues, coins, lamps, the lot. We'll have to clear out the library to display them.'

Philip had gone back to his breakfast, but he looked up from his kipper. 'You won't be allowed to keep anything you do find,' he said. 'It'll all belong to the state, be heaved off to the museums.'

Victor looked at him in disbelief.

'Not my finds.'

'I thought they didn't dig anything up nowadays,' said Polly. 'They just use electronic probes and computers and things, and draw what's there, and leave it all where it is.'

'Don't be foolish,' said Victor. 'What's the point of that?'

'To save it for future archaeologists who will have more advanced technology and techniques, I believe, Pa,' said Don, inspecting the dishes and spearing a sausage with a handy fork.

'Not my site, they don't,' said Victor. He bounded forward as Hester came back into the room.

'Don't loom like that,' said Hester. 'I'm afraid there's no reply.'

'No reply? What do you mean there's no reply?'

'I mean that the telephone rang and rang, and nobody answered it,' said Hester.

'That's odd,' said Don. 'They usually leave a message on the answerphone. They're probably out in the garden.'

'Perhaps with the expert from Cambridge, looking at their Roman remains,' said Hester.

'Then someone must go there immediately,' said Victor, thwarted. 'This very minute. We must have that man, or his telephone number, as soon as possible.'

'I'll ring again in half an hour or so,' said Hester.

'No, no, not a minute to be wasted,' said Victor.

Don knew his father in this mood. 'Where are your car keys, Pa? I walked over, but I'll drive to Heartwell and see if anyone's on the prems. Shan't be long.'

Lisa looked up as Don strolled back into the room. 'Archaeologist in tow?' she asked.

'Afraid not. The owners are away, and Dr B has gone to ground in Cambridge.'

'So there was no one there after all?'

'Um, there's a friend of theirs staying in the house,' said Don noncommittally, giving Philip a quick look. Philip's attention was elsewhere.

'I'll go down and see what Alec and Victor are up to,' he said.

'Good idea,' said Don, falling in alongside Philip to lend a hand if needed. Lisa waited for the inevitable rebuff, but, strangely, Philip didn't seem to mind Don.

They stood and looked at the heaps of earth and holes all over the sunken garden. Victor had dug like a giant burrowing creature, here and there as impulse took him.

'You see where this wall runs,' he said, delighted to have an audience. 'There's the corner there. We're going to follow it as far as it goes, and of course that will lead us into other areas of the villa, reception rooms, living area, domestic quarters, bathhouse. It's all here.'

Looking at the rough stonework so far unearthed, Lisa thought Victor's enthusiasm was a triumph of hope over experience.

'Found any pottery, yet?' asked Philip.

'Lots,' said Alec. 'I told Victor he has to leave it where it is.'

'Ridiculous,' said Victor with a frown. 'Pile it all up on the side, I say, but Alec won't have it. Very bossy, this boy of yours, Philip.'

'Alec, pipe down, will you?' said Philip. 'It's hardly your business to go telling Victor what he should do.'

'Oh, but he's quite right,' said Don. 'Pa, you'll get into terrible trouble with the archaeologists if you scrabble about like this. If there's anything there, they'll want a pristine site.'

'They can want away,' said Victor. 'It's my land, nobody believed me when I said the Romans had been here, and I'm going to show them all. Just wait till I get to the mosaics.'

'I believe the excavation of a Roman site, if this is what it is, takes years and years,' said Philip. 'You don't want all those people careering over your land, you know, Victor. Drive you mad. Cover it up, if I were you, forget about it. That's my advice.'

Victor waved his spade around in a dramatic fashion. 'You're supposed to be a man of science, Philip. Can't go covering the evidence up, you know. And,' he added cunningly, 'the reason these digs take so long is because they never have any money. Now, I have plenty of money, and we can summon a whole lot of idle types up from the job centre if need be.'

Victor clearly thought he was in Egypt in the thirties, with hordes of eager locals – preferably, no doubt, in flowing robes – waiting to heave baskets of earth hither and thither. Lisa couldn't help feeling that digging for Romans wasn't high on the list of preferred occupations at the job centre.

There was a shout from Alec, and Victor leapt out of one pit and into another to see what he'd found.

'I think it's silver,' said Alec eagerly. Lisa's heart lurched when she saw that look on his face, the desperate keenness of youth with its belief in miracles. She found herself praying that his find wouldn't turn out to be half a Victorian chamber pot, tossed out by a guilty housemaid.

'And who are you praying to?' Don stood beside her.

She laughed. 'Was it that obvious? Jupiter, perhaps.'

'No need,' said Don, his face suddenly becoming very alert. 'Good heavens, I think that boy of yours really has found something this time.'

Victor wasn't having any of this leaving finds untouched, not when he'd set eyes on what Alec had unearthed. There was a small curved piece of what – pottery? . . . metal? – jutting out of the spot where Alec had just dug. Victor seized it with both hands, and gave it a good tug.

He let out a roar of triumph, wiping the earth off it, and brandishing it in the air. 'Silver,' he shouted. 'A silver plate. There now, what more do you want?'

Philip was impressed. 'Well, Victor,' he said, taking it and looking at it closely. 'Do you know, I think that it might turn out to be silver. Alec, here, tuck it back where you found it.'

'What?' Victor couldn't believe his ears. 'No way does that go back. Guy can clean it, and I shall eat my dinner off it tonight. There, what do you think of that?'

Hester, a recent arrival on the scene, thought nothing at all of that. 'Out of the question, Victor. Alec, do as your father says. And Victor, this has gone quite far enough. There's to be no more of this careless digging out here.'

Before Victor could explode, Philip stepped in to pour oil on the blaze. 'Come along, Victor, face facts. You need the experts now. You'll get into a deal of trouble if you carry on with your random excavations; yes, I know it's your land, but that's got nothing to do with it.'

He turned to his wife. 'Lisa, that young woman you've rescued and left with Toby. What did she read at university? Wasn't it archaeology?'

Lisa stared at Philip in amazement. How did he know these things? 'She went to a northern university,' she ventured.

Philip gave her a look that might have been withering if he'd had two eyes. 'As you're always telling me, there's nothing wrong with the north. Ring her up, Lisa. Ask her if she knows anything about archaeology, get her down here. She can have a look at this lot, unofficially. If it's her field, she'll have contacts.'

Victor was still booming away in the background. 'Do shut up, there's a good fellow,' said Philip irritably. 'Otherwise I'll ring up some local government office and tell them what's going on here.'

'You'll what?' Victor was visibly astounded. 'A guest, and old friend, treating me like this? Threatening me with some tinpot official? Philip, I feel very badly let down.'

'Rubbish,' said Philip briskly and unsympathetically. 'You can't steamroller me, Victor. I'm a guest all right, but I'm a scientist as you mentioned. You have to do this in the proper way, or you'll bugger everything up. And, incidentally, land yourself in court.'

'Quick,' said Don. 'Back to the house with you, Lisa, and get on the phone to this young woman. Before Victor bursts a blood vessel.'

Lisa was doubtful about the whole idea. 'She's probably out. And if she's in, she probably isn't an archaeologist at all. And if she is, why should she want to come all the way to Heartsease?'

Don was sanguine. 'Philip's usually right, isn't he? Has to be accurate in his line of business. And why shouldn't she want to come to Heartsease? Lovely place.'

Lisa refrained from saying that a dose of the Cordovans right now might be too much for poor Fanny, and contented herself with pointing out that she was a young woman with her own life to lead.

'Tell me about her,' said Don, steering Lisa inexorably towards the house. 'Is she pretty? Sexy? What does she do? How old is she?'

'She's twenty-six, Don, and would be pretty but she doesn't look after herself. She's just been dumped by her long-standing man, she's lost her job; I don't think she needs to come face to face with Victor right now.'

'On the contrary,' said Don. 'Does she have a sumptuous bosom? Julia's away, Victor's in need of some delightful and compliant company.'

What a Pandarus. Mind you, thought Lisa, Victor on form was almost irresistible. Even if he was old enough to be Fanny's father. It might take her mind off that ridiculous Gerry character and his unscrupulous girlfriend; Claudia, stealer of lovers, saucepans and valuable pictures.

She didn't want to think about anyone called Claudia.

CHAPTER 20

Toby had been listening for Fanny to come back, and he called out as soon as he heard the front door open and close.

'Fanny?'

There was no reply, but a dripping Fanny, clad from head to foot in a nasty plastic mac, opened the office door and stood there.

Toby closed his eyes in pain. 'Fanny! Where did you get that horrible item? From a sex shop, one would hazard a guess. The section catering for cling-film fiends, perhaps?'

'From a stall in Oxford Street,' said Fanny, extricating herself from its clammy folds. She sank into a sofa. 'Phew, it's hot out there. Hot and wet. Jungly.'

'Hardly surprising in that garment of yours. Now, Fanny . . .'

'Now, I'm going to get myself a long cold drink,' said Fanny, pushing herself forward ready for a heave off the sofa.

Toby pushed her back with a surprisingly strong arm. 'No,' he said. 'Wait a minute. Lisa rang.'

'Oh?'

'She says, did you read archaeology at university?'

Fanny looked puzzled. 'Yes, I did. Why does Lisa want to know that? Is she job-hunting for me? I wish she wouldn't, I hate owing her.'

'That remark shows your immaturity,' said Toby severely. 'You don't owe her, she's just helping out. Be grateful. One day you'll return the favour.'

'Oh, very likely,' said Fanny. 'I can just see that.'

'It seems,' said Toby, who was much intrigued by the whole business, 'that they have made some discoveries down in Heartset.'

He paused for a reaction. Fanny just stared at him. 'And?' she prompted. 'What kind of discoveries? Vicar has sex orgy on graves? Mrs Tootle at the shop is carried away by aliens?'

Toby was affronted. 'Really, Fanny, you have got a sordid mind. We're talking old here. Roman, they think.'

'Oh, you mean they've turned up a bit of Samian ware while doing the gardening. It happens all the time. There were quite a few Romans dotted about in that part of the world, if I remember rightly. But it's clean out of my period, you know.'

'What?'

'I specialised in the early bronze age. Anyway, what do they want to know?'

'We aren't talking a few sherds here, duckie. More like walls and silver plates, and heaven knows what else besides. It's terribly, terribly exciting. All got to be kept under wraps, of course,' he added.

'If they've found a cache, they don't need me, they need to tell the authorities,' said Fanny, giving her left shin a good scratch.

Toby's expression grew more pained. 'Must you rasp?' he said. 'Now, why don't you give Lisa a ring? She can explain.' He pulled a phone out of his drawer and handed it to Fanny with a flourish. 'And there's the number,' he said, passing her a slip of paper, with numbers written in exquisite italic form. 'You just have a little chat.'

Toby stood listening outside in the hall for a few seconds, and then opened one of the doors to a tall cupboard. A moment's reflection, and he decided on a bulgy bag in navy. This he took to Fanny's room, where he deposited it on the bed.

Back to the office, where Fanny was still on the phone, a perplexed look on her face.

'Buonamici? Yes, I went to some of his seminars. He teaches at Cambridge now, at Wenceslaus. Well, you could ring him up and explain . . . Yes, I do see that it would be better to make sure. All right. No, it's okay, really it is.'

'I've put a bag on your bed,' said Toby. 'Seeing as how that snake used yours to cart away her stolen goodies along with your man. I'll find a map, and rustle up a sandwich or two for the journey.'

Fanny said not to bother, that she'd stop on the way, but Toby was firm. His memories of his journey down with Philip were fresh in his mind. 'Take it from me, best to have your own sustenance.'

'It won't take that long, surely?'

Toby looked at the clock on his desk. Being of an original

design, it took him a little while to calculate what the loops and spirals meant, timewise, but it seemed to be ten past eleven.

'You should get there some time after three, if you're lucky.'

'Four hours? It can't take that long; it's less than two hundred miles.'

'Wait till you see the roads for the last forty miles or so. Not to mention the tractors, the level crossings, the cows, and for all I know, the annual Thrubmet Magna goose race. And you can't pretend your car is a fast one.'

Fanny, under the impression that she was saving the environment, drove a Deux Chevaux.

'You should be there in time for tea,' said Toby encouragingly. 'Even allowing for getting lost several times, which you will.'

'Tea?' said Fanny.

'Tea. An institution there, so Guy told me.'

'Guy?'

Toby's face took on an almost mystical expression. 'Guy. God, he's gorgeous. We're going to get together sometime when he's in London.'

'That kind of gorgeous,' said Fanny.

'Beauty is beauty,' said Toby. 'And I gather there's lots of scope for all tastes with that particular family. Watch out for Victor, he's a big, demanding type, lots of go in him, one gathers.'

'I'm off men,' said Fanny sadly.

'Victor will do you the world of good. Now run along and pack, and make sure you take all those delicious clothes you bought.'

Fanny showed her surprise. 'What, for the depths of the country, and a muddy field with bits of fallen-down barn in it?'

'Is that what you reckon? You could be surprised,' said Toby. 'Magic, that place, so you just do as Uncle Toby tells you, and pack some nice things.'

He could see doubt and stubbornness creeping on to Fanny's face. 'Just think if it were a really big find,' he said cunningly.

Fanny hesitated. 'It's not very likely,' she said, weakening.

'The regret, if you missed it. And if it's a wonderful find, you'll need to look smart, think of the publicity there'll be.'

Fanny sighed.

'It's something new, Fanny. New place, new people. Who knows what could come of it?'

'Nothing, I should think,' said Fanny dolefully. 'You don't want me here,' she added.

'Too right,' said Toby to himself, as she trailed off to pack.

'No, Rudi,' said Toby twiddling the aerial on his phone. 'Fanny is not going to drive into a tree. Or another car, or lose her way and find herself in Scotland.'

Rudi wasn't convinced. 'She'll start crying. They'll play something sad on the radio, and she'll be off. Why, there's that piece by Albinoni, that Adagio; well, I only have to think of it and I weep. Yes, weep. What if they play that?'

'Self preservation,' said Toby. 'Basic human instinct, not to drive into, under or through things.'

'She may feel she has nothing to live for.'

'She has plenty to live for. You can see she's curious about this discovery they've made down there.'

'That's to do with the mind, not the heart.'

'You underestimate how strong an emotion inquisitiveness is. It involves both heart and mind, and you take my word for it, Fanny isn't going to do away with herself until she's had a look.'

That wasn't the end of Rudi's concern. 'It'll be depressing for her to be with that family.'

'What, observing a happy marriage at close quarters? Thinking of what might have been?' Toby gave a rude laugh. 'I don't think that's very likely.'

'No, no, being at close quarters with those screwed-up people, it's enough to put anyone into therapy.'

'They aren't screwed-up,' said Toby indignantly.

'Built on glass, that marriage,' said Rudi cynically. 'You mark my words.'

'I'm an optimist,' said Toby. 'Speak to you later, bye.'

'I shall never be optimistic again,' said Fanny tragically, as she dragged her bag across the hall.

Toby went over to give her a hand. 'God almighty, Fanny, what have you got in here?' He unzipped it before she could stop him. 'Books! Fanny, are you mad?' He pulled out a couple of fat tomes. 'Poetry. Definitely, absolutely not. Last thing you need, sighing over a lot of heart-rending poems.'

'I like poetry. I went out and bought them specially.'

'Give me the bill,' said Toby.

'What?'

'They're going back, all of them. No poetry, no gloomy music, no wallowing, Fanny. I'll get a credit note, and when you come back to London you can go round and pick out some juicy reads. Or cookbooks, or accounts of single-handed Atlantic crossings. Anything, but not this. Wordsworth, indeed. What a really, really bad idea. Honestly, Fanny, you're not fit to be out on your own.'

Fanny was too bruised to fight Toby's bossiness. He staunched her tears, thrust packets of paper tissues into her hand and ushered her down the steps to her car. Then he slung the now much lighter bag into the back, and closed the car door in his precise way.

'Got that map?'

Fanny nodded, not trusting herself to speak.

'Off you go, then. And do cheer up, Fanny. The last thing Lisa needs right now is a Dismal Daisy drooping about the place.'

A final howl and a screech of gears, and the little car trundled off.

'Goodness,' Toby said to the cat as he darted back into the house. 'Such trauma. Now, what I need is a stiff drink. Then I'll settle down to some peaceful work, such bliss on my own, at least for a few days. And,' he went on, as he stretched out luxuriously on Lisa's large sofa for a few minutes' rest and relaxation, the cat beside him, 'it's nice to know that Lisa's out of trouble. No chance of Philip getting up to whatever he has been getting up to, not while he's down in the depths of Heartset, isn't that right, puss?'

CHAPTER 21

Hester waylaid Don as he and Lisa came out of the library. 'Who's staying at Heartwell House?' she asked him. 'Anyone we know?'

Lisa was amused to see that calm Hester was as interested in her neighbour's doings as the rest of them.

'No,' said Don. 'Never seen her before.'

'Young?' Lisa asked, as Hester went on her way.

'Mmm,' said Don.

'You're hiding something, Don.'

He swung round and looked straight at her. 'I'll tell you what's lurking at Heartwell House. A loin-stirrer. A come-hitherer of the most basic and mesmeric kind. Huge, burning eyes and a sensuous hunger that sucks at your soul.'

'Are you serious?'

He nodded.

'What does this astonishing creature look like?' Lisa said, quite crossly. 'Blonde and big tits? Just right for Victor?'

'Victor is never vulgar,' said Don reproachfully. 'No, she's quite elegant, in a very sexy way. It isn't overt, she's quite thin, no particular figure. Not beautiful, but a compelling face. Not unlike you in colouring, actually, Lisa. But taller, and well, just . . . ' Don shrugged and made an expressive gesture with his hands. 'Well, you know.'

Lisa hated her.

'What is this piece of exotica doing in these parts?'

'Heaven knows,' said Don. 'However, I have a strong feeling she may be going to head in this direction. After she'd given me the quick once over – I've never been undressed by a woman's eyes like that before, do you know that?'

'Get to the point,' Lisa said coldly.

'Ah, yes,' he said. 'Anyway, she asked who I was, and when I said I was a Cordovan, she said, from Heartsease? I said yes, and she was very interested. Was it far? Were there many people staying there?'

'Nosy,' Lisa said. 'Perhaps she's a private detective, and those burning eyes are on the lookout for scandal and sin.'

'Mock not,' said Don. 'I'm impervious to such charms, because I don't have a fancy to be sucked dry and left for dead, however great the intervening pleasure. Others may not see her in that light. They may not have my experience.'

'Lucky for you.'

'Indeed.'

'So you think this piece of virtue is going to turn up on Victor's doorstep, touting for trade?'

'Touting doesn't come into it. I suspect she has a victim all lined up and waiting.'

'You're being fanciful, Don. What's her name? So that I can avoid her if she does turn up?'

'You won't have any doubt, not after my masterful description,' said Don. 'She's unmistakable. And very dangerous; I speak as one wise in these matters.'

'And called?'

He didn't need to tell Lisa, of course. She knew.

'Claudia.'

CHAPTER 22

Lisa had taken her work and specs and a jug of Maria's special lemon cocktail out on to the terrace. There was a slight breeze, so she looked around for something to weigh her papers down. There were some glossy pebbles lurking round the base of a palm; they would do. So much at Heartsease was larger than life, she thought, looking up into the extravagant leaves of the palm.

She settled down to work, but it was hard to concentrate, with the summer noises buzzing about in the sun, and the sound of excited diggers' voices drifting up from the sunken garden.

Philip had gone back to his horses, with Polly for company. It was perfectly obvious that he was planning to ride, but he brushed aside Lisa's concern.

'If I feel up to it, I'll do it, otherwise I won't.'

'Go on, then. Fall off a bloody horse, and make yourself really ill.'

'You're being hysterical. If I fall off, it'll hurt like hell, so what? In any case, I'm not going to fall off. I very seldom have a fall.'

'It's different with one eye.'

Philip didn't need both eyes, his single-eyed scornful look was quite sufficient.

Lisa wondered if Philip had smiled since he came to Heartsease. Not while she was around, in any case. He might be full of mirth and merriment down among the horses, who could tell? But then, he'd been distant for weeks. If anything, he was better when he was in hospital. No man's land, she supposed.

Polly glared at her mother, hating her for antagonising Philip, as she saw it. She was too young to realise that it was Philip who was behaving strangely, not Lisa. Polly sensed things weren't right, and loathed it.

'There's a really wild stallion,' she went on, at her most

aggressive. 'Daddy won't ride him, no one can. He won't let anyone near him.'

'I might buy him,' said Philip. 'Good line.'

No asking what Lisa was working on, what else she was going to do, whether she'd like to come and see the horses. Not interested; the message came across very clearly.

And that wasn't like Philip at all. Philip was inquisitive, had a keen interest in other people's doings.

Philip was feeling guilty, Lisa was sure of it. Some men would be over the top with kindness and little attentions. Others would provoke flaming rows, so that they could justify whatever it was they were up to.

Not Philip. Philip's way was to pretend that he and his wife were indifferent strangers, thrown together by chance.

Philip was up to some serious mischief.

Lisa sighed and went back to the text she was working on, reading the same lines for the tenth time, making no sense of them. This was a 3D book of a city, the first of a series. It could have been a city in a distant galaxy for anything she knew. Or cared.

She gave up, shuffling her papers together in an unruly way and banging her specs down on top of the pile. She stood, yawned, stretched. The day had shed its mists and high cloud, and was as perfect as you could ever get in the English countryside. She strolled along the terrace, looking out over the wide grass ride which stretched away from the house, up the hill.

A turn, another view, and there was the sea, an inviting silvery glimmer in the distance. The wind must have been blowing from that direction, because there was a tang of salt and seaweed on the breeze.

Lisa decided to go for a walk. She would exercise the fidgets and the worries away.

First stop, the sunken garden.

It was extraordinary how much mess one man and a boy could make in such a short time. It was also extraordinary how harmoniously they seemed to work together, Victor issuing instructions in his commanding way, Alec challenging everything he said while getting on and doing it.

They were discussing Roman footwear. Alec was well up in this, he'd recently done a project on Roman clothes. Victor wasn't having any of it.

'Extremely sensible chaps, these Romans. You wouldn't have found them poncing about in strappy sandals. No, no, much more like boots, think of the marches.'

'That was soldiers,' said Alec, chest deep in yet another hole. 'Fifty miles a day, forced marches were. Imagine! With packs weighing fifty pounds on their backs. About twenty-five kilos.'

Victor wasn't interested in kilos, and he was sticking to his point. 'Sturdy chaps, must have been. Not tall; well, the Italians aren't, are they? But plenty of muscles, kept themselves in good trim.'

'They lived on vegetables, mostly,' said Alec.

'Are you telling me that Roman soldiers, centurions, legionnaires, tough guys like that, were vegetarians? Nutburgers for dinner, and feeling sorry for the poor little lambs in the fields? Not very likely, when you think about it. Absolute rubbish, in fact.'

'But true,' Alec muttered into his ditch. Then he saw Lisa. 'Hi, Mum.'

'I hate to interrupt your labours,' she said, 'but don't you think it would be better to pause until Fanny gets here? In case what you're doing isn't exactly what the experts want?'

Victor frowned. 'The more we uncover, the more she's got to go on. Besides, she won't be here much before tea. We can't waste all that time, got to get on.'

In proof of which he hurled several shovelfuls of earth into the air at great speed.

'What about the fish?' Lisa asked. 'Won't they be getting bored in the tank and longing for their pond in the sun?'

Victor went on shovelling. 'Don's coming over, going to give Jarvis a hand fixing it. Should have done it this morning, but he's got to spray or something. Full of chemicals, that wine he makes, if you ask me.'

Alec couldn't let that pass. He told Victor more about grapes and fungal attacks and wilts than Victor could possibly want to know. But Victor took it in good part. 'Amazing, what this boy's head is stuffed with,' he said genially. 'Far too much education they get these days. Never taught us about grapes when I was at school.'

'He did a project on it,' Lisa said weakly.

'Keep 'em ignorant, stick to the classics and maths,' said Victor. 'Fit them for anything. And music,' he added unexpectedly. 'Can't do without music if you're going to call yourself civilised.'

What a surprising man Victor was.

'Do you play anything?' he called across to Alec.

'The oboe,' said Alec, peering over a pile of earth.

'Excellent,' said Victor. 'You can have a tootle while you're here. I shall enjoy that.'

Lisa gave up her attempts to save Roman this-and-thats for posterity, and turned her nose towards the sea.

She had taken her watch off when she was working on the terrace. Trying to work, that is. So as the afternoon went on, she had no idea what time it was. She had walked for what seemed like miles along rutted lanes between high and ancient hedges, following the smell and the sound and the occasional sight of the sea. Then the ground underfoot became sandy, the grass dry and tufty, and the path she was on narrowed and went down in a series of zig zags to a deserted cove.

An idyllic place, a cove from childhood, with rocks and enticing pools and a curve of sand. She took off her shoes and padded down to the water's edge. It was calm, and greeny-blue, with idle little waves toppling over in fragments of foam. Gulls mewed overhead; behind her, insects buzzed.

The water wasn't as cold as she had expected. In her childhood, Lisa had bathed off the icy coasts of the north, where even on the hottest summer days a chill breath hung over the sands. There was none of that there in the cove. I must bring the children, she thought. They would love it; even Polly might find it pleasant enough to forget her endless woes and worries for a few pleasurable hours. We could bring a picnic.

How her life had been turned upside down, all in a matter of days. Who was this Claudia? Where had Philip and Rory met her? Anywhere; for all Lisa knew, she was a waitress at their club. Not very likely, she told herself, remembering the waitresses she had seen on her rare visits there.

Philip's life, she would have said until recently, was an open book. Home, work, more work, home. Evenings out together, to the theatre, to see a film. Dinner with friends, often at a restaurant. Rarely at home; Philip disliked dinner parties. Visits to Titia.

He took time off work for the children, arriving with perfect punctuality at school plays, parents' evenings and other events.

Although he had missed recently, when he had failed to turn up for Polly's sports day. He'd apologised afterwards, but it was the first time it had happened. Polly had noticed, and stored it away in her growing file of evidence that Something was Wrong. Too many of her friends came from split families; she had a terror of Lisa and Philip parting.

Rightly so. Of course they weren't about to go their separate ways, Lisa told herself forcefully.

Or were they? It only took one to go a separate way, and the deed was done.

Lisa moodily draped a strand of seaweed over her toes; it had been washed up at her feet by a rogue wave. It smelt salty and fishy and felt rubbery. A symbol of her life. She conceived a mad plan; she would go to this neighbour's house, confront Claudia, assess her, measure her up as an enemy.

Lisa knew quite well it would be pointless. If Claudia was staying nearby, it was for a purpose, and you'd have to be very dense not to guess what that purpose was. No need to stalk out her opponent, she was on her way.

She clambered on to an inviting rock, which had a flat, smooth patch ideal for sitting on. She duly sat, clasping her hands round her knees, relaxing in the hot salty air. Lisa was lucky, she'd inherited her father's dark colouring, which took the sun, rather than her mother's pink and white fairness, which didn't.

Even so, she could feel her skin reddening; time to be going back. For a moment she imagined staying there, on that tiny beach, camping alone and untroubled under a cloudless, starry sky.

In reality, the midges would bite, the tide would come up, the night air would be cold and damp, and no doubt weasels and stoats would come down from those woods to prowl around.

No, time to get back and face the human weasel that was prowling about their bedroom door.

CHAPTER 23

Don was attacking a row of vines with vicious delight, but he paused when he heard the familiar throb and roar of Harry's bike.

'Zoë gone into labour?' he enquired, pulling off his mask and drawing his arm across a perspiring brow.

'No, no. Far too soon,' said Harry.

'I want to know what it's like being an uncle,' said Don. 'My range of relationships is painfully limited. Brother, yes. Far too much so, when you think of it. Eight is excessive. I am also a grandson, and a nephew, and that's it.'

'Get yourself a wife,' said Harry. 'Much to recommend it. Then you can be a husband and a father.'

'And an adulterer and a divorcé, and possibly even a widower,' said Don cynically.

'That reminds me,' said Harry. 'I met a piece of perfection, an houri, a vision from one's dreams – or, possibly, nightmares – this morning while calling in at Heartwell. She's staying at Heartwell House. A widow, so village rumour has it. She wants me to pick her up this afternoon and convey her to Heartsease.'

'Why?' said Don.

Harry shrugged. 'Who knows? Wants to call on the squire, perhaps. Has heard of Guy's astonishing looks and wants to seduce him. Collecting for the widows' and orphans' fund. Mine not to enquire, but to do as I am bid.'

'Why can't she drive herself?' said Don. 'Why does she need to go cadging lifts from you?'

'Apparently she doesn't drive.'

'Doesn't, as in never learned, or as in has too many points on her licence?'

'She told me, in an artless way, that she had never learned to drive, because she'd never found any problem in getting people to take her hither and thither.'

'Such as you.'

'Indeed.'

'Mugs, in fact.'

'Very likely.'

'I'd leave her alone if I were you, Harry,' said Don. 'Speaking as one who has a large acquaintance among women of a sort that you've never acquired.'

'For various reasons.'

'You don't want to upset Zoë at this delicate stage.'

'No,' said Harry, a tinge of regret in his voice. 'There is that, of course. But she really is something.'

'Cat among the pigeons is what she'll be if she calls at the Hall. You couldn't forget to pick her up, I suppose?'

'I think she'd simply find someone else to take her,' said Harry. 'I get the impression that she's a single-minded type, and what she wants, she gets.'

'I very much fear that you're right,' said Don. 'Well, I'd better get on with this; clearly reinforcements are going to be necessary, so it's tea at the big house today.'

'Pa said you were going to give Jarvis a hand with the pool.'

'Oh, hell, yes, I forgot.'

'I'll tell the houri that I'll have to take her back to Heartwell by six as I have other commitments. That's only an hour, there's no harm in an hour.'

Don gave a derisive whoosh of his spray, Harry pulled his helmet back on, and the peaceful sounds of the countryside were heard once more as the generator and a two-cylinder engine surged into action.

'Where's Lisa?' asked Victor, as he helped Alec to a generous helping of potato salad. 'No, no, you can manage all this, you're a growing lad. Guy, go and see if she's on the terrace.'

'She isn't,' said Alec with his mouth full. 'I looked.'

'Alec, if you're going to eat like that, you can go outside,' said Philip. 'Stuffing food into your mouth.'

Alec went scarlet, and choked on a spring onion.

'Leave the boy alone,' said Victor. 'Nothing wrong with the way he eats.'

'He's not fit to be in company,' said Philip coldly.

Polly looked up anxiously from her small plate of cucumber and tomato salad. She hated it when Philip and Alec argued. Which seemed to be all the time, these days.

Hester noticed her anxiety, as she noticed everything, and she moved Alec away from his father's line of vision. 'Lisa went for a walk,' she said. 'I expect she went further than she had intended. There's no problem, since it's a cold lunch, she can have some when she gets back.'

'She won't want it,' said Polly. 'She doesn't eat much these days.'

'A country walk will give her an appetite,' said Hester.

'Bloody rude,' said Philip, determined to get worked up about something. 'Guests shouldn't just walk off without saying when they'll be back. It's most inconsiderate, quite busy enough in the kitchen, I expect, without my wife giving them all extra trouble.'

'It's no trouble at all,' said Hester. 'I would feel ashamed if Lisa didn't feel she could wander off when she wants.'

'There aren't any cliffs or anything, are there?' said Alec.

'Your mother's a sensible woman,' said Victor heartily. 'Far too much sense to go dropping off cliffs.'

Alec looked unconvinced, and nibbled at some home-cured ham in an unenthusiastic way.

'None of that,' said Victor. 'Stop fretting, we've never lost a visitor yet.'

'I don't like the tension,' said Guy, as he carefully washed and rinsed the crystal in the sink, a green apron protecting his immaculate trousers from stray splashes. Not that there were any, Guy was quick and neat in his ways and rarely spilt or splashed anything.

'Tension?' said Maria. She gave the rectangle of pastry set in front of her on its marble slab a half turn. 'What tension?'

'The Mafficks,' said Guy.

'He is a sick man, such an accident,' said Maria, waving her rolling pin for emphasis. 'It takes time to get over this, and the pain makes him bad-tempered, perhaps.'

'Perhaps,' said Guy. 'I think it's more than that. I think he's got something on his mind. And he isn't nice to Lisa, not at all. Very hostile, I should say. They weren't like this at all last time they came.'

'A lot can happen in two years.'

113

'He's very harsh with Alec, too.'

'Fathers with sons of that age are always harsh,' said Maria. 'Like old bulls and young ones.'

'Philip Maffick is hardly a bull.'

'All men are bulls,' said Maria, slapping her pastry into shape. 'Or think they are. No doubt this Philip has been up to something, or maybe he thinks Lisa has, or he wants her to do something which she doesn't want to do. Or he has lost his skill in bed, with only one eye, and this makes him cross.'

'I hardly think an eye would affect him like that,' said Guy.

'Men and women, and what goes on in bed between them, what do you know about it?' said Maria with scorn.

'Enough to know when there's trouble brewing,' said Guy with foreboding.

Lisa went back to the Hall a different way. Not intentionally, but because she could see the old house in its superb setting on the hillside, and she thought another lane would be a more direct route. In fact, it brought her out among rows of vines, a Mediterranean sight in this most English of landscapes.

There was a strange figure working among the vines. Neither English nor Mediterranean looking.

A Martian, Lisa decided.

The Martian unravelled his hose and spray and face guard and protective clothing and turned into Don, red-faced and breathing deeply.

'Lisa,' he said, with that lurking smile. He wiped his brow and upper lip. 'You look hot and tired, and so do I. Let's go up to my house and have a glass of wine. And I can tell you the latest on the harpy.'

'Oh.'

'Bad news, I'm afraid. She's on her way to the Hall. For tea.'

'For tea?' said Lisa, stunned. Then she began to laugh. 'How very proper.'

CHAPTER 24

She had the most compelling eyes Lisa had ever seen.

Stunning eyes; dramatic, sparkling with life. Don was right, you wouldn't call her beautiful. Not even obviously attractive, not at a passing glance. But as soon as Lisa saw those eyes, she knew that this was big trouble.

And the utterly charming way she flirted with Lisa's husband. She was devouring him with her attention, her eyes fixed on his, her body leaning towards him.

And the completely charmless way he responded, lapping her up, his single eye hazy with desire for her.

Yuk.

'Claudia,' he said, putting out a hand to touch her arm. 'How good to see you. How kind of you to come.'

Had Lisa been less well brought up, she would have made being sick noises. Look at him sitting there, she thought crossly. Gooey-eyed, heedless of his wife and children. He was totally taken in by this woman's wiles and guiles.

No woman would have been deceived for a moment. Lisa could tell at once what Claudia was.

Claudia moved on, leaving Philip dangling breathless on her hook. She had a caressing remark for Victor, a warm, inviting smile for Harry, a come-hither flash of her long eyelashes for Don's benefit.

Alec, even, was gazing at her with undisguised admiration, thoughts too old for his tender years making his blood stir. And Claudia was happy to draw him into her net, with a teasing word, a warm glance of her lovely eyes.

Hester might seem lost in domesticity, but she was no fool, and Lisa could see that one glance had told her what Claudia was up to. And Polly, well, her glare would have stopped anyone else in their tracks. Bravo, Polly, thought Lisa. You may only be ten, but you can suss out what's what.

Claudia was so secure of her sensuous appeal, her youth, her charisma, that she clearly felt no need to win the approval or liking of other women. In that she was unlike others of her kind Lisa had met over the years. They often seemed almost as fond of their women friends as the men in their lives.

Lisa was prepared to bet anything that Claudia had no women friends.

Claudia took a cup of tea from Hester, murmuring her thanks without looking at her. Her eyes were on Philip.

'She has ugly feet,' hissed a voice in Lisa's ear.

She turned to look at Don, who was sitting beside her. To her surprise, he wasn't gazing at Claudia with a doting expression on his face. He merely looked amused. And relaxed; here wasn't a man stiffening his sinews, his stomach muscles and other parts of his anatomy in the presence of a dazzling woman.

Lisa looked at Claudia's feet, encased in soft leather pumps. 'How do you know?' she whispered back. 'They look fine to me.'

'She was barefoot when she answered the door to me at Heartwell,' said Don. 'Ugly feet, believe me.'

'To match her soul,' Lisa said. 'The witch.'

'She's bewitching Harry, but Victor isn't succumbing.'

Now there was a surprise. If ever there was a man susceptible to feminine charms, it was Victor. He had an immediate and robust way with women, if he could get away with it, but was also prepared to lay siege over quite a long time. All this while keeping Julia at bay; you had to admire him for it.

But Don was right. Victor was enjoying Claudia's tricks, you could see that, but it was as a connoisseur, not as one who would like to draw up his chair and sup at that particular table. Unlike Harry, whose dark eyes under his slanting brows showed more than passing interest.

'It's too bad of Harry,' Lisa said. 'With a pregnant wife.' Lucky Zoë, not to be here, seeing Harry leering at Claudia in that obvious fashion, she thought.

Don sighed. 'Don't be naive. Wives, pregnant or otherwise, don't come into this.'

How right he was. She'd never seen Philip look so besotted. All right, she had. But not in these circumstances; had he no pride?

'No room for pride where types like this Claudia are concerned,' said Don, sotto voce. 'She expects and gets total attention, total devotion; she's the sort who wants to own a man body and soul.'

'You're making me come out in gooseflesh,' Lisa said.

Don looked at her arm. 'So I am,' he said. 'And is your stomach churning?'

She nodded. It was.

'Flight or fight?' Don said with a particularly wicked smile. 'Which is it to be?'

He was enjoying all this.

Lisa wasn't.

Guy replenished the teapot with a flourish and a quick, contemptuous glance at Claudia. Naturally, Guy was impervious to Claudia's attractions, and despite Claudia's flicker of interest when she first saw Guy, she had soon realised that this was no prey for her.

The chug-chug of a car drifted through the window. That would be Fanny, thought Lisa. Only Fanny's car sounded like that.

Guy glanced out of the long windows which ran along one side of the splendid drawing room, and was out of the door in a flash. As Fanny's disreputable vehicle drew to a halt, Guy was there, helping Fanny out, removing her bag from the boot.

Lisa didn't recognise Fanny for a moment. Her hair! What an improvement. Clothes that fitted. Well-cut trousers, a silk top. Lisa blessed Toby, as she got up to welcome Fanny as she came across the room.

Fanny went white, an apology dying on her lips as she saw who was sitting beside Philip on the sofa.

Literally, and that was something Lisa had never seen happen before. Don took one look, and sprang to his feet, reaching her just in time to tuck a supporting arm under her elbow before she crumpled to the ground. He guided her to a seat.

'Claudia,' she said in an icy and despairing whisper.

Claudia wasn't in the least perturbed. 'Oh, hi, Fanny. What are you doing here?'

'Blatant,' said Guy, banging the tray down on the table in a most uncharacteristic way.

'What?'

'Who,' said Guy, lips pursed. 'That woman. Claudia, she calls herself. A whore, nothing more or less. That's what she is.' He

117

opened and shut several cupboard doors very rapidly and noisily, to show the strength of his feeling.

'Ha.' Maria was intrigued. 'Is she a guest?'

'Not here, thankfully,' said Guy. 'At least,' he added, 'not yet. I wouldn't be at all surprised if she moved in. I wouldn't be surprised if when I took the Mafficks their morning tea, she was in bed there with him and Lisa was outside in the passage, on the floor.'

Maria made a very Spanish noise, indicative of shock and horror.

'Where is she now, this *puta*?' enquired Maria, as she crafted little pastry shells with deft fingers.

'Gone back to Heartwell,' said Guy. 'Harry took her, on his bike. I think she expected Victor to offer to drive her back, but he didn't. Too much sense, Victor. I expect she's had her hands all over Harry by now.'

Maria didn't like the sound of that. 'He is married, now, with a young wife. A pregnant wife. How can he do this?'

'She's bewitched him. In passing, mind you. Of course, the one she's really after is Philip Maffick.'

'He is ill.'

'It makes no difference.'

'He has a wife, two young children.'

'And so?'

'*Ave Maria purissima*, such wickedness. What is the world coming to?'

'I tell you, Maria, if this Claudia is the one I think she is, there's worse than that to her.'

'No!'

'Yes,' said Guy.

Claudia was discontented as Harry zoomed along the lanes to Heartwell. This wasn't what she had planned or expected. Victor Cordovan, who should have been a walkover, was almost unfriendly. Then he had been all over Fanny, boring on about Romans, how rude, when she was there. And no chance to be alone with Philip, not with his nasty, sharp-eyed wife watching them like a gaoler.

Claudia dismounted outside Heartwell House, and handed the helmet back to Harry.

There was always Harry. She gave him a charming smile. 'Come inside,' she said. 'There's no one here but me.'

Harry followed her in through the door, to be brought up short by the uncompromising figure of Mrs Slubs, who did for several of the houses thereabouts. She had her hands placed on substantial hips.

'Good evening,' she said. 'You'll be wanting to get back to your wife, Harry, that you will, before she starts worriting about where you might be. It's not right for a lady in her condition to fret and carry on, so you just get back there on your scooter outside, and make sure she have a proper meal. She do need good victuals the way she is.'

Lisa was left comforting Fanny while an impatient Victor kept on popping his head round the door, eager for Fanny to come out and be an archaeologist. Finally he could bear it no longer, and surged into the room.

'Now, now. What's going on?' he said, offering the gulping Fanny a large, blue-spotted handkerchief.

'That woman who was here' – Lisa couldn't bring herself to mention her name – 'ran off with Fanny's boyfriend.'

There was a wail from Fanny.

'They were going to be married,' Lisa explained. 'Wedding arranged, house chosen, children planned. Then *she* got her hooks into Gerry and off he went.'

'Ho,' said Victor in a deep and disapproving voice. 'A delicious number, I can tell that at a glance, but she belongs in a brothel, not in one's sitting-room.'

Fanny howled even more; Lisa supposed she didn't like having to face the fact that Gerry had gone off with a slut, however glamorous and beautiful. And Victor wasn't quite right there, in Lisa's opinion. Claudia was too focused to be a mere slut.

And what about the picture? 'She must be short of money,' Lisa said.

'She isn't,' said Fanny, subsiding under Victor's vigorous pats and strokes into a series of depressing sniffs. 'She's terribly rich, although that doesn't stop her being really grasping. Her husband died, and left her a lot of money, and she already had some from her father. He was a Thackeray, and very wealthy.'

'I expect she poisoned him,' Lisa said.

'What, her father?' said Victor, intrigued.

'Maybe,' Lisa said. 'I was thinking of the husband, actually.'

Fanny seemed to be marginally less tearful, so Lisa drew Victor away. 'Give her a few moments, Victor, she needs to pull herself together.'

'Time is short,' said Victor. 'We need her in the trenches.'

Lisa's mind was elsewhere. 'What I'd like to know is why I've never come across this Claudia before. If she's been drifting around London, rich and well-connected, and making off with people's boyfriends – and husbands, clearly – I should have heard about her.'

'She's been abroad,' said Fanny, who had reached the hic-coughing stage.

Victor cast an expert eye over her and went across to where some decanters stood on the side. He poured out a generous brandy. 'Drink up,' he said. 'All in one go, there's a good girl.'

Victor was so large and avuncular and sympathetic, that Lisa could see Fanny was about to go off again. 'Yes, it'll do you good,' she said quickly.

'I don't drink spirits,' said Fanny dolefully.

'Oh, yes, you do,' said Victor, and such was the power of his personality that Fanny drank the brandy in obedient silence, looking rather startled as it glided down her throat.

She gave a belch, and looked surprised. 'That was wonderful,' she said, holding out her glass for more.

'Just a drop,' said Victor. 'You can have some more when you've been round the site.'

'Abroad?' Lisa said. 'Where?'

'America,' said Fanny. 'Or Australia, maybe. She went off with a tycoon. He was going to marry her, but then he didn't, so she came back.'

'Wonder who that was?' said Victor, interested. 'Lucky escape, if you ask me.'

'He's in a home,' said Fanny. 'He had a breakdown.'

'Hardly surprising,' said Lisa.

CHAPTER 25

Victor had led a slightly woozy Fanny away to his earthy heaps. He'd urged Lisa to come, 'You must be in on this, Lisa,' but she had a more disagreeable encounter ahead of her than one with ancient Romans.

Philip.

He'd buggered off, of course he had. To the horses, possibly, but she thought she'd try their room first.

There he was, stretched out on the bed, murmuring into the phone. No prizes for guessing who he was talking to.

Lisa yanked the phone away from him, told the husky little voice at the other end to fuck off, and sat down hard on the bed.

'Really, Lisa,' said Philip, in his coldest voice. 'You know that hurts my eye. And why do you have to be so bloody rude, bursting in here when I'm on the phone? Let alone making obscene remarks to my friends.'

'I didn't burst in here, I came into my bedroom through the door, in a perfectly normal way.'

'Angrily,' said Philip unemotionally. He had shut his un-bandaged eye, and lay there in a world of his own.

Lisa wanted to hit him.

She didn't. 'You were talking to Claudia.'

'You were so offensive, getting Victor to hustle the poor woman out of the house like that. She's all on her own at Heartwell; Gareth and Lori are away for several days. She would have liked to stay to dinner.'

'No doubt Lori doesn't trust Gareth to be in the same house as Claudia for five minutes.'

'You always were spiteful,' said Philip. 'Spiteful and petty-minded.'

'Unlike warm-hearted Claudia.'

'I'm not prepared to talk about Claudia. She's a very good

friend, she's been through an awful lot, and she needs sympathy and understanding, not your open hostility.'

'What has she been through?' Lisa asked. 'The trauma of running away with Fanny's boyfriend?'

'Claudia is a beautiful woman,' said Philip, still in that flat voice as though he was a teacher addressing a dull class. 'Naturally, men throw themselves at her. It doesn't mean she encourages it. Or likes them to do it.'

'No?'

'Don't be sarcastic, Lisa,' he said annoyingly. 'It doesn't suit you. Now, I'd be grateful if you'd leave me alone, because I'm feeling tired.'

'Bet you are,' Lisa said under her breath. Then, aloud, 'In that case, I'll draw the curtains and turn the lights off. And I'll take the phone with me, you won't want to be disturbed, will you?'

That was one thing to be grateful for. Philip couldn't drive, and was too weak to walk; there was no way he could get himself over to Heartwell House, which was clearly what he would have liked to do.

It crossed Lisa's mind that he might try to slink out and get a taxi. Poor man, he needed his rest. So she thoughtfully removed the key from the door, and silently thanking Hester for her good housekeeping, which meant that the locks were all oiled and efficient, she quietly locked the door behind her.

Lisa had a lot on her mind that evening, and Polly was so subdued she wondered if she was going to be ill. Nonetheless, dinner was a feast, and a joyous feast at that.

'You see,' said Victor, drawing the cork out of a bottle of champagne with firm-fingered ease. 'I was right. Now, all you Jeremiahs, you doubting Thomases, drink up, celebrate.'

'Pour a libation, first,' said Don, sprinkling some frothy drops on to the floor. 'One, two, three; this world, the underworld, and the one up there. Best to keep them placated, don't you think?'

Polly watched, startled, as he poured some more into the long stemmed glass and handed it to her. 'First sip for you, Pol,' he said. 'Being the youngest and so on.'

Lisa managed a discreet word with Fanny. 'Is it anything serious, this site?'

Fanny's eyes were shining. The lure of a find, and the pleasure in using her expertise had vanquished her lamentations for Gerry, at least for the moment.

'Amazing,' she said. 'I can't believe it. Mind you, Victor shouldn't have gone on beavering away, but he's struck gold.'

'Gold?'

'Figuratively,' said Victor.

'There's Roman masonry, all right,' said Fanny. 'And from what I've seen, I think he's unearthed what's going to be a big site.'

'Fishbourne?' asked Alec.

Fanny laughed. 'No, Alec. Fishbourne was a palace, and I should think what you've got here is a prosperous villa. Just as much worth finding.'

'So what happens now?' Lisa asked, drinking her champagne rather too quickly, hoping to dull the ache inside her.

'I've rung Salvatore,' she said. 'He wasn't in, but I left a message.'

'The tops, Fanny says,' said Victor with simple pride. 'She'll have got him really excited, he'll be here tomorrow, driving down first thing, I dare say. Ah, Hester,' he went on, 'we'll need a room for Dr Buonamici. A *good* room.'

'When's he coming?' asked Hester in her calm way.

'Soon, soon,' said Victor.

Guy took the bottle away from Victor and handed him another one. 'Excellent,' said Victor. 'And I hope Maria is giving us a specially good dinner tonight; I'm ravenous.' He looked around the assembled company and frowned. 'Philip not joining us?' he asked.

'Philip's not feeling too well this evening,' Lisa said.

'Shall I take him something on a tray?' Guy asked.

'No, he's taken a painkiller, and they make him very sleepy. Best to let him sleep.'

And he would be asleep, because while having that very unsatisfactory conversation with her shut-eyed husband, Lisa had dropped a painkiller and a sleeping tablet into the glass of lemonade beside his bed. Lisa knew he would drink it before long; Philip was a thirsty man.

CHAPTER 26

Lisa couldn't believe her eyes. She was sitting on the deep, curved ledge beneath the window of the tower room, looking out on to a misty landscape. But it wasn't the landscape which held her interest. Closer at hand, completely at her ease, was Claudia, walking along, chatting with Harry as though she had known him all her life.

She was looking, Lisa had to admit, peculiarly fetching in a dress splashed with giant cherries that not one woman in a thousand could carry off. Lisa knew she couldn't; she wasn't tall enough, and she didn't have Claudia's cloud of dark hair, damn her great sultry eyes.

She uncurled a fist, and looked down at where her nails had left little marks in the palm.

Worse and worse.

Not only was Claudia making a beeline for Lisa's husband, but she was leading her to self mutilation.

Lisa wasn't going to have it. Claudia must be got rid of; tipped out of Philip's orbit, sent off with some other hapless man who didn't know a bloodsucker when she was spitting out his flesh.

Gerry. Why couldn't Claudia stay with Gerry? Where was Gerry? If it was a fling, it was a very short one, and what had happened to all Fanny's possessions? And why had Claudia taken all those things? It showed a very grasping nature, as well as a vindictive one. And there was the matter of the Harriety.

Poor Philip. Whatever he'd done in a previous existence, he didn't deserve to end up victim to a Claudia. Mind you, thought Lisa, she had noticed that the nicest men often ended up with awful women. But they were usually awful because they were harridans; or authoritative bossyboots; or drains, those women who leave their husbands, lovers and anyone else who passes by feeling depressed and at odds with the world.

Claudia was none of those types. She was a Lilith. A seducer, a destroyer, a mocker of men. How did Lisa know this? Because you only had to see her drooling over Philip, in full view of his wife, his two children, his oldest friend and assorted others to know what she was.

This was not normal behaviour.

Had she fallen wildly in love with Philip? Was this an all-consuming passion, was he the man for whom she had been endlessly seeking? Was she the embodiment of all Philip's dreams, the ultimate woman?

If so, tough.

Lisa considered herself to be very tolerant, but tolerance has its limits.

Quite suddenly, Lisa made a decision. She would go to London. Then, that very day. She had to get away by herself, and think. And have her hair done, and buy some new clothes . . .

She felt sure the day was going to be hot, once the early-morning mist had burned off, and the prospect of roads clogged with fuming cars and drivers offered little joy. 'I'll drive to Heartsease Station and catch a train there,' she called through into the bathroom where Philip was engaged in the slow process of getting himself up.

'Does Heartsease have a station?' said Philip. 'It seems rather improbable.'

'It does,' said Lisa.

'And the train goes direct to London?' asked Philip, his voice muffled as he tried to track a clear path through the shaving foam liberally applied to his chin.

'No, but there's a good connection at Heartley Junction,' said Lisa. 'Wouldn't an electric shaver be easier?'

Philip didn't answer. He'd always used a razor, and no distorted vision was going to make him change his ways. 'It's only a matter of practice,' he said. 'Getting used to a different perspective.'

Lisa tucked a few more things into a small suitcase and zipped it up.

'How long are you going to be away?'

'A couple of days at most.'

'Oh.'

Not long enough for you to get up to any major mischief, thought Lisa.

'What about the children?'

'Hester is going to keep an eye on them. Polly will be with you mostly, won't she?'

'Um, yes,' said Philip, who had invited Claudia to come for a ride, and didn't want Polly around.

'I'll tell her to stick with you,' said Lisa, who suspected something of the kind.

'Um,' said Philip again.

Lisa dropped a quick kiss on the back of his handsome neck before he could duck, and, pausing only to pick up a book, went to find out where Jarvis had hidden the car.

'Behind the hay bales in the long barn,' she said. 'I see.'

'Wasn't sure if you'd be wanting she,' said Jarvis.

'Well, I am.'

'Going far?'

'To the station.'

'I'll run you there,' said Jarvis. 'Then they bales can stay. That'll be the ten nine you're after.'

'Yes,' said Lisa, realising that she would have to accept Jarvis's offer. She wasn't up on hay bales, but there was a substantial pile of them, and they looked as though they would take some shifting. She looked at her watch. 'How long does it take to get to the station?'

'Don't you go worriting about that,' said Jarvis. 'She's always late, that darned train. And if I sees the train a-rattling along that line, why, I waves to the driver, and then he waits for us.'

Lisa had her doubts about this, knowing that under the new improved railway system the train companies took a delight in not holding trains, thus causing endless missed connections.

''Tis different in these parts,' said Jarvis.

Fanny was distressed to see Lisa go. 'I could drive you up,' she said. 'I'm not needed here.'

'No, Fanny,' said Lisa firmly. 'Hester says you're to stay here as long as you want, she's taken a great liking to you. And you can help look after Alec while I'm in London.'

'Huh, shoe's on the other foot,' said Alec. 'Fanny's not fit to be out, she's fallen into three holes this morning already.'

'Only because Victor had covered them up with twigs and leaves to hide them.'

Lisa couldn't help laughing. 'More holes? This Dr Buonamici

isn't going to be very happy when he does finally get here. I'm sure Victor should leave well alone.'

'*If* he gets here,' said Fanny. 'He's very elusive.'

Lisa looked at the moonscape which was the sunken garden. 'Julia's going to have a fit when she comes back.'

Victor surged towards them. 'What's that? Julia? Ha, I had a letter from her. She's going off to stay with a Swedish friend on a remote island, up all night in the sun, I dare say. She won't be back for a while, and by the time she is, we'll be in full swing here. As long as that damned chap turns up; I can't think why he isn't here yet.'

'Give my love to Toby,' said Fanny, her anxious face appearing at the car window. 'Do you think Claudia will come here again?'

'Fanny, she's already here. Even now, she's probably at the stables, waiting for Philip. I gather she has a passion for horses.'

'How surprising,' said Fanny.

'Not surprising at all,' said Lisa.

'I hate her,' said Fanny, her face suddenly full of venom.

'Quite right, too,' said Lisa. 'See you in a couple of days.'

Lisa liked train journeys, and this one started very promisingly, with a gentle trundle along a single line through idyllic country-side. The train chugged up a green tunnel, rattling out at the top of the slope to give a view of an endless, undulating landscape.

The carriage only had two other occupants, a snoozing mother and her small son, who amused himself by pulling faces at Lisa over the back of the seat. This began to irritate her, so she pulled a gruesome face of her own, causing the little boy to tumble down, suitably chastened, into his own seat and mercifully out of sight.

It took Lisa back to the days of her youth when she used to pull faces to keep men at a distance while at parties, or on the road. She sighed. Gone for ever, she thought wistfully, was the time when her trim but curvy figure and lively, attractive face had drawn men to her like bees round the proverbial honeypot.

Huh, she thought, in those days she could have given Claudia a run for her money. Or perhaps not. Claudia had a fascination about her that clearly turned men's bowels to water. She was like something out of the Old Testament, or, no, something from the classical world. In any case, she belonged in a wilder landscape, where emotions were rawer and the stakes higher than was the case in contemporary England.

Or so you would have thought, but there she was. In Heartset, now, damn her eyes.

'Hussy,' said Lisa out loud, startling the sleeping woman into wakefulness.

Probably thinks it's a station name, said Lisa, gazing out of the window and musing on the otherworld places the train went through. They had left Corda Episcopi, and were now running alongside the Heart Gorge, breathtakingly lovely. Then came Little Ease and Long Ease, before the train started the complicated manoeuvres which would allow it to change direction completely and draw into Heartley Junction.

Wonder where Heartbreak is, thought Lisa gloomily, as she jumped down to the platform and turned to pull her bag down after her.

'This train terminates here,' bellowed the guard, and a few more recalcitrant passengers tumbled down on to the platform.

'Platform 1 for the London train. This will be the 11.17, calling at . . .'

Lisa sat down on a pleasingly wrought but highly uncomfortable bench to wait for the London train.

Limbo, she thought. Really, it would be a good life just to be endlessly in transit, the cares of one part of your life safely left behind; the troubles and concerns of your destination pleasantly out of immediate reach.

The train clattered into the station, and she got on it.

Toby heard the taxi coming round the corner. He flew to the window, saw that it was indeed Lisa, and was on the steps to greet her and take her bag.

'It's so quiet here without you,' he complained as he flicked through the important post, passing letters to her with comments and queries. 'And without Fanny. How is she?'

'Mmm,' said Lisa, deciphering a quote from an Italian printer.

'Coffee,' said Toby, clearing a space on her desk, and putting the cup and saucer neatly down. 'Fanny?'

Lisa pushed the papers away and sat back in her chair. 'I can leave all this to you, Toby.' She blew reflectively on her coffee, sending little ripples across the steaming black surface. 'Fanny's all right. Fine, in fact. Victor has his eye on her; what a difference now that she's lost that unbecoming plait.'

'Eye?'

'It'll be more than eye shortly, if I know Victor. And Julia's away, so Fanny will have to watch it.'

'A man of appetites, Victor?'

'Definitely.'

'But our Fanny still hankers for Gerry?'

'I'm not so sure about that,' said Lisa. 'She misses him, of course she does. They've been together for five years, they're a couple, she's used to him.'

'Time for a change,' said Toby. 'Perhaps Victor will widen her horizons.'

CHAPTER 27

Fanny's horizons were temporarily bounded by several rose bushes and an irate Jarvis. She was explaining that no, she didn't plan to dig up any roses; all right, any *more* roses. She was merely measuring, and yes, she was sorry if she was disturbing the plants, she was being as careful as she could, and if anything, she pointed out, looking at a deep scratch on the inside of her arm, the roses were doing better than she was.

Victor was impatient with all this orderly activity. 'You won't find out what's down there by running around the gardens with tapes like a demented surveyor,' he said.

'We have to make a record of what you've done so far,' said Fanny patiently. She could imagine Salvatore's face if he arrived and found out what Victor had been up to, and how haphazardly everything had been done. 'It would be good if we can get it mapped before Dr Buonamici arrives. Then we can fill in the holes.'

'Fill in the holes? What are you talking about?' Victor was horrified. 'We'll need to extend them, not fill them in. Take up the whole area.'

Fanny wondered how you got a man like Victor to appreciate modern archaeological techniques. 'It doesn't work like that,' she explained. 'It's slow work, but then, if there's a proper excavation, it's got some of the basics already done. And grass grows back; Dr Buonamici will need to make sure that if the site is ever excavated, the team know exactly where everything is.'

'If? Grass grows back? Good heavens, he must get his people down right away. Grass growing back, indeed. No, no, we can't have that.'

'You don't quite understand,' said Fanny, wiping her eye with her arm and leaving a muddy streak mingled with blood across her face.

'You've hurt yourself,' said Victor.

Fanny looked down at her arm, surprised. So she had. 'It's only a scratch. From the roses. I think the gardener put a curse on them.'

'Off to the house with you. It needs antiseptic, you'll have got dirt into it. We're bound to have a first aid box in the house. Try the kitchen.'

Fanny put her head nervously round the kitchen door. Guy was sitting at the table reading *The Times*, and he looked up. Fanny nearly fled; she didn't feel up to a crowd.

'You've hurt your arm.'

Maria emerged from the large pantry with an eager look on her face. '*Pobrecita*,' she said. 'I have some cream here, but first you need to wash it.'

'Coffee?' said Guy. 'Or perhaps a cold drink?'

'That would be lovely,' said Fanny, who was longing for something to drink. Her enthusiasm for the dandelion version of the brew, as served in her office, had vanished with her job. 'Thank you. But I only came in for some antiseptic; I didn't mean to interrupt your work.'

'Not at all,' said Guy. 'Tell us how the digging is going.'

Fanny was touched by their polite interest. She little knew that Guy and Maria were consumed with curiosity about Victor's finds.

'The neighbours will have to pipe down about their kiln,' Guy had said with satisfaction when Victor had unearthed his remains.

'Ha, but Victor won't have the people from the newspapers and television down like those others did,' said Maria with some regret.

Guy hadn't been so sure, but Victor, although hugely proud of his discovery, had been fairly cagey about future developments.

Now they could find out from Fanny exactly what was going on.

Fanny shifted as their eyes fixed themselves on her. They didn't have to say anything; their faces spoke for them.

Fanny would know.

'Ah, Hester, I was looking for you.'

Hester was doing some quiet gathering in the herb garden, but she paused in her labours as Don came across the springy turf towards her. 'Let me,' he said, taking her basket, and crouching down to attend to a furry clump of thyme. He scrunched it in his strong fingers, wrinkling his nose at the powerful aroma. 'Wonderful stuff, thyme,' he said, standing up.

'Why were you looking for me?' said Hester.

'About Philip. Lisa's gone to London.'

'I know.'

'I think we need to keep an eye on Philip.'

Hester said nothing, but her expression was alert. 'And?'

'And to discourage that Claudia from haunting the place.'

'It's difficult, if Philip invites her. And Harry's very keen for her to come here.'

'Silly idiot,' said Don. 'The trouble with Harry is that he cut his teeth on young men, and so he's never learnt about the likes of Claudia.'

'Is she such a threat?' asked Hester mildly. 'I can see that Philip's smitten; is it any more than a middle-aged fancy?'

'Philip isn't the same sort as Pa, is he?' said Don. 'With Pa it's zest for life and an over-sized ego, and outsize lust. All in a very pleasant way, however, and none but passing fancies.'

'Rather like Claudia.'

'No,' said Don. 'Not at all like Claudia. Claudia can have as many lovers, flings, one-night stands as she likes. That's her business, and each to their own and good luck to her. No, the trouble with Claudia is that she's vicious. She's out to gain power over her lovers. She's a destroyer, not a bringer of joy.'

'Philip and Lisa are grown-ups. They have to cope with this matter in their own way.'

'They have children.'

'Yes,' said Hester, a rare frown wrinkling her forehead. 'They have children.'

'Vulnerable ages, ten and twelve.'

'Yes.'

'I don't mean we should interfere, exactly,' said Don, mendaciously; he had every intention of interfering. 'Just make it a little difficult for Philip to spend much time alone with Claudia.'

'That sort of thing,' agreed Hester. 'I didn't know you were such a good friend of Philip's.'

'I'm not. I like him well enough; when he isn't gasping in the coils of love, he's a lively, witty chap, good company. But I don't care to see Lisa being treated like this. She deserves better.'

'Few of us get what we deserve,' said Hester, spying an intrusive weed peeping out from behind the mint and making a dive for it.

'Just as well, then,' said Don.

They walked back together to the kitchen.

'Fanny's in there,' said Don as they passed the window.

'With Maria?'

'With Maria and Guy. Now, Fanny has tangled with this Claudia, so Lisa tells me. She could be very helpful.'

Hester paused in the little cobbled courtyard outside the main kitchen door. 'I believe Claudia ran away with Fanny's young man. The one she was going to marry. I expect she's feeling very sore about Claudia. It's a sensitive subject, at the least.'

'Pooh,' said Don. 'No flies on Fanny, if you ask me. And if she's got an ounce of fight in her, then she'll be more than keen to lend a hand.'

'Spy on them, you mean?' said Fanny, shocked.

'No,' said Hester.

'Yes,' said Don.

'That's right, spy,' said Maria with a passion. 'Watch them, every minute of the day. And night,' she added, flicking away a fly with the tea towel.

'It's a tricky one,' said Guy, sounding very doubtful.

'No time for petty morality,' said Don. 'This has to be nipped in the bud. Philip mustn't be allowed to do anything irrevocable. He must be thwarted. Starting today. Right now. Well, when we've had coffee.' He took a cup from Maria with a nod of thanks, tipped a spoonful of brown sugar into it, and stirred it vigorously. Don was a fidgeter, who had to be doing something with his hands when he was thinking. Or plotting and planning.

'Thwarted,' said Fanny thoughtfully. 'I don't care about thwarting Philip, but I'd do anything to thwart Claudia.' She spat the name out.

'Tactics,' said Don, leaning his arms on the table. He eyed Fanny, sure that she was less fragile than she appeared. 'I'm sorry if I touch any nerves here, Fanny, but we need to know the enemy. Now, how does this Claudia work?'

'Work? She doesn't work as far as I know. She's got pots of

money, which leaves her lots of time and energy for having the hots for men.'

'No, no. Her modus operandi, how does she go about ensnaring her men, separating them from wives and girlfriends and so on?'

Fanny sighed. 'I'm not sure. She just crooks a finger, and whoosh, they're off. Sex appeal, I suppose. I can't say.'

'How well do you know her?'

'She wasn't ever really a friend,' said Fanny quickly. 'More an acquaintance. She lived in the flat upstairs from us. When I was with Gerry,' she went on with a sad sniff.

'Was it her flat?'

'No, she'd rented it from the usual occupant, who'd gone abroad. Because her house – she has a house of her own, left to her by her late husband – was being pulled apart. Dry rot, I believe.'

'And that was where she met Gerry?'

'Came to borrow some coffee, like that terrible ad on the telly.' She mimicked Claudia's slightly husky voice: ' "I've just moved in, and I'm dying for a cup of coffee, and not a bean in the place." '

'So Gerry, the fool, looks deeply into those eyes, and goes all neighbourly: "Come in, I'll make some coffee, have it with us." '

'Claudia tanked straight over me, I might as well not have been there. Then she swept Gerry off to help her with some plugs.' Husky and helpless voice again: ' "I'm so hopeless with anything electrical, how sweet of you." '

Fanny looked reflective. 'It could have been a fatal move, that, because Gerry doesn't know one end of a plug from the other. Unfortunately it wasn't, and after that she was always flitting in and out, and cooing over Gerry.'

'Didn't any alarm bells ring?'

'I didn't like it, but I thought it was just her way. Good heavens, she had troops of men up and down to see her, all day long. And half the night. When she wasn't out with them, that is. And honestly, I can see the men all falling over themselves, but I don't know why, really. She isn't even pretty.'

'Was there anyone in particular? Apart from Gerry, that is.'

'I don't think she had any kind of feeling about Gerry at that stage. Her most persistent suitor, if you can call him that, was George Sermion.'

Don pricked up his ears. 'The poet?'

Fanny nodded. 'He's a real sweetie. The nicest man I ever met, and she was just sucking him dry.'

Don banged a fist down on the table, making them all jump and causing two stray teaspoons to rattle together in surprise. 'Got it,' he said. 'You know the poem he wrote, in that book of love poetry. It must have been written about her.'

'Oh?'

'It begins, "Fuck you, Claudia, a thousand times."'

'Hardly a love poem,' said Guy.

Maria had cast her eyes heavenward, and was making disapproving noises. 'The shame of such a woman,' she hissed.

'Poor guy,' said Don. 'It's the most bitter poem I ever read. And the other ones about his mistress are bitter, too, all except for a few early ones.'

'I wish she'd just been content with George,' said Fanny.

'So what made her up and off with Gerry?'

'She's acquisitive. I chatted to her, the way one does. About our plans. House hunting; we were getting married, we were going to start a family. She obviously thought, I can take Gerry away from all this, just like that.' Fanny snapped her fingers and made a loud hiccuping noise. 'And she did.'

Hester rose and went round to where Fanny was sitting. She patted her on the shoulder, as the others made sympathetic murmurings.

'Well rid of him,' said Don brutally.

'I loved him,' Fanny snuffled into her handkerchief.

'Yes, probably. But you've got a trained mind, Fanny, use your brain. Much better for Gerry to take a runner with Claudia *before* you were married.'

'If we'd got married and moved he might never have met her.'

'Okay, not Claudia. But a similar.'

'She's unique,' said Fanny vehemently. Anger took her sniffles away, Don saw with approval. 'Most people never come across a Claudia. But God help you if you do.'

'Doesn't impress me,' said Don. 'Despite her subtle ways. She's like the classical tart, thrilling in the dining room, chilling in the bedroom, I bet you.'

Guy found that very funny. 'Victor doesn't think much of her,' he volunteered.

'That's because she isn't well-endowed in the bosom line,' said Don. 'Pa's big on tits, you know that, Guy.'

'No need to be vulgar. Or disrespectful.'

'Animals,' said Maria angrily. 'While poor Fanny sits and weeps.'

'Not any more she doesn't,' said Don hastily, seeing signs of more tears. 'You're too cross to cry, aren't you, Fanny?'

Fanny nodded her head.

'So,' said Don. 'Philip's caught the Claudia, and so has Harry.'

'You make her sound like a disease,' said Hester.

'And so she is,' said Fanny.

Maria was furious. 'Huh, that woman, winding Harry round her little finger. And Harry running about after her, what shame. Have these men no pride?'

'No,' said Fanny.

CHAPTER 28

Lisa would have recognised that lean and hawkish profile anywhere.

'Sara!'

They were a comical pair, Sara, an Ethiopian, nearly six foot tall, and built like an elegant reed; Lisa so small in comparison, so compact and central European.

'Lunch?' said Sara. 'I like the hair.'

'I've just had it done,' said Lisa. 'Lovely suggestion, lunch.'

'How long before you rush back to work? Or can we have a proper lunch?'

'I have the time,' said Lisa, 'if you have.'

They were ushered to a table in a corner, not out of the way, but not exposed and as though one were in a traffic jam, as Lisa put it.

'How come you aren't in a hurry?' enquired Sara over a preliminary glass of wine.

'I'm on holiday,' said Lisa.

'In London? Why not Maffick? Or abroad? No, I forgot, Philip isn't very keen on abroad.'

'He travels for work,' said Lisa. 'A lot, so he prefers not to for holidays. We were going to Spain, to a remote spot, but Philip had an accident.'

'Ah, the eye. I read about it in the papers. I tried to ring you, but all I got was Toby.'

'He didn't say.'

'He wouldn't, you know how he loathes me.'

'Only because you frighten him.'

Sara shrugged, amused. 'So how is Philip? Coping, no doubt.'

'Coping,' said Lisa, after a tiny pause.

Sara raised an inquisitive, expressive eyebrow. 'And?'

'And . . .'

Sara sighed, and ate a mouthful of fish. 'A woman, I suppose,' she said. She looked at her fork with surprise. 'What a lot of bones. Come on, Lisa, out with it.'

Lisa and Sara went back a long way. Sara had been brought back to England from Ethiopia by a redoubtable Yorkshire woman who had been helping with famine aid. It had caused a stir with the authorities, but Barlow Empton was more than a match for them.

'She's an orphan, all her relations have died. If I'd left her in Ethiopia, she'd be dead too. No, I don't care what colour she is, and no, she's not going back. Josh and I are going to give her a home here, and there's an end of it.'

Lisa had been enchanted by Sara from the day she turned up, all eyes and wary disbelief, at St Austin's Junior School. Sara, as her teachers and everyone else soon discovered, had an outstanding brain. Lisa sidled into the grammar school through luck, when two girls higher on the list had left the area. Sara sailed in at the top.

They had stayed firm friends all through Getley Grammar. Sara was good at everything, but had a particular flair for mathematics. It was one of the reasons why Lisa had opted not to go to university from the sixth form.

'For Sara, it's effortless,' she had said. 'There's nothing I can do in the way she can do maths.'

The teachers had drawn in a collective breath. That sounded like envy, or at the least a counsel of despair. If Sara was a certainty for Cambridge, that didn't mean Lisa shouldn't try for a less demanding course at an appropriate university.

Lisa had been impatient with them, but Sara had understood. 'You want to wait until you find a subject to study that you can do the way I do maths.'

'That's it,' said Lisa. 'Although I doubt if I ever will find it.'

Sara had pooh-poohed that. 'You've got plenty of brains. Ten school subjects, that's not much. Lots of things they never teach you at school, one of those will be what you want to do.'

Sara had been right. Lisa had gone to London University a few years later, to take a degree in History of Art. And had enjoyed every moment, as she reported back to Sara.

Sara, making a fortune as a computer analyst of a rarefied kind, was pleased. 'Getley Grammar was fine for sound girls doing sound subjects,' she said. 'But you can't pretend they encouraged the arts.'

'Just as well, it would have put me off for life.'

Lisa came out of a haze of memory to see Sara sitting on the other side of the table, twirling her glass and with a calculating look on her face. 'Do you remember Snorter Porter?'

'Snorter Porter? Goodness, yes.'

'Roger Porter, he was really, wasn't he?'

'Yes.'

'He ran off with the French *assistante*.'

'So he did.'

'Always reminded me of your Philip, old Snorter.'

'Sara, no, he wasn't a bit like Philip.'

'Yes he was. Very good at his job, tolerant, funny, good marriage, two interesting kids.'

'And blew it.' Just like Philip is trying to, thought Lisa.

'He stayed with Felicité for less than a year, did you know that?'

'I didn't hear. Did he go back to his wife?'

'Nope. She didn't want him back.'

'No forgiveness, no tearful reconciliations?'

'No. Because after Felicité had finished with him, he wasn't the Roger that his wife had fallen in love with and married. He was a shell. The wit, the humour, the authority – all gone.'

'Good heavens, I never knew that. What happened to him in the end?'

'Went into a monastery. Trappist order, I believe.'

'How desperately sad.'

'So, Lisa, truth time,' said Sara. 'Who's Philip got himself entangled with? What is it, mid-life crisis? Bored with his work?'

'Hooked by a witch,' said Lisa, twirling cream into patterns over the plate of summer fruits.

'A witch? Lisa, you're being unrealistic. That's what angry wives always think of their husbands' fancies; it's an immature statement of the way the situation is in actuality.'

'No, in actuality, she's a witch,' said Lisa flatly. 'She's made a dead set at Philip, nearly got him killed, fighting that duel with Rory, and she's determined to have him. At any cost.'

'Let's get something straight. You and Rory didn't have a thing going, did you?'

'Not seriously. A flirtation, nothing more . . .'

Sara was brisk in matters of the heart. 'The mistake you made, way back, was getting married. It makes everything so complicated. Legally.'

Sara lived happily with her current lover and her daughter by an earlier friend. 'Nobody else can have any claims on Becky; if Jules gets troublesome, I throw him out, life's very straightforward. Now, with you, if you leave Philip, you're in trouble.'

'I don't want to leave Philip.'

Sara took no notice. 'First thing, you need a good lawyer. Yours, not Philip's. Someone who knows about child custody cases. I assume Philip will fight to keep the children.'

'Sara, I'm not splitting up with Philip.'

Sara gave Lisa a cool and knowing look. 'Lisa, the way I'm hearing it, you aren't going to have any choice. Philip's going to do the splitting, and you're going to have to pick up the pieces.'

'I don't think he'd hurt the children.'

Sara made a derisive noise. 'What's new? Is Philip a member of an alien species? This bint he's taken up with has got under his skin. If she says jump, with or without kids, then he'll jump. These middle-aged passions are peculiarly destructive.'

'Thanks a lot,' said Lisa, thoroughly depressed.

'I can see why you're unhappy about chucking Philip. All that charm, and such good company. Good in bed, too, you used to say.'

'Huh,' said Lisa, thinking of Philip's turned back.

'Too busy getting a leg over the floozy to give you the time of day, is that it? Ditch him, Lisa, make yourself a new life. Change the locks on your house, tell him to bugger off, him and the ladyfriend, and find yourself a proper man.'

'Philip was a proper man. Is. And I can't toss away years and years of marriage just like that. And the children would be wretched. And besides, thick and thin, you know.'

Sara was unimpressed. 'I know what I'd do if it was me.'

'It wouldn't be,' said Lisa. 'Your life is different, lucky you.'

'It's never too late.'

'To start leading a different life? Change one's whole emotional and moral baggage? Oh, but it is.' Lisa gave her coffee a savage stir. 'If the children were older, it might be easier.'

'They aren't, so it's a waste of time thinking about it.'

Sara changed the subject. 'Nice jacket, don't spill coffee on it.'

Lisa looked at her wobbly hand. 'Nerves,' she said dispassionately.

'Worry,' said Sara. 'Is it new? The jacket, I mean.'

'I got it this morning. There's a chill wind blowing, which was unexpected, so I nipped in and saw this. I wanted to do some shopping anyway.'

'It'll make you feel better about yourself, even if Philip doesn't notice,' said Sara brutally. 'Is Philip's fancy very sexy? Elegant? Motherly? Interesting to know the type he goes for.'

Lisa sighed. 'Pots of money, from her first husband, who popped it. So wonderful clothes.'

'What did he die of?'

'Exasperation. Or a broken heart, when he realised Claudia was about to seek fresh woods.'

'Claudia,' said Sara, sitting up very sharply. 'Did you say Claudia? Claudia who? Lisa, you can't mean Philip's fallen into the clutches of Claudia Sutcliffe?'

Lisa stared at her friend, astonished at the change that had come over her. Gone was the laid-back wise woman; Sara looked as though something had bitten her. 'That's her name, yes.'

'I had no idea; that's quite a different matter, it couldn't be more serious.'

'You *know* Claudia?'

'By sight, and by reputation, which couldn't be worse, let me say right away. She was eyeing Jules up at one time, but fortunately someone more interesting came along. Good gracious, she's a mad nymphomaniac with no morals whatsoever. And deadly, look what she's done to poor George.'

'George? I met a George. At her flat; he was looking for her.'

'The poet,' Sara said, shaking her head. 'George Sermion. They had a big thing going, oh, it was a flaming affair. It inspired him, and he wrote some wonderful poetry about her. He was eaten up with being in love with her; all worship and delight. Such passion, I can't tell you.'

'And?'

'And she got bored. Too much devotion, no challenge any more. Besides, she'd ruined him, made him unfit for normal life.'

Much as Lisa disliked Claudia, Lisa wasn't convinced about this. 'You make him sound quite wet.'

'George isn't wet at all,' cried Sara. 'Just gripped by this

141

enormous passion. Oh, it's such a shame. If ever there was a man who should have married and had a family, it's George.'

'I thought you were anti-marriage,' said Lisa waspishly.

'In the right circumstances, and for the right people, marriage is fine. It would have been for George, but he'll never get over Claudia, in my opinion. Your case is different. You aren't a George.'

Friends are such a comfort, thought Lisa, as she bid Sara an affectionate goodbye outside the restaurant. Rather like having an icy shower on a wintry day, in fact.

She'd ask Toby to get the locks changed, though.

Just in case.

CHAPTER 29

Philip was beginning to feel hounded. All he wanted was some blissful time alone with Claudia, and it just didn't happen. Here he was, in the depths of the countryside, and he might as well be in Piccadilly Circus for all the privacy he got.

For a start, there was Polly. She clung to him like a limpet, anxious about his well-being, not wanting to let him out of her sight.

'Get rid of her,' Claudia cooed in his ear.

'I don't want to hurt her feelings.'

Claudia would cheerfully have kicked Polly into the nearest ditch, but she was far too wily to criticise Philip's daughter. 'Dear little girl. Bribe her.'

'I've tried, nothing doing.'

'Why is she so clingy? Does she have a problem? Is she abnormal?'

Philip didn't like that at all. 'No, certainly not. I think it's that Lisa told her to look after me.'

'Oh, Lisa,' said Claudia, with a complete lack of enthusiasm. 'Well, I have an idea. We'll go out for a ride together, and then you and I can gallop off. She won't be able to keep up with us on that little pony.'

'I can't just abandon her in the middle of the country.'

'Why not? The pony will take her home, they always do, you know, longing to get back to their stables and a net of hay.' Claudia fixed her fatal, glowing eyes on Philip. 'Don't you want to be alone with me?'

'Claudia, you know . . . Yes, Polly, what *is* it?'

Then, when he had managed to escape from Polly for even a few minutes, Hester would appear. Philip had thought that her domain was the house, and all her time was taken up with running the large household with busy competence. Yet here she was, in the garden, on the terraces, in the orchard, at the stables, with some domestic query, an offer of refreshment, a message from the nurse.

If she vanished for a few merciful moments, Don would be there. Philip liked Don, but why the hell couldn't he be somewhere else? Minding his vineyard, for instance.

'Plenty of time for that,' said Don unperturbed, when Philip mentioned this to him. 'Fancy a walk to the Bunch of Grapes?'

Philip didn't fancy a walk anywhere with Don. And Guy was just as bad, how could Victor employ someone who was so ubiquitous? Philip would have sworn he appeared out of the ground, mostly at the most inconvenient moments.

All it needs is Lisa back, and I might as well be in a lunatic asylum, brooded Philip. Let out into the grounds for a walk, but watched for my own good.

'He's quite right,' observed Don when he reported back to the team. 'Since he is indeed suffering from a kind of madness, he needs watching. And Claudia's getting rattled.'

Maria was unconvinced. 'Not her,' she said. 'She'll have some scheme working away in her nasty mind, you wait and see.'

CHAPTER 30

'Busy tonight, Toby?' Lisa was restless, disinclined to rummage in the freezer. If she stayed in, she'd inevitably end up in the office, working. Better to leave it to Toby; if she was away from her work, then *be* away, she told herself.

'I might meet Rudi,' said Toby cautiously. He liked to know what was on offer before committing himself.

'Any new restaurants opened?'

'At this time of the year? Hardly.'

Toby flicked at his calculator and then relented. He was worried about Lisa, she was more thoughtful than usual, and lacked some of her usual ebullience. 'Rudi and I were planning to try the Phoebus.'

'Greek?'

'Good Greek.'

'Let's go.'

'I'll ring Rudi.'

They sat peacefully round a huge dish of fishy offerings. Toby uttered flutterings of enthusiasm, while Rudi simply got his sleek and exquisite head down and concentrated on the food.

Lisa watched the two men, amused. Once they had eaten, they settled down into some bitchy gossip, mostly about people Lisa didn't know. She listened idly, until a name suddenly caught her attention.

'Claudia? Claudia who?'

Rudi gave her a wilful look. 'Lisa, darling, there is only one Claudia, divine Claudia. Unique, in her way.'

Toby was flashing warnings across the table at Rudi, but Rudi, who knew perfectly well why the name had aroused Lisa's interest, settled down to what he thought of as a gentle tease.

'Irresistible, you know. The men fall down like ninepins, they simply pant for her. Women too, one gathers, although she isn't interested. Not rich enough, I should guess.'

'Is she only keen on rich men?'

'She loves rich, married men, so that she can entice them away from their wives. It's a game, one she never loses; such an expert, one has to admire, you know.'

'Inflated reputation, I'd say.' Toby sounded peeved. 'Even if she's madly attractive, so are lots of wives. Why should every man she fancies throw up that for a whore?'

'Not a whore,' said Rudi, lowering his voice dramatically, and savouring the word. 'No, she loves where she fucks, truly she does.'

Toby made a derisive noise. 'Not from what I hear. And not so good in bed either, rumour has it.'

'That's precisely why she's so potent,' said Rudi with a little crow. 'It's not just a physical thing, do you see? She eats into men's souls; oh, she's so clever.'

'And what about the children of these men she so happily and cleverly devours?' asked Lisa crossly.

'Darling! Children! This is the modern world, my pet. Grown-ups have to think of themselves first and foremost, we've earned the right to our happiness. The poor little dears just have to manage with their abandoned mamas; it happens all the time, they survive.'

'Oh, balls, Rudi,' said Toby.

'Now, you mustn't get so heated,' said Rudi. 'It doesn't affect you and me, after all, does it? Neither of us is going to be ensnared by the divine Claudia. Oh, but it is such fun to watch *normal* men so entangled in her coils.'

After dinner with those two, Lisa was not in a happy and relaxed mood as she stood at the door of Granny Paget's flat. What kind of friends did she have, each more ruthless or dispiriting than the last? Why didn't her friends go in for cosy times, full of sympathy and easy comfort?

She listened to the manic dongs of the Victorian bell inside as it jangled away. Granny P always took her time to answer the door; she liked her clients to be a little on edge.

'Come in, come in,' she said. 'Such a busy evening, so many clients, such turmoil in everyone's lives. Now, I was just brewing a pot of tea, so I'll get that, and then we'll settle down for a good talk.'

'It isn't talk I need,' said Lisa as Granny P came back into the room carrying an ornate tray laden with cups, jugs, an extra saucer for the cat and a samovar affair she used to top up the pot. It all sat on a rich wine-red velvet cloth, and took Lisa back to her childhood. Granny P had always had trays of tea just like this, although the china was getting finer and finer, she noticed.

'Business good?' she asked, as Granny P poured out some milk into a saucer for her huge, green-eyed tabby.

'Not just this evening, dear, but all day. All week. Everyone needing to know, wanting advice. Aren't people's lives a muddle, and isn't it a good thing for me that they are? Now, if not talk, what?'

'Practical help,' said Lisa, putting her cup down and leaning forward. 'I've got to get rid of this woman who's floated into Philip's life.'

'Murder?' said Granny P. 'Lisa, you wouldn't.'

Lisa was laughing at Granny P's horrified expression. 'No, no, of course not, although I'd certainly like to attend her funeral, that's how strongly I feel about her. I'd send flowers, too,' she added wistfully. Then she sharpened up. 'No, I want to know how I can send her packing, or cure Philip of his obsession and preferably both.'

Apart from the help she got from the spirits, Lisa knew Granny P to be a shrewd cookie who had learned a lot over her years of card spinning and crystal ball gazing. 'Tell me everything,' she said with a sigh. 'I knew this was coming, I saw it in your cards.'

Lisa told.

Granny P's face grew foxier, her eyes more calculating. 'I've come across this creature before,' she said. 'She's caused a lot of trouble, one way and the other. Dear, oh dear, it does sound as though she's sunk her talons into Philip good and proper. Now, I would have staked my reputation on him not succumbing to a trollop like this. He has a sense of humour, and that's usually a strong protection against the siren type.'

She absentmindedly crunched a biscuit, scattering crumbs which the watchful cat licked up in a nonchalant way.

'Well, well. Now, let me think, and I'll just lay out the cards while I do. Don't say another word; we don't want you disturbing the ether.'

CHAPTER 31

'Goodness,' said Fanny, who had escaped from Victor's roars to sanctuary in the kitchen. 'Is he usually like this?'

'Far too often,' said Hester crossly. 'He has absolutely no control over his temper.'

'Salvatore is doing his best to come; I rang him again last night. I'm sure he's interested in what Victor's found . . . But he is a very busy person, Victor should appreciate that.'

Hester was amused. 'That has nothing at all to do with it. Victor wants something; he senses that Dr Buonamici isn't going to drop everything and rush to his assistance; ergo: Victor's in a rage.'

'These things take time.'

'I'm sure they do,' said Hester. 'I'm equally sure that if Victor's determined to dig up a mosaic, then he will.'

'We can't be sure there is a mosaic floor.'

Hester made a humming sound. 'Oh, I think there probably is, you know. I quite look forward to seeing it, now I've given up hope for the lawns.'

Don had dropped into the kitchen to catch up on the news. Naturally, he was used to Victor. 'Pa and his tantrums,' he said. 'What he needs is a good session in bed with a buxom lady; how about it, Fanny?'

Fanny went bright pink.

'Don,' said Hester warningly.

'Pa has his eye on Fanny, Hester, you can see that. Julia's away, so no connubial felicity; Victor's feeling his oats.'

'All this digging is very good for him,' said Hester obscurely.

'Now,' said Don. 'So far, so good. Philip's under close scrutiny, no scope for any mischief there. Another frustrated soul. I wonder if he has tantrums, too.'

'About Claudia, do you mean?' said Fanny, looking worried.

Mrs Slubs was attacking a pile of ironing in the corner. There was a perfectly good laundry room, but Mrs Slubs preferred to be where the action was.

'Gone to Bath with Harry, that Claudia has,' she observed. 'Zoë's quite upset about it. I told her, you wants to rest right now, and not fret, and there's no harm in Harry giving a young lady a lift.'

Hester frowned. 'Did Zoë believe you?'

'No,' said Mrs Slubs, getting vicious with the iron.

Don didn't need telling that. Zoë had looked strained and unhappy when he'd dropped in for a chat. She'd been told all about Claudia from one quarter or another, and didn't at all like what she heard. I don't blame her, thought Don, wondering if he should have a word with Harry.

'T'ain't Harry she's after,' said Mrs Slubs, subduing one of Victor's shirts. 'Tis that Mr Maffick who's staying here at the Hall. With his wife and two children; a shame, that's what it is.'

'She may not be after Harry,' said Fanny, sampling a chocolate biscuit. 'But Harry's after her. Which comes to much the same thing in the end.'

'No good will come of it,' said Mrs Slubs in a sepulchral voice.

Hester rose and gathered up the cups.

Mrs Slubs didn't want to see people go. 'News from Heartsbane,' she said. 'Sybil's got a visitor coming. A young man.'

'It's her godson,' said Hester.

Mrs Slubs was unimpressed. 'I know he. A good-looking young man, I'll give you that, but idle! Well!'

'He's a poet,' said Don, amused.

'A poet, and what's a poet? That's no living for a grown man, however handsome. What does he live on, I'd like to know?'

'He's a famous poet. I expect he earns lots of money.'

'Famous is as famous does,' said Mrs Slubs. 'We need no poets in these parts, stirring up folks with their lamentations and rude ways.'

Down at the paddock, attention was focussed on another beautiful male creature; one with four legs.

'He's smashing,' said Polly. 'Just lovely. Are you going to buy him, Dad? You could keep him at Maffick, there's lots of room.'

Philip and Polly were hanging over the paddock fence, watching the Arabian stallion flying into a series of wild but elegant bucks.

'The trouble is, no-one can get near him,' said Philip.

'Geraghty does.'

'He bred him, raised him as a foal.'

'Mum would like him,' said Polly eagerly.

'What? Lisa?' Philip's face took on the reserved look which Polly had come to know and fear. 'Oh, I don't think Lisa minds about horses one way or the other.'

'Unlike that Claudia,' Polly muttered under her breath.

'Claudia?' Philip's voice had a reverential tone. 'Claudia's wonderful with horses. She has such an instinct for them, and she's a superb horsewoman.'

'Yes, and the sun shines out of her arse,' said Polly before she could stop herself.

Philip couldn't believe his ears. He stared furiously at Polly. '*What* did you say? No, don't repeat it, and never let me hear you saying anything like that again. It's unspeakably vulgar, and to use that sort of language about Claudia . . . How dare you? And wherever did you pick up that foul expression?'

Polly's chin went up. 'From Claudia, actually,' she said.

'And you're a liar, too,' said Philip.

'I am not,' shrieked Polly. 'Claudia's all sweet and lovey dovey when you're around, but she isn't like that with other people. Not unless she fancies them, like she does Harry.'

That was Polly banished, and she ran with tears of fury pouring down her face to the orchard, where she flung herself on the ground in paroxysms of sobs. An inquisitive pig came lumbering over to see what all the fuss was about, and Polly scrambled to her feet as she felt a touch on her shoulder.

'Oh, pig,' she said, sniffing and gulping. 'I thought you were Dad. I hate him, I hate him, and I'm glad it was you.'

The pig looked up at Polly with bright little piggy eyes.

'Yes, and I hate Claudia. I'd like to kill her. I used to hate Mummy, in fact I still do, but I wish she'd come back and that horrible Claudia would go away.'

The pig shook its large head, losing interest; this was no fun, not like Victor and the holes. She went back to her companions, and Polly, after a moment's hesitation, took the path back towards the other side of the paddock. Her father might have ordered her into the house, but she wanted to watch Geraghty put the horse through his paces.

To her surprise, Alec was there, hanging over the railings. Alec loved horses, but he had been so tied up with Victor and the excavations that he had hardly been near the stables or paddock.

'Hi,' he said. 'What's up?'

'Nothing,' said Polly, dragging an arm across her face and leaving a smear of grime behind.

'You look very messy,' said Alec critically. 'Where's Dad?'

'I don't know, and I don't care. He's a beast. He's over there, watching. And all he can think about is how Claudia would appreciate the horse. Yuk!'

'Claudia? What's she got to do with anything?'

Polly curled her mouth up in a very annoying way. 'You just don't notice anything, grubbing about with Victor. Dad's dead keen on Claudia, who's a horrible cow. He spends hours with her, and he's glad that Mum's gone to London, because then he can spend all day making gooey eyes at her.'

Alec looked a good deal shaken at this item of news. 'I haven't noticed anything,' he said defensively.

'Well, everyone else has,' said Polly.

'He's alone now, look, he's over there.'

'That's because Claudia's gone to Bath with Harry. Dad's cross about that, he's in an awful mood. That's why I'm on this side of the paddock.'

'I expect you've been rude again,' said Alec with a sigh, and got a hefty thump for his pains. 'Oh, go away, you silly little girl.' He swung a leg over the paddock railing and slipped down on the other side.

'I'm not a silly little girl. And where are you going?'

'To have a ride on that horse.'

'Alec! Come back! Nobody can ride him.'

Alec took no notice, but walked steadily towards the horse, who was keeping a watchful eye on him.

'Alec! He's a stallion. He's dangerous, really wild. Come back, you'll get hurt.'

Jarvis's tale had the kitchen enthralled. He had been coming past the paddock with the lettuces for the kitchen, when he'd heard young Polly a-yelling and screaming, because her brother was walking, calm as you pleased, towards that dangerous brute of a horse that Geraghty was so mad about.

Jarvis had expected to see the lad kicked to kingdom come, especially when he remembered how the stallion had lashed out at one of the boys in the stables. But not a bit of it. Alec had gone slap up to the horse, and started talking to the animal. Jarvis was contemptuous about talking to a horse, or to any animal. Jarvis was a flowers and veg man.

And no, his father hadn't gone to his aid, although Jarvis reckoned he'd been about to, but before he could swing himself over the fence and into the enclosure, the boy Alec was up on the horse's back.

Maria wrung her hands. 'Aie! What happened? Tell us! Is Alec injured?'

'Not a bit of it.'

'Did the horse throw him?'

'No, he did not. Not for want of trying mind you, he rear up and thrash out, the way they horses do. But Alec, he just sit there, calm as anything, until the horse get his four feet down on the ground, looking all surprised like because the boy's still there.'

'And?'

'And then he ride him over to his dad.'

'What did Mr Maffick say?' Hester wanted to know. 'Was he angry? Did he shout at Alec?'

Maria made clicking noises. 'Why would he shout? He would be proud of him.'

'I wouldn't say that,' said Jarvis. 'You couldn't tell whether he were proud or not. All he does is says to Geraghty, "I'll have that horse."'

The assembled company let out its collective breath.

'Polly'll be pleased if her father buys the stallion,' said Guy, who had struck up an unlikely friendship with her. 'She dotes on that horse.'

'Good for Alec to have a horse of his own,' said Hester, getting up from the table. 'Give him an interest in life. And good for him to have a bit of admiration from his father; I sometimes think Philip's forgotten he has children.'

Murmurings of agreement all round the table.

'He was a very good father before,' said Hester fairly. No-one asked before what. 'Very lively and full of fun. He had a running game going with Polly, I remember, all about a ghost under her bed. And he got on well with Alec, took an interest in what he was doing.'

'Well, he's doing the right thing there, buying that horse,' said Jarvis. He finished his beer and wiped the foam off his moustache with the back of a brown hand. 'Back to work,' he said, with a quick look at Hester.

'Yes,' said Hester. 'Back to work.'

CHAPTER 32

'Wake up, sweetie.'

Toby was in Lisa's room, shaking her awake.

'Ugh?' said Lisa, surfacing reluctantly from an unrefreshing sleep.

'All hell's broken out. Press ringing constantly; they'll be at the door soon. Heartsease is all over the front pages.'

'What? Why?'

'Roman remains, rich aristocratic family – so they say, but *I* know how Victor's grandpa made his heap – and the near-mortally wounded Philip Maffick. This wicked capitalist sinner, they say, is using Heartsease for a love nest, so that he can be with his intimate friend – their words, not mine – Claudia Sutcliffe. Long distance lens, duckie, and you aren't going to like the piccies.'

'Shit,' said Lisa.

'And Emilia's in the sitting-room.'

Lisa, who had struggled to a sitting position, slumped back on her pillows. 'No, spare me that. Get rid of her, please, Toby.'

Too late. Emilia opened the bedroom door without knocking and sailed into the room. '*Well*,' she said, determined to have a go at someone. 'Really! If this is what goes on . . .'

'Nothing goes on,' said Toby, sidling out past her. 'Truly, Emilia, Lisa's virtue is utterly safe with me, you know how it is.'

'No, I don't,' said Emilia as the door closed behind him. 'It's all most unsuitable, and makes a very bad impression on the children.'

'The children aren't here,' said Lisa wearily. 'Toby came in to wake me out of pure kindness. He knew I'd switched the bedroom phone off.'

The door reopened, and with a winning smile for Emilia, Toby deposited a cup of tea beside Lisa's bed. 'Coffee's brewing,' he said. 'For when you want something stronger.'

Lisa swung her legs on to the floor, and stood up. Then, as Emilia opened her mouth to share a few more of her views, Lisa fled into the bathroom. She firmly locked the door and turned the shower full on, drowning out the all too penetrating tones of Emilia's voice.

What am I doing here? Lisa asked herself. She winced at Emilia changing gears in a cacophony of noisy screeches as she dived through the London traffic.

Why aren't I on that lovely, peaceful train, tickety-tacketting through a green world?

Because Emilia had the bit between her teeth, that's why.

'I've spoken to Hester, first thing. Of course, she's so shocked about the papers, she says the house is under siege, and Victor's been out with his gun.'

'Did he bag any?'

'Any what?'

'Reporters?'

'Darling, don't be silly. It was just to threaten, you know.'

Lisa could see the picture in the next day's paper, Victor in a hat with his gun. That'd really calm everything down.

'Are you staying at the Hall?'

'Of course,' said Emilia. 'I need to be on the spot, so that I can make sure Philip doesn't do anything he'd regret.'

He already has, thought Lisa, gazing out of the window at a row of dilapidated shops selling second-hand parts and assorted ironmongery. Hours in the car with Emilia, why had she allowed herself to be bullied into it?

'You can't possibly go back on the train, so risky, train travel. You'll almost certainly catch something, think of all the people who've been in those carriages.'

'I came up on the train.'

'The danger, exposing yourself to all those germs like that. You should think of your children. No, you're coming with me.'

Perhaps it would be better if she arrived at the same time as Emilia; she could keep an eye on her. Emilia would only make matters worse.

What could she say to Philip, after the picture that had appeared in the paper that morning? Blurred, but unmistakably Philip, with his bandaged eye, hovering in a very close way over a recumbent Claudia.

Ultimatum time? 'Choose, her or me?' No contest; he'd be off into the sunset with Claudia wrapped round him. No, she thought, subtlety and a dose of Granny P's medicament to keep us going. There was no way she could match Claudia's soul-gripping appeal. No wife of fifteen years' standing could hope to compete with that.

Emilia hooted and braked as she jerked her way on to a stretch of dual carriageway from a side road. Lisa closed her eyes.

What do I have on my side, she wondered.

The children? Philip was so intoxicated by Claudia, he would probably think she would be a splendid mother to them. And that'd be them off to boarding school before you could take a breath.

Home and hearth? What a joke. Philip took his house and creature comforts for granted, like all men, but he could perfectly well have a new home complete with Claudia curled up on the mat in place of the cat. Money wouldn't be a problem.

Loyalty? Philip was known for his loyalty, he stood by his friends and colleagues in good times and bad. Normally, you could trust Philip; but not while he had stars dazzling his eyes.

Lisa opened one eye and inspected the vigorous figure sitting bolt upright in the driving seat. With her immaculate blue-white hair, the pink floral silk dress and the ugly glasses, she was the very model of an Englishwoman of her age and generation. Surely she would defend the family and the status quo?

Lisa passed on that one. Emilia had always disapproved of her, but when push came to shove, would she be happy to see Claudia carry Philip off? Possibly; Claudia was rich.

Lisa gripped her safety belt as Emilia skidded and accelerated into a bend. The key question was, what was Claudia after? Flowers, flattery, adoration, some determined screwing, a scalp on her waist, a drained lover and on to the next victim?

Or did she fancy another spot of matrimony?

Either way, Philip wouldn't last, any fool could see that. Lisa could sit it out, give him enough rope to hang himself, and then pick up the broken pieces.

Would she want the pieces? It was a poor exchange, when you'd had the whole man for years and years. And when you'd loved him as he was before all this, damn him.

Emilia took a dramatic lurch to the left and rolled into a petrol station, sending a hapless forecourt attendant diving for cover. 'You see to the petrol,' she told Lisa. 'I'm going to find a loo.'

I need allies, Lisa thought as she paid for the petrol and headed back to the car.

'Get out the map,' instructed Emilia. 'There's bound to be a short cut.'

'I know the way,' said Lisa.

'There'll be a better one,' said Emilia, infuriatingly.

A struggle like this was best not tackled on one's own. Lisa felt sure that she could count on Don; she was certain he would enjoy being in the thick of any intrigue or skullduggery that might be going on.

Then there was Toby. He thought the world of Philip, but despite his own cruising lifestyle, he had strangely old-fashioned ideas about marriage. He was a Catholic, for one thing, and very attached to the children for another. And to Lisa.

Hester and Victor hadn't seemed very struck by Claudia, although Harry had clearly fallen under her spell. Then there was Fanny, an intelligent person when she wasn't boo-hooing. Lisa had to admit that Fanny the expert was a very different fish from Fanny the howler. Much more her mother's daughter than she had at first thought.

And there was Granny Paget. A mine of spiritual and practical help.

'And you still haven't got the map out,' said Emilia snappily, as she got back into the car. 'Sharpen your wits, Lisa, dear, this is hardly the time for daydreaming.'

CHAPTER 33

Fanny had escaped to a shady, secluded spot for a little soothing gloom. And to get away from Victor's grumbles about Dr Buonamici.

Fanny didn't think Salvatore minded having long chats on the phone with her. Her end was paying, and he was quite ready to have a good gossip about intrigues and scandals in the Ancient Roman Society.

Fanny supposed that when you were as knowledgeable about Roman history as Salvatore, you weren't bothered when Victor seized the phone from the person you were talking to and interrupted your conversation to have a good thunder at you. After Nero and Tiberius and so on, Victor must seem quite tame.

She had mentioned this to Victor, but he was unconvinced. 'These archaeologist chaps don't know the first thing about history,' he said. 'They can date a pot or what have you, but can't tell you that Caesar was murdered on the Ides of March. Bloodless lot, these academics.'

Fanny heard crashing noises, and sighed. Victor came thudding through the undergrowth in search of his prey, and for a report on Dr Buonamici's planned movements.

'Ah, here you are.'

Why are you looking at me like that? wondered Fanny. As if she didn't know.

'I made a few phone calls,' he announced. 'I finally got hold of Olivia. My eldest daughter, you know. Works at Cambridge, when she isn't gadding off somewhere abroad. She's back in the country, at last. Knows your Dr Buonamici, and she was very keen to hear what's been done here at Heartsease. She's going to have a word with the head of the gang up at Cambridge. Having dinner with some big cheese this very evening, says she'll see what she can do.'

Oh great, thought Fanny. 'I'm not sure how Salvatore will feel about that,' she said tactfully.

'Family has its uses,' said Victor. 'Sometimes,' he added, remembering the not infrequent times when he thought very differently about his numerous offspring. 'Such as Harry,' he said, thinking out loud. 'Making an ass of himself over that woman, Claudia. Very hard on Zoë, but you can't tell him anything. "Leave me to mind my own affairs, Pa," he says. All very well, but he's managing them extremely badly.'

Fanny's lip started to quiver; she simply couldn't help it; the mere mention of that woman's name was enough to set her off.

Victor took no notice. 'If we aren't careful, Zoë'll be on the phone to her mother, and the next thing we know, she'll be down here on our doorstep. And I can't be doing with mothers-in-law, terrifying breed.'

Fanny gave a valiant hiccup.

'Don't see why she couldn't stay with that other young man she's supposed to have run off with, that friend of yours, what was his name? Gerry? Something like that. Idiotic chap, gave up a nice girlfriend, so they say. No future in a woman like this Claudia, deadly, that type.'

Fanny couldn't contain herself any longer, and she gave way to great gulping sobs.

Victor stared at her, puzzled. 'What's the matter with you?' he demanded. 'Have a handkerchief,' he offered helpfully. 'It's clean. Now, Fanny, you've got to get back on to Cambridge and get things moving there. Time presses, we want to make the most of the summer.'

Fanny pulled herself together with a few sniffs. She knew exactly how the conversation would go. 'My dear Fanny, I think this all sounds most interesting. It may be worth looking at, at some point. However, you must appreciate that there is a long list of excavation work waiting to be done. There have been no outstanding discoveries here, such as would . . .'

Victor wasn't having that. 'What about my silver bowl?' he roared at Fanny when she tried to explain yet again. 'What about the mosaic, it'll be one of the finest in the country?'

'A tessera or two doesn't make a mosaic.'

'But I know it's there. What more do you want?'

'Well, of course, if one uncovers artefacts, large artefacts, then that can make a difference to a site's potential. So Salvatore says.'

'Artefacts?'

'A wall. And stone fragments, marble even. Such as part of an altar, or a bench, or possibly . . .'

'Plenty of marble and stone things at Heartsease,' said Victor impatiently. 'I mean, you're sitting on a marble bench at this very moment.'

Fanny looked at Victor, and then down where she was sitting. She got up, backing away from the bench. No. Surely not. It couldn't be . . . 'Victor, where did this come from? Did you buy it at an auction?'

Victor was insulted. 'No such thing,' he said huffily. 'That's always been there. Dozens of marble bits and pieces around the place. If you want to admire all that sort of thing, go ahead. Lots of stone this-and-thats in the conservatory, and dotted around the garden. Italian, you know. They've always been here.'

'Good heavens.' Fanny had become animated, quite over her sobs and tears.

'I don't understand it,' said Victor. 'You pay no attention to my silver bowl, and then you get all worked up about a lot of uninteresting pieces which are mostly fairly mothy. Broken noses, arms missing. Scruffy.'

Fanny was almost dancing with excitement.

'Show me, now. You don't seem to realise, Victor, that this bench is Roman.'

'Yes, yes, quite possibly. Renaissance Italian, but just as likely to be from northern Italy as from Rome, you know. They turned out this stuff all over the place, country was teeming with sculptors and masons in those days. Made things for the Popes. Catholics you understand, plenty of money about then. Corrupt as hell, I dare say.'

'Victor, you don't understand. Not that kind of Roman. *Ancient* Roman.'

Victor took a lot of convincing. 'No, no,' he kept saying. 'You don't want to go making a fool of yourself,' he went on, as he led Fanny from bust to nymph to column. 'These were copies, all the rage back in the eighteenth century, pop over to Italy, bring back a few bits and pieces to put about the place. Added an air of classicism, you see.'

Fanny wasn't sure. 'All these may have come from here,' she

said, gazing at a detached hand which lodged in a niche by the conservatory pool. 'Unearthed in earlier times, what a shame.'

'Why is it a shame? There's no pleasing you,' said Victor, annoyed. 'Oh, I suppose you think Salvatore would rather have the glory of digging them up.'

'Scholars aren't interested in personal glory,' said Fanny naively. 'It's just that archaeological finds are of no use outside their context.'

Victor patted a nearby goddess on her bottom in an affectionate way. 'Context?' he said. 'What context?'

'Now, we must draw up a complete list and description of all these – and you said there are more?'

'About the grounds, yes, plenty,' said Victor.

'You see, if these came from here, then there might be more which haven't been discovered. What a find!'

'I told you so.'

Fanny shook her head, and sighed. 'It's not very likely, though, is it? I mean, it's much more probable that these were brought over from Italy in past centuries.'

Victor was exasperated. 'That's what I said, and you wouldn't have it.'

'They would still be Roman,' Fanny explained patiently. 'From ancient Rome, originals, not later copies.'

'You mean they're all a lot older than I thought, wherever they came from.'

'Yes, if I'm right.' Fanny couldn't be certain, but she had a strong feeling about it. Her only previous boyfriend before she met Gerry had had a passion for Roman sculpture and she had learned a lot from him.

'Don't you *know*? Don't they teach you anything at the university these days? Whatever we find, or I want to do, you say, "I'm not an expert". It seems the only thing you are an expert on is not letting me do what I want.'

'Roman art is a very specialised area. We need someone who really knows about it to have a look. I'll have to ring Salvatore again.'

'I might as well ring the Pope,' said Victor, deeply disgruntled. 'For all the good it will do.'

CHAPTER 34

'Heartsease,' said Emilia with satisfaction as she twirled the steering wheel to shoot her car through the gates and on to the long Hall drive. 'Such peace, such calmness. Hester is so wonderful, it's always like heaven staying here.'

Lisa staggered out of the car, vowing never again to travel as far as the next traffic lights in a car driven by Emilia. To her surprise, there was no Guy bounding out to help with bags, no welcoming Hester.

Instead, definite sounds of altercation were coming from within. Lisa went through the open door and found herself in the midst of a family gathering. A domestic crisis was clearly stirring.

Is Hester going to lose her temper? thought Lisa. I never imagined she would. Or could. But she looks so extremely annoyed.

'Really, Harry, this is more than I'm prepared to put up with.'

Harry, flushed, his wiry body taut, his chin up, was defending the indefensible. 'You've always said to us, ask your friends, whenever you like.'

'That was when you lived here, Harry. The situation is quite different in this case. And I hardly think she's a friend, you've only known her a few days.'

Victor came into the hall at top speed, making Lisa feel as though several electric light bulbs had just been switched on. He stopped dead in his tracks at the sight of several members of his family all glaring at each other.

'Friends?' he said. 'Harry's friends are always welcome. What's the problem?'

'Thank you, Pa,' said Harry. 'I rest my case.'

'Victor, please keep out of this,' said Hester. 'This is a domestic matter, and it's not a question of friends.'

'Enlighten me, then,' said Victor, folding his arms and looking, so Lisa thought, particularly large and magnificent.

Harry opened his mouth, but Hester ignored him. 'Harry has asked Claudia to stay here, at Heartsease Hall.'

Lisa's jaw dropped. Was Harry mad?

'Ah,' said Victor. 'Um. Yes, well, I think I'll just go along to my study, there are a few things . . .'

'You will stay here,' said Hester firmly. 'I have been explaining to Harry that we do not have room for another visitor.'

'That's rubbish,' said Harry hotly.

'Emilia is coming shortly,' began Hester.

'She's here, actually,' said Lisa. Guy, who had been hovering around in a concerned manner, looked very put out, and vanished out of the door to attend to the new guest and her luggage.

'Emilia is staying for a few days,' said Hester. 'Then Fanny is here, as you know, and the Mafficks.'

'Dr Buonamici never arrived,' said Harry. 'Claudia can have his room.'

'Wrong,' said Victor. He spoke with pride. 'I and Fanny have just made some very important new discoveries, and he'll be rushing down.'

Fanny made a sound of protest, quickly stifled.

'What was that?' said Victor, displeased, but his eyes softening as they did when he got an eyeful of Fanny.

'Nothing,' said Fanny hastily. 'I, er, I just thought I was going to sneeze.'

Lisa breathed a sigh of relief. Definitely house full signs up at the Hall; she couldn't imagine anything worse than having Claudia here morning, noon and night.

Harry was looking sulky. 'Well, you'll have to think of something, Hester, because I've invited her, and I've promised to get her; in fact I should be collecting her right now.'

'Then I'm afraid you'll have to ring her up and explain,' said Hester.

'What about Sybil?' suggested Don, who had been following the proceedings with great interest.

He loves all this, thought Lisa, noticing his barely-suppressed laughter. She felt almost angry with him; how could he find this so amusing?

He gave her a quick wink, as though reading her thoughts, and turned his attention back to Hester.

'Sybil's godson is visiting her,' she was saying.

'Why can't Claudia stay on at Heartwell House?' enquired Victor. 'Seems the easiest solution.'

Hester rounded on him. 'Because they don't want her there any more.'

'If Harry's so keen to find her somewhere to stay,' said Don outrageously, 'he can have her at the Lodge.'

Indrawn breath all round.

'No,' said Hester quickly. 'Not with Zoë as pregnant as she is.'

'Fanny could stay with us, and Claudia can have her room,' suggested Harry.

Lisa could see that Fanny was about to volunteer to leave at once; she willed her not to make the offer.

In vain, but Victor came to the rescue. 'No, no,' he said. 'That's a bad idea. We need Fanny here. For the work on the excavation. This is my house, I invited Fanny, and she stays. And that's final.'

'Well done, Victor,' said Lisa under her breath.

'So, Harry, you see that it's quite impossible,' said Hester. 'I'm afraid your friend will have to make other arrangements.'

Harry lost his temper. 'God, just because she's an attractive woman, you're all against her. Spite and petty-mindedness, that's what it is. Why can't we put her in the tower? Alec,' he said, spying the boy who was lurking in a doorway, 'you wouldn't mind moving in with Polly, would you? So that Claudia can come and stay?'

Lisa watched her daughter's lip curl as she launched herself into the fray. Good for you, Polly, she thought.

'I don't care whether Alec would mind or not. *I* would mind, very much indeed. I'm not doing anything to be nice to that Claudia, because I think she's ghastly, if you really want to know.'

'Hear, hear,' muttered Alec from the sidelines.

'And besides, it's indecent, brothers and sisters in the same room. That's incest, practically,' said Polly in a very moral tone of voice.

Victor let out a shout of laughter, and Don gave Polly a hug. 'You tell them, Polly.'

Harry spun round to attack his older brother. 'Why don't you have one or two of the guests from here, to free up a room? Not Claudia, because I can tell you don't like her.'

'On the contrary, I think Claudia's charming, but would my virtue be safe with her? And think of her reputation – I assume she does have a reputation – if she were to stay alone with a single man. Heartset is old-fashioned in its ways, Harry.'

'Oh, bugger off,' said Harry. He looked defiantly at Hester. 'I'm sorry, but I'm not going back on my word. I've asked her to come and stay, and she's going to come. She can have Esme's room until something better comes up.'

Esme, Lisa wondered. Who was Esme?

'Australian au pair,' Don whispered in her ear. 'Big girl, fond of other girls. Quite a character. Left a few weeks ago.'

'I hope her room is really horrible. Rats and so forth.'

'I'm afraid not. Simple, compared to the state which Harry would like for Claudia, but wholesome.'

'Pity.'

'Harry would have put her in Aimeé's room if he could, but it's being redecorated while Aimeé's away. Do you remember Aimeé's room?'

'Wall paintings,' said Lisa. 'I remember those, or was it tapestries? All on amorous themes, is that right?'

'Mmm,' said Don. 'We must wander up there some time and have a look.'

If I weren't in the middle of Philip's mid-life stupidity, I'd say you were feeling seductive, thought Lisa. And for a brief but revealing moment, she thought what fun that might be.

The impasse was broken by the arrival of Claudia and Emilia who were doing a kind of tango at the door. Emilia naturally expected to go through the door first; but politesse wasn't part of Claudia's make-up.

'Harry, I waited and waited, and in the end I had to call a taxi. It's too bad of you, when you'd promised. I rang your house, and I must say, your wife or whoever answered the phone wasn't at all helpful.' She turned her lustrous eyes on Hester. 'It is so kind of you to invite me here. Can someone show me where my room is?'

CHAPTER 35

With Emilia and Claudia in residence, the atmosphere at Heartsease changed dramatically. The household was divided, with Harry and Philip firmly in Claudia's camp. Emilia, misled as so many others by Claudia's glossy appearance, had been prepared to forgive Claudia's little lapse of manners on her arrival. 'Poor thing, everyone so unwelcoming,' she said and treated her with the respect due to one in her condition of life, viz, a rich young widow.

'She counts as a pro-Claudia,' said Don, who had disliked Emilia for years.

Fanny skulked. She longed to pack her bag and leave, but then the statuary that was coming to light in the oddest places was a sore temptation. Clean out of her period it might be, but she knew all about classifying and describing, and it wasn't as though she had anything else to do. Besides, she was coming to rely on the large and reassuring presence of Victor, so kind, so endlessly helpful, as she told Maria.

Maria adored Victor, but she had no illusions about him. Her eyes narrowed. 'He is not to be trusted in matters between men and women, because he is not faithful to his wife and enjoys many other women.'

'At once?'

'It is a serious matter,' said Maria reprovingly.

'Anyway,' said Fanny, 'why does his wife go off like that? Doesn't she know about him straying?'

'She knows all about it, and it puts her into a terrible temper. Mother of God, the scenes! But every so often, she has had enough of him, and Heartsease, and she goes away. She is a doctor, you know.'

Fanny hadn't known. 'I can't see Victor marrying a doctor,' she said, surprised.

'She wasn't a doctor when they married. It was many, many years ago, when she was just out of school.'

'That can't be right; I know Victor's been married more than once.'

'Three wives,' said Maria, waving a wooden spoon in a dramatic manner. 'Julia was the first.'

'Huh?'

'Then he left her and married another, and then another, and then Julia came back.'

'He's married her twice, then. He must be fond of her,' Fanny added, a touch of regret in her voice.

'No, they weren't married again,' said Maria. 'For Julia, there is no such thing as divorce. To her, marriage is sacred. And so it is,' she said with spirit, 'or would be, if this were a Christian country.'

'And the children? Whose are they?'

'They have various mothers,' said Maria grandly. 'They know their mothers, too, except for Olivia, and nobody knows who her mother was. Except Victor, maybe, but he never says.'

'It's all very irregular,' said Fanny, looking puzzled.

'They are happy,' said Maria. 'Have a biscuit.'

Jarvis was in a fury. 'It's that bloody creature, she up and at him, and he flapped off into the bushes; it'll take all day to entice he out.'

Hester, on her way to check out what her unwelcome house guest was up to, sighed and asked Jarvis who exactly had done what. Was Philip lurking in the bushes, she wondered, with Claudia prowling round in the undergrowth? Or Harry, perhaps, with a justly incensed wife; although Zoë was far too large and pregnant to be involved with bushes.

Jarvis enlightened her. 'That peacock,' he said, impatient with her slow understanding. 'That new one, which Victor had to go and buy from that advertisement in the paper. I said that bird would be trouble, and trouble it is. And what's the sense in getting a male, and no females for him to frolic with?'

'The females will be coming,' said Hester. 'Who upped and at the peacock, then?'

'That dratted tabby.'

'Oh, surely not, Jarvis. Electra never bothers the peacocks, she's far too stately for that.'

'Maybe, but maybe not when that silly fool go up and peck she while her's lying in the sun.'

'Ah,' said Hester. 'Won't the peacock come out of the bushes in his own good time?'

'Not he,' said Jarvis with scorn. 'Lost is what he is, won't see him again if we don't go and winkle him out pretty smart. Leave him too long and he'll flap all over the place, out of sight, out of reach. Then the fox will get him, and a dang good thing too, only Victor will carry on so.'

'Victor's very taken up with his archaeology at the moment,' said Hester consolingly. 'I don't suppose he'll notice.'

'Him? Not notice?' Jarvis gave a disbelieving and mirthless laugh. 'Eyes everywhere, Victor, especially when it's his possessions is threatened.'

Hester had to admit the justice of this, and gave in to the inevitable. 'Which bushes, Jarvis? Do we need a net?'

Philip couldn't believe his luck. He had taken to lurking in the vicinity of Claudia's room, which was slightly away from the other bedrooms and main rooms of the house, constructed as it was above some old stabling. In his normal state, his sense of humour would have got the better of him, and he would have laughed at his schoolboyish behaviour. But he was in the grip of an ancient and terrible passion, in which there was no place for humour or self-knowledge.

So far, he had been singularly unlucky, never managing to get Claudia to himself. It was extraordinary how there were always people around the house, just as there seemed to be out in the gardens, or down by the paddocks. He looked cautiously around, sure of seeing Hester appear with an armful of linen, or Guy in his long grey apron, carrying a vase of flowers or some rolls of loo paper for the bathroom.

No-one.

'Claudia,' he whispered, trying the handle of her door. 'Can I come in. There's no-one about.'

The handle turned.

'Really no-one?' said Claudia. She had a mind above what other people thought or could see, but even she had to admit that the constant surveillance was rather wearing.

'No, for once there's no-one at all,' said Philip, falling into Claudia's arms as Alec turned into the passage from the other end. He watched his father clasped in a close embrace, caressing Claudia's hair and devouring her with kisses. Neither of them saw his white, shocked young face as Claudia drew Philip into the room and shut the door.

Alec heard the key turn. Enraged, he flew at the door, banging and hammering in his frenzy. 'I know you're in there, I know what you're up to. Come out, I know you're there.'

Lisa hugged the quivering boy closer to her. She was sitting beside him on the swinging seat on the terrace, trying to make sense of his jangled outpourings.

'He was in there?'

Alec nodded his head violently. 'Yes, and in the end he had to come out. He was furious, shouting and yelling at me. He grabbed hold of me, and was shaking me, but he only had my arm and I got away.'

Lisa could see the trouble in his young face, and her heart went out to him. Bad enough for her, to have Philip panting round after Claudia, but what would be the effect on vulnerable Alec?

All his sophistication had deserted him. 'Mum, he's never, ever gone for me like that. He's horrible, and I hate him. I'd like to kill him.'

Lisa didn't protest at his vehemence; in recent days, she'd had an urge to fly out at Philip herself, bandaged eye or no bandaged eye.

'Mum, is he going to go off with Claudia? Leave us? Divorce you?'

Lisa's mouth was firm. 'No way,' she said. 'Your father's in the grip of a kind of madness, Alec. It's very difficult for you to understand, but it's really almost as though he was ill.'

Alec wasn't having that. 'It's all very well, but people's fathers do run off with women. It doesn't matter if they're mad or not, they're gone. They aren't there any more. It happened to Hamish at school, and his father's moved in with his girlfriend. Hamish has to go round and see him on Saturday afternoons, when she isn't there. And they never do anything together any more.'

'Lots of families split up, Alec,' said Lisa. 'We both know that. All I'm saying is that it isn't going to happen to me and Philip. I will see to it that it doesn't.'

'How?'

'Darling, if I told you, you wouldn't believe me.'

Alec had got over the worst of his gulping sobs, and was brooding on the iniquities of his father. 'I'll tell you what I hate most,' he burst out. 'Dad being such a pillock!'

Lisa fished out his handkerchief and dabbed at his hot, damp face. 'No, he's not a pillock. He's just behaving like one.'

'What's the difference? Oh, Mum, he used to be such fun. And I was really looking forward to coming down here, and being with him. I thought he might be like he used to be, when I was younger, even if he wasn't very well.' A gloomy look came over his face. 'Do you know, I don't think he's smiled once since we came to Heartsease? Except that sloppy grin when he's looking at horrible Claudia, ugh, it's revolting.'

'Hush, darling,' said Lisa. 'I think I can hear Emilia.'

'I hate her, too,' said Alec, swiftly getting to his feet and heading for cover.

'Where are you going?' Lisa called after him.

'To ground,' said Alec.

'Alec's manners,' said Emilia. 'Running off like that, and then shouting back at you, it's disgraceful.'

'He's rather upset at the moment,' said Lisa.

'Upset about what?'

Lisa longed to tell her, but habits of loyalty die hard, and anyway, who could tell how Emilia would react.

Emilia settled herself on the seat, shading her eyes against the light. 'This should be round the other way, the sun shines straight into one's face.'

'I like sitting in the sun,' said Lisa.

'It's very bad for your complexion. And at your age, Lisa, you really do need to take care of your skin.' She paused, ostentatiously trying to pull the canopy down. 'Claudia, now, have you noticed how white her skin is? She has a lovely complexion. I expect she never sits in the sun.'

No, thought Lisa, she spends too much time on horizontal pursuits. White skin indeed, pinky grey would be more like it.

'She has the advantage of youth, of course,' Emilia went on. 'You can't hope to have that sort of bloom when you reach your thirties.'

CHAPTER 36

Lisa was still fuming from Emilia's barbed remarks and tactless comments as she walked across the sunken garden. She was on her way to find Alec, but was stopped in her tracks by a head emerging, mole-like, from a heap of earth.

'Fanny! What are you doing down there? Heavens, what a hole!'

'I'm awfully glad to see you,' said Fanny. 'Could you possibly give me a hand out?'

'Do you mean you're stuck down there?'

'I was,' said Fanny, heaving herself out with Lisa's help, and banging her legs and torso to get rid of the trails of clinging earth. 'Victor would have rescued me in the end, but goodness knows where he's got to.'

Lisa peered down into the hole. 'Is that a sensible way to dig?' she asked doubtfully. 'It seems a bit shaft-like.'

'It is not,' said Fanny. 'Victor isn't sensible, however, and so he just burrows away.' She sighed. 'I do hope there isn't a wonderful site under here, because I'm going to come in for a lot of stick from the powers-that-be if there is. They're bound to blame me.'

'Victor seems certain that there are wonders below ground.'

'Oh, Victor has no doubts at all,' said Fanny, her voice warm with affection. 'He's marvellous. Only not very scientific in his approach.'

'I see,' said Lisa. 'What do you think?'

'I know there was Roman occupation here. That's beyond any doubt. And Victor has turned up one or two interesting finds. And there are these statues and urns and so on dotted about the place. Could they have come from here originally?'

'More likely brought back as booty on early Cordovan tourist trips, don't you think? The grand tour and so forth.'

'Mmm,' said Fanny, as she fell into step beside Lisa, who was heading once more for the wilder part of the gardens. 'I can't say, but I have explained it all on the phone to Salvatore.'

'Is he ever coming?'

'I hope so.' Fanny frowned. 'The trouble is that in the meantime he's trying to despatch another expert from Cambridge. To look at the above-ground Roman relics.'

'That's good.'

'No, it's bad,' said Fanny. 'The expert is Dr Quelper, which won't mean anything to you, but I can tell you that she's simply terrifying. She has bulging muscles everywhere, and well, you know, likes women.'

Lisa burst out laughing. 'Poor Fanny. Are you afraid of her?'

Fanny stopped and looked at Lisa. 'It's serious, Lisa. She was a lecturer at my university for my second year. She *jumps* on girls.'

'On you?'

Fanny nodded.

'What did you do?'

'Squealed and kicked her and ran.'

'Did she leave you alone after that? Having got the message that her attentions weren't welcome?'

'Not a bit of it. It was dreadful, you had to be careful when you went past storerooms and so on. Lots of my friends had bruises, I can tell you.'

'Why didn't you report her?'

'Come on, Lisa, a feminist lecturer? One word and that would be your chances of a decent degree. I can tell you, that place was full of weirdos, and they all stuck together.'

'You mean they were all lesbians?'

'Oh, good gracious no. Apart from anything, most of the department were men, and so . . . But they all seemed to have been up to something, so they didn't want to rock the boat. You know how it is, once one sordid tale gets out, people start sniffing round, and then the whole lot might have come to light.'

'We never had anything like that at my university,' said Lisa.

'You were a mature student; it's not the same.'

'I hope she doesn't jump on Polly,' said Lisa.

Fanny pondered. 'I don't *think* so,' she said finally. 'I never heard her called a pederast. Lots of other things, but not that. I should think Polly's a bit young and, well, prepubescent for her.'

'I'll watch her, though,' said Lisa. 'Thank you for the warning.'

As if I didn't have enough to worry about, she thought, as she headed for where she could hear rustlings in the undergrowth.

Fanny resolutely followed her into the bramble patch. 'Ouch,' she said. 'Are we here for a particular reason, may one ask?'

'I'm looking for Alec,' said Lisa, trying to duck the wild branches of a ferocious elder. 'He was upset about something, and then his grandmother came along.'

'And he got even more upset,' said Fanny with sympathy. 'She's a difficult one, isn't she?'

One way of putting it, thought Lisa.

'I can hear Hester,' said Fanny, surprised. 'Is she looking for Alec?'

At that moment Alec, looking positively cheerful, came crashing through the trees. 'Hey, have you seen the peacock? It came this way.'

'Peacock?'

'Yes, Victor's new one. Jarvis and Hester and I are trying to catch it.'

'It'll die of shock if you go after it like that,' said Lisa. 'Where did you last see it?'

A superfluous question, for at that moment there was a raucous cry from above their heads as the silly bird, perched high on a branch, decided to brag about its brilliant escape.

Jarvis was there in a flash. 'Got the bugger,' he said in triumph, advancing with a huge angler's net. He made a great swipe at the bird, knocking it off the branch, and it fell squawking with indignation on to Hester.

'Hold he,' cried Jarvis, rushing to the rescue. 'And don't you go a-pecking of me, you bird, because I don't like it. Pot's the place for you, and no fussing.'

'Jarvis, you wouldn't,' said Alec, shocked, but bright-eyed with the excitement of it all.

'No, of course he wouldn't,' said Hester, dusting herself down and regaining her breath and dignity. 'Take the wretched bird back to its pen, Jarvis. I'm going to have a word with Victor about it.'

'And I'm going to have a word with him about these pits here,' said Fanny indignantly. 'He swore I'd seen all his diggings, and look at these.'

'T'aint Victor, not they holes,' said Jarvis fairly, keeping a firm grasp on the peacock which was penned under his jacket. 'They just appear in the ground, subsidence or something it is. Danged nuisance; that's why this part of the garden's all overgrown. T'ain't safe to clear it and plant, and to my knowledge it never has been. You look at old maps of the land, from centuries back, and this was untouched. Underground streams, I dare say.'

Fanny looked thoughtfully at the dents visible in the slight clearings between the dense vegetation of trees and bushes. 'Funny, that,' she said.

'Funny ha ha, or funny strange?' asked Alec.

Fanny gave him an abstracted look. 'There are lots of nettles,' she said inconsequentially.

'Yes, we'd noticed,' said Lisa.

'Jarvis, were there ever any buildings here? Outhouses, animal sheds? Or an old house?'

'Like I say, you can go back to King Richard and before, and there's nothing here but squiggles for trees. Ask Victor, he's got all the maps and old papers stashed away. Mind you, I have wondered, because I do find a lot of bricks and stones here.'

'Bricks?'

'Yes, but they aren't no use. Small uns, no good for anything around here.'

'Red?'

'Oh, yes. Thin, mean-looking types, but proper brick-coloured.'

'Are you thinking they might be Roman?' said Alec.

'Let's go and have a look,' said Lisa, holes, lesbians and nettle stings forgotten.

CHAPTER 37

Lisa was perched on the stone balustrade round the pond, trying to decipher Granny Paget's handwriting. She had never believed the folklore about how every child used to come out of school at fourteen able to add up and write a neat hand, and here was proof. Granny P was a living testament to a deep-seated English capacity to resist education.

Lisa squinted at the straggling, uneven letters. Perhaps I could just tip the whole lot in, she thought. Then she dismissed the idea; start with a small dose and work up, had been Granny P's advice.

She felt an arm slip round her waist, and looked up startled. Physical gestures of affection were not at present forthcoming from Philip.

It wasn't Philip.

'Don,' she said, sliding out of reach.

'I like your hair up in that loose way,' said Don appreciatively. He liked the look of her altogether, that liveliness was intriguing and most appealing. What of Claudia? Had she given up on her rival? Surely not. 'Where's the witchwoman this morning?' he asked. 'Why aren't you keeping an eye on her?'

'Don, I can't go creeping round after her all the time.'

'Then she'll go creeping off after Philip, and you'll never see either of them again.' And good riddance. Then he relented. 'No need to worry, in fact; Guy and Hester are on the job this morning.'

'On the job?'

'Mmm, just keeping an eye on things.'

'I can manage my own affairs.'

'Yes, of course you can,' he agreed.

Lisa fell silent, looking down at the orange and golden fish as they swam lazily and regally among the lilies.

'Look at that fine fellow there,' said Don. 'I expect he's a descendant of an imperial fish at the court of the Emperor of Japan; he looks grand enough. No, don't move away, it's very unkind of you when I get such pleasure in being so close to you.'

'Exactly,' said Lisa, but she didn't move any further away.

'Now, what are you trying to decipher? Love messages?'

'No, it's a . . . a recipe.'

'Let me see.'

He twitched the piece of lined paper from Lisa's fingers, consumed with curiosity. 'I'm very good at this kind of thing,' he said with assurance. Then he looked closer. 'On the other hand . . . Are you sure this is English?'

'Yes. Look, that word is "three".'

'Could be. But there are other numbers written as figures. That word could be tree, or trout, or tous, even. I think it's French,' he said, handing it back. 'Or possibly Greek.'

'I'm sure it says three spoonfuls,' said Lisa. 'I'll try that to start with.'

'Three spoons of what size?' asked Don. 'Are we talking genteel coffee spoon size, or one of Maria's serving spoons?'

'Teaspoons,' said Lisa firmly. 'You can't go wrong with teaspoons.'

'Am I going to be obliged to eat this?' inquired Don. 'Are you handing it over to Maria?'

'It's not that kind of recipe,' said Lisa, suppressing a laugh. 'And I think it would be better if you didn't eat it.'

'You're up to mischief,' said Don, looking at her intently. 'You suddenly look years younger, and as though you had a toad in your pocket. Come on, Lisa, what are you up to?'

'Up to?'

'You're planning something.'

'Maybe,' said Lisa, her face lighting up, and some of her sparkle coming back. 'But I'm not going to say a word about it until I see whether it works or not.'

'Works?'

'I'm biding my time,' Lisa told him. 'Watching for the right moment, you know. Who lives may see, but it might do some good.'

Entrancing woman, thought Don. What's she up to? Something to do with Claudia? It must be, but I wonder what. And what's she thinking about, with that intent look on her face?

Lisa looked down at the scrawled instructions once more.

The only problem, she told herself, is how and when I can administer it.

'I wish you'd tell me your secret. I'm perfectly trustworthy, you know.'

'I don't trust you an inch,' said Lisa. 'No, you'd laugh at me, and I don't know if it's going to work.'

'When will you know?'

'Soonish, I hope.'

'Most unsatisfactory,' said Don.

I must look casual, Lisa told herself as she walked stiffly into the kitchen. It was difficult to look casual when you felt you had the word 'poisoner' emblazoned across your forehead.

Maria greeted her with friendliness, making Lisa feel even more uncomfortable and criminal. 'Hester says you and your children will not be having lunch at the Hall today, because that woman will be there, and you prefer not to sit with her.'

'Um,' said Lisa, taken aback. 'I just thought . . .'

'No need to explain,' said Maria. 'I see this woman, and I know her for what she is, she should be out in the streets, with nothing on, and people shunning her.'

Lisa wondered if shunning was what would happen to a naked Claudia, but she felt encouraged by Maria's uncompromising attitude. 'Women like this should be shamed, and driven out.'

Lisa found this altogether a pleasing idea. 'Sadly, that doesn't happen much in Heartset, I don't think,' she said.

'No, because this is a barbaric country,' said Maria with satisfaction, consulting a long list pinned up on a cork board. 'Where are you having lunch, you and the children?'

'I thought I'd take them over to Heartsbane. Don says there's a very nice pub there, with a garden.'

'The Bunch of Grapes, yes, quite nice food. For English cooking.'

'Is everyone else in for lunch?' Lisa tried to sound indifferent.

'Harry, who should be at home, Hester, Don, he lunches today. And the whore, with her mean little pots of yoghurt.'

'What?'

'But yes. This Claudia, she cannot eat my puddings and sweets. No, no, impossible, she says, so bad for her. Bad for her! So we have to buy, especially for her, this disgraceful little pot of goo, no fat, no taste, no goodness.' She gestured towards a packet of

177

yoghurts standing on the table. 'We have to buy them from the milkman, and he can't believe it. "Are you sure you want these?" he says. Pah!'

'Shall I put them in the fridge for you?'

'In the fridge over there,' said Maria, gesturing with her hand. 'Push them to the back where I do not have to see them every time I open the door.'

'Is she having one for lunch?' asked Lisa, holding her breath.

'But yes, every meal, the silly woman.'

'I'll leave one out in front then,' said Lisa, and went to the fridge, where she extracted one of the pots from the back. At the same moment, she whipped out the twist of powder from her pocket.

There. She'd done it.

CHAPTER 38

George didn't realise it was Fanny at first, so flushed and streaked with mud as she was. Then recognition dawned.

'God, Fanny, what are you doing here? And why are you so dirty?'

'Hello, George,' said Fanny, wiping her face and making matters even worse. She felt mildly pleased to see George; she liked him. 'I can't tell you how exciting, I think there may have been a hypocaust here. And, possibly, a bath house.'

'Bath house?' said George, uncomprehendingly, as he gazed about his bushy surroundings. 'Why ever would anybody put a bath house in a place like this?'

'It wasn't like this then.'

'Then?'

'Romans.'

'Ah. We're talking about a *Roman* bath house.'

'A *possible* Roman bath house.' Fanny concentrated, and returned with an effort to the present day. 'If it comes to that, what on earth are you going here, George?'

'I've come to find Claudia,' said George.

'Oh,' said Fanny, feeling no more than a mild prickle in her eyes at the thought of Claudia. 'Is that wise?'

'Wise? What's wise to do with it? Fanny, I've got to see Claudia. I must make her understand how I feel.'

'I expect she already knows how you feel.' And doesn't care, she said to herself.

'She can't,' said George bleakly. 'If she did, she wouldn't be with Gerry.'

Fanny looked at him with surprise. Could he really not know that Gerry had swiftly been discarded? Had only been a passing fancy, along with several others, while Claudia was training her guns on her present target?

'If you'd been kinder to Gerry,' George began.

'Kinder!'

'There must have been some reason why he left you. I don't want to pry, but things must have gone wrong. I mean, if he turned to Claudia for comfort . . .'

'Comfort. Comfort! He did no such thing,' said Fanny, roused to unwonted fury. 'No, and it wasn't because I was frigid or neglected Gerry for my work or didn't put him first or any other stupid reason. Your Claudia enticed Gerry away purely because she couldn't bear to see two people – that was me and Gerry – who had a life together and were happy with each other.'

What a self-centred man George was, thinking that she was responsible for Claudia's evil doings. Look at him standing there, with his magnificent profile and unruly black locks, blaming her, *her*! for Claudia's wickedness. 'Marriage, children, affection, growing old together, you know the scenario.'

'Are you suggesting that Claudia tried to get Gerry to leave you just because of that?'

'Just, nothing,' said Fanny. 'Claudia saw a man attached to someone else, and thought "I'll have him". And so she did. Don't ask me how, you must know better than me what her special attractions are. As far as I'm concerned, she's a spiteful nymphomaniac.'

'Fanny!'

'Don't you Fanny me. Claudia dumped Gerry, and the reason she's here at Heartsease, in case you want to know, is because she's after someone else's husband. She's the most destructive person I've ever known, and you'd be doing everybody except yourself a big favour if you could prise her out of here.'

'You're a bitch, Fanny.'

George's blue eyes were blazing; even in her temper, Fanny had to admit that with his white face and dark hair, he was especially good-looking when being dramatic.

'Oh, and while she isn't sniffing round Philip – that's her prey's name; he has two children, what a shame – she's giving one of the Cordovans the hots. Pity about him, really, so hard on his wife, expecting a baby at any moment.'

George turned on his heel and left without another word, leaving Fanny fuming with rage and resentment. Whether with Gerry or Claudia or George or herself, she couldn't have said, but a tall and familiar figure suddenly appeared beside one of the pits.

'Oh,' she wailed, hurling herself at Victor's manly chest and dissolving in waves of tears.

Victor wasn't too keen on the tears, nor on the mud and general twigginess which was transferring itself on to his shirt; nonetheless, he found that Fanny made an extremely satisfactory armful.

'Calm down,' he commanded. 'Now, come with me, you badly need a wash before lunch, and then you can tell me all about it.'

CHAPTER 39

'Ah, lunch,' said Victor a little while later, coming into the dining room in his usual overpowering way and rubbing his hands together. 'Excellent.' He looked at the company present and frowned. 'Where are the others? Where's Lisa? And the children?'

'They've gone over to have lunch in Heartsbane,' said Hester, sitting down and unfolding her napkin.

Victor cast his eyes around the table. 'Ha, you're here again, Harry, are you? A little more of your free time spent at home with Zoë would be appropriate, you might as well not have got married the way you're carrying on.'

'I came to have a word with Jarvis,' said Harry defensively.

'I don't see Jarvis here among us.'

'I saw him earlier, so I thought I'd stay for lunch.'

'Much earlier,' said Victor nastily. 'Since he left for Heartbury at eleven, and isn't back yet.'

Harry pulled a bread roll apart.

'What's Jarvis doing in Heartbury?' Don asked, taking momentary pity on his younger brother; what an ass he was making of himself.

'Peacocks,' said Victor. 'Females, to go with the white peacock. Time he had something to occupy himself with, always escaping, gave the cat a nasty fright this morning so I hear.' He took a substantial mouthful of Maria's splendid steak and kidney pie. 'Fine for birds,' he went on, 'peacocking around with various females. I don't approve of it in people, however, not under a civilised roof.'

The hypocrite, thought Don, remembering his father's attentions to Fanny. He glanced across at her, but Fanny was wrapped in a Roman daze, oblivious of the dangerous currents swelling around her.

'Especially married men, with wives in situ.' Victor glared at Harry and Philip; Harry went bright red, Philip was unfazed.

'I think I can manage my own affairs, thank you, Victor.'

'I dare say you can. It's the right of every man to make a mess of his life, as long as he doesn't expect others to pick up the pieces.'

'Plenty of messes in your life, Victor.'

'Not at all. I conduct my amours with discretion and style. And, at present, I have no wife, and no young children. Or babies in the womb,' he added, giving Harry another ferocious look.

Philip bit silently into a stalk of broccoli.

Claudia turned her huge eyes on Victor. 'I think you're getting at me,' she said in her husky voice. 'It's not my fault, you know. I can't help falling in love.' And she bestowed her best smile on Philip, who had never taken his eyes off her. Then she flashed a quick, lesser smile at Harry and gave Don a conspiratorial wink.

Hester choked into her glass, and Victor rose to give her a thump on the back which nearly sent her flying. 'Crumbs,' he said. 'You have to watch it with crumbs.'

'Thank you, Victor,' said Hester weakly.

A hovering Guy watched the lunchers eat their way silently to the end of the course; I hope those two get indigestion, he said to himself. Sitting there, devouring that woman with their googly eyes. He darted in to clear the table, putting a big bowl of fruit salad and the jug of cream in front of Hester, and then, with distaste written all over his face, a plate with the pot of yoghurt and a spoon in front of Claudia.

'What's that?' said Victor. 'What are you eating? What's wrong with the fruit salad?'

'I never eat anything except yoghurt to finish a meal,' said Claudia.

'Rot your stomach, nothing but chemical muck, that stuff,' he said.

'I like it,' said Claudia, wondering why it tasted a little strange. She was tempted for a moment to summon Guy, demand another one, but she wasn't at all sure about how Victor would react.

They pushed their chairs back and rose. Claudia led the way out. 'I'm going to explore that delightful rose garden,' she said. 'Coming, Philip?'

Victor glowered, and put out a hand to restrain Philip. 'A word,' he said.

It looked for a moment as though Philip would shake off Victor's large hand, but he hesitated, and then told Claudia to go, he would join her in a few minutes.

'Coffee?' said Victor amiably.

'Thank you. What is it, Victor? I wasn't really intending to have coffee.'

'We go back a long way, been friends a good while,' said Victor, handing Philip a cup of coffee and holding up the decanter. 'A glass? Or does it interfere with whatever medicine you're still taking?'

'I won't have any now,' said Philip, who hadn't sat down, but was standing over by the window, looking to see if he could catch a glimpse of the loved one on her way to the rose garden. Probably with Harry in tow, damn his eyes.

'Lisa's not very happy,' said Victor.

Philip shrugged. 'She seems all right to me. On holiday, fresh air, plenty of time with the children.'

'Not much time with you.'

'Preaching, Victor?'

'I'm fond of Lisa.'

'Lisa is very self-contained, you know, Victor. Leads her own life, busy career. She doesn't want me hanging around her all day long.'

'No, and I dare say she doesn't want you hanging around someone else all day long, either. Come on, Philip, apart from anything else, it's bloody bad manners to come here, welcome though you are, and then make sheep's eyes at some little slut who's panting for you.'

'Victor!'

'If your friends won't say anything, who will?'

CHAPTER 40

'Got you,' said Victor, advancing on the hapless young man. His blood was up, and he held a gun at a threatening angle. 'Trespassing! Where's your camera, eh? Got one of those sneaky jobs, I suppose, tucked away in your buttonhole.'

George stared at Victor in alarm. 'What?' he said.

'What, indeed. Now, just turn round and take yourself off. I've got you covered, and don't think I won't use this. I've peppered poachers before now, so go.'

'Let me explain,' George began.

Victor looked balefully at his victim. Scandalous, what these papers got up to, sending down well-spoken young men, imagining that he'd be taken in because he'd be looking out for some tired old hack in a seedy jacket. Ha, this chap would be claiming he worked for *The Times* in a minute; saying he'd come to do a piece on the Roman remains, no doubt.

'Don't try any of that on me,' he said, his voice full of menace. 'I know you aren't here about the Roman finds.'

'Roman finds?' said George in astonishment. What was this huge, bearded lunatic on about? 'I'm not interested in Roman remains.' He had a flash of inspiration. 'I was speaking to a friend not long ago, though, and she was very excited about some Roman bricks and tiles she'd just come across.'

'Friend?' Victor was still deeply suspicious.

'Fanny Jenson, she's staying here.'

Victor lowered his gun a fraction. 'Fanny? You know Fanny?'

Hester swept across the grass, and told Victor to put his gun away, at once. 'Terrifying the poor man like that. What will he think of you?'

'I don't care what he thinks of me,' said Victor, exasperated. 'He's one of those press types, and he's on my land. Within view of my house. It's an outrage!'

'Don't worry,' Hester assured George. 'It isn't loaded.'

'It bloody well is. This is the gun I've been keeping loaded for this very reason.'

'Yes, Victor, but I unloaded it in case you got up to anything silly. Which you have. This is Sybil's godson, George Sermion. He's staying with her, and came over to see his friends.'

'Sybil should be more careful about her godsons,' said Victor, uncowed. 'She should know better than to have anything to do with the press.'

'But I'm not . . .' began George, his voice rising swiftly into the falsetto register.

'George is a poet, Victor,' said Hester. 'A *poet*. One of our foremost young poets. Nothing to do with newspapers.'

George nodded violently in agreement.

'Poet? What, like Keats and that one who drowned?'

'Shelley,' supplied George helpfully.

'That's the one,' said Victor. Only half convinced, he broke his gun, inspected it with a subdued growl as he discovered that Hester had spoken the truth, and tucked it under his arm. 'Poet, eh? Do you make a living from that?'

'Of sorts,' said George. 'And I work for a publisher, and do some lecture tours.'

'I don't know about poets,' said Victor. 'But if you're a friend of Fanny's, that's all right. Boyfriend, are you?' he added crossly.

George was quick to reassure him. 'Oh, no, nothing like that. We were neighbours, that's all. And I know Claudia.' His voice lingered on her name.

Victor's glare increased. 'Another one of her followers, are you?' He snorted. 'You're a fool, then. She's worse than a bitch on heat, that woman, with all of you sniffing round her like a pack of dogs.'

George was incensed. His dark eyes grew intense and he launched into a passionate panegyric in defence of Claudia.

'I can see you're a poet,' said Victor, the benign side of his personality returning like the sun from behind a thundercloud. 'You've got a way with words, I will say that for you. You're quite wrong of course, that woman isn't worth five minutes of anyone's time. Except for one thing, and I expect she gets a lot of that.'

'Victor,' cried Hester, seeing the agony in George's face. 'That's quite enough. No, you're not to say another word.' She turned to the poet. 'George, you're very welcome. I don't know where Claudia is, but she'll probably be in for tea. How long have you been here? Did Sybil give you lunch before you came out? No? Then come along with me to the kitchen, and we'll see what we can find for you.'

Deaf to George's protests, and ignoring Victor's bellows – he had a lot more he wanted to say about the folly of men who were taken in by the likes of Claudia – Hester bore George off.

'Ho,' said Victor, baulked of his prey. I know, he said to himself. I'll go and find Fanny. Some words of George's returned to him. Roman bricks? Tiles? They hadn't figured on the list of finds so far. Had Fanny made a new discovery, and if so, why hadn't she told him about it? At once.

CHAPTER 41

Lisa was glad to see Alec and Polly run off towards the paddock; keeping up a lively and light-hearted front wasn't easy. Damn Philip. It should have been an idyllic summer here, with so many warm days to be passed in the lush greenness of Heartset. There was the sea close at hand, the pleasure of being in such an old house.

Bath and Salisbury were within easy reach, only she could summon up no enthusiasm for any gadding or shopping or theatre or cinema-going. Not when at the back of her mind was the nagging question of what Philip might be up to in her absence.

In her presence, if it came to that. Claudia had no shame. She was openly affectionate and caressing to Philip; a hand on his shoulder as she went past, tucking an askew collar into place, and always, always, listening to him, focusing on him, making him the centre of her attention.

Naturally, she threw off glances and winning smiles at any other susceptible male who came within reach, but it was pure reflex. Philip was her target. Even her flirting with Harry was done to attract Philip's attention and make him jealous.

'Ugh,' said Lisa.

'I hope you're not commenting on your lunch,' said Don, falling into step beside her. 'Did you go to the Bunch of Grapes?'

'We did, and it was a relief not to be here, I have to confess. Or was it a feast of joy and pleasantness?'

'Not at all. Victor had a go at Philip, told him he was making a fool of himself. Got himself into quite a roar.'

'What, in front of Claudia?'

Don nodded. 'Who, as you can well imagine, wasn't a whit perturbed. Went on chewing her greens and swallowing down her revolting yoghurt as though all we were talking about was the weather.'

'Yoghurt?'

'Yes, ghastly stuff in a pot. Made Pa mad, he hates faddy eaters.'

Good, thought Lisa. She's eaten it; let's see if it works. Four or five hours, Granny P said, if taken on a full stomach. If she had it for pudding, that would be right.

'And George has appeared.'

'Will that annoy Claudia, I wonder?'

'I expect she'll just tank over him like she does everyone else. Your esteemed ma-in-law wasn't there for lunch, where's she gone?'

'To look up a crony who lives in these parts, Little Oath, could it be?'

'Barney Manor,' said Don instantly. 'Yes, Vanessa Rackrent would be a friend of Emilia's, she's a foul woman with a tongue like a viper. Ha, I bet she brings Emilia up to date with all the local gossip, and I don't suppose Emilia will like it very much.'

Lisa pulled a face. 'Are they talking about it much?'

''Fraid so. There are still two press men hanging about, and that keeps the story going.'

'I don't think I want to know.'

They walked on in silence, Lisa tense and Don relaxed as always. 'Of course,' he said, as they reached the doors which led into the library, 'you could always make Philip jealous, couldn't you?'

'How?'

'An amour. An enjoyable one, naturally, obligations carried out without pleasure are not on the agenda.'

'But you are?'

'Of course. Think how it would enrage Philip to see you swept off your feet by a man so much younger than he is.'

'And such a charming one,' said Lisa appreciatively. 'It's very kind, Don, but it wouldn't work.'

'Kind?' Don was affronted. 'Kindness doesn't come into it. Desire, sweet lust is what I'm talking about.'

'Don, in the state I am at the moment, neither desire nor lust figure at all.'

'That's because you're depressed. Rejected by Philip, belittled, made to feel of no account, it's quite natural.'

'I'm glad you realise this.'

'But some dalliance, some pleasures of a new kind, think how that would restore you to a better mood.'

'It will take more than that, Don. I need to see Claudia rolled up, foot and guns, and sent packing out of Philip's life. Nothing less will do, and I don't see how it's going to happen, whatever I do.'

Don opened the doors and bowed Lisa in. 'You prefer your work to me,' he said gravely. 'I'm broken-hearted.'

Lisa's laugh rang out, causing Jarvis to raise his head from a row of lettuces, and Hester to feel a sudden lilt to her spirits.

'It's good to hear you laugh, Lisa.'

Philip, making up one of an uneasy quartet in the rose garden, heard Lisa's laugh, and for a moment his heart was lifted and he was, in a flash, in another time and another place.

Paddington Station. Nearly twenty years ago, when it still looked grubby and postwar. No wide station lawn, no brooding bronze figure of Brunel, no little shops selling anything a traveller might or might not need. No good coffee, and a legendary giant cat, which he had never seen, but so many of his women acquaintances had. It lived, they assured him, in the Ladies, in a huge basket.

He had been standing by the entrance to the subterranean Ladies when he had heard that laugh, floating up the stairs. Before he even saw her, he knew, with absolute certainty, that this was the woman he was going to marry.

When he saw Lisa, her face still alight with laughter, walking in a way that betrayed an irresistible joie de vivre, he knew he had met his fate.

She was with a tall, dramatically beautiful black woman; Philip barely gave her a second glance. Without thinking, he followed the pair. Two men were waiting by the Bristol train; Philip watched an ecstatic greeting, hugs, kisses, more laughter, with hatred in his heart. Close enough to hear snatches of their conversation as they boarded the train, he gathered that they were going to stay with friends for the weekend.

A name drifted through the dust-speckled air. Freshford Castle. He was filled with a desperate sense of relief. He knew Freshford Castle, a gothick folly near Bath; had friends who were well-acquainted with its eccentric and arty owners. He could find out who this glorious young woman was, wangle an introduction . . .

'Philip!'

A discontented voice sounded in his ear. 'Darling, why did you wander off like that? I told you to wait for me, and you left my luggage just sitting there on the platform.'

Philip stared at her as though he had never seen her before. Then, with an effort, he jerked himself back to reality. What was her name? Oh, yes, Celia. And they were going away for a romantic weekend together at a hotel in Cornwall. Good God, he couldn't go to Cornwall, or even to the first stop along the line with this woman now.

'Celia,' he began.

And then he was back in the rose garden, with Claudia's dark eyes on him, and Harry and this black-haired young fellow glaring at him. 'Darling,' she said, in a voice husky with hidden invitation. 'Darling, you mustn't be rude to George, he's such a pet, one of my most favourite men.'

Philip extended a hand. 'How do you do?' he said shortly.

George eyed him warily, but took his hand. 'George Sermion,' he said. 'And you're Philip Maffick.'

'The poet,' said Philip. He wasn't a great reader of poetry, but George was sufficiently well known to be a familiar name even to philistines.

'You deal in money, don't you?' said George. 'You have an instinct for currencies, make fortunes overnight by betting against the franc and so on.'

'That kind of thing,' agreed Philip.

'Darlings, not business here,' said Claudia. 'This is not the place, so dull to talk about work.'

Philip hadn't been in touch with his office; doctor's orders, and his wife and the office had seen to it that he obeyed the orders strictly. Now he felt a stirring of irritation; damn it, he would ring his office, insist. It was his concern, after all. His eye was better, he was feeling quite fit. He was out of touch; true, it was summer, when currencies were sluggish while their masters holidayed. Nonetheless, some vital piece of information might have slipped past in his absence, some indicator of which markets were going to greet the autumn with a spectacular tumble or startling rise.

'Darling,' said Claudia. 'You look quite severe.'

'Philip isn't young and carefree like us,' said Harry cruelly. 'He has responsibilities and duties.'

'And you don't?' Philip, stung by the reminder that Harry and George – and Claudia – were half his age or less – hit back. Bloody Harry, as if he hadn't got a thriving business which he was currently neglecting. *And* a young wife about to have a baby.

Harry flushed, and George was quick to seize his chance. 'While you two have a business talk,' he said, 'I'll just take Claudia for a stroll about the grounds, it's ages since I've seen her, and there's lots of gossip for her to catch up on.'

Claudia's eyes lit up. 'Nasty gossip?'

George sighed. Nothing had changed, Claudia was still the same eminently unsatisfactory person she had always been.

And he was still as hopelessly in love with her as ever.

CHAPTER 42

Emilia wasn't interested in gardens. A city person through and through, she could cheerfully pass the whole year without walking on damp lawns, spraying this and that, or crouching down to inspect a fine specimen.

But manners are manners. Vanessa was an ardent gardener who rarely ventured out from her village and the surrounding countryside. There were infrequent sorties to Salisbury or Bath and she made an annual visit to London to go to the dentist. That was invariably followed by a show and dinner at the Gay Hussar.

'Why the Gay Hussar?' Emilia had asked on one of these trips.

'Years and years ago, you wouldn't remember it, Philip was little and you still lived in the Fens, I had a fling with a Hungarian. I ate a lot of Hungarian food then, and I still love it. I cook it, sometimes, but it's heavenly to go to a Hungarian restaurant. And there aren't many near Little Oath.'

Emilia found it difficult to think of Vanessa having a fling with anyone, although this had happened in the days before gardens figured so largely in her friend's life.

City-dwelling Emilia pitied Vanessa, despite a friendship dating from their schooldays in a particularly cold and wind-swept Yorkshire boarding school. What a waste, she thought as she followed Vanessa along the beautifully kept paths and recalled Vanessa's flaring beauty at eighteen. On the other hand, she looked very happy. 'Children well?' she enquired, as Vanessa, trowel in hand, made a quick pre-emptive strike at a lurking weed in the border.

Vanessa straightened up. 'Yes, six grandchildren now, would you believe it? The boys seem to be in the pink, and Caroline's business is going very well, so she tells me. And Philip? Still making money in that extraordinary way? Incredible to think that any child of Charles's should have such a gift.'

Emilia stiffened. 'Incredible? Why is it incredible?'

'Emilia, Charles was hopeless with money, you always said so. It was touch and go whether you'd keep Maffick in the family. Not that you'd have minded that much, would you? You never cared for draughty old houses in the Fens.'

'Philip's fine,' said Emilia, feeling she was on uncertain ground as far as her late husband was concerned. 'Alec's doing very well at school.'

'And Polly?'

'You always had a soft spot for Polly. I think she's very badly brought up.'

'Got a lot of character, Polly has. How is Philip recovering from his injury? A terrible thing, to lose an eye.'

'You know about that?'

Vanessa led the way to a grotto with rustic benches and a sturdy table. 'The whole world knows about it, it was all over the papers.'

'And I suppose you've seen the latest horror in the papers, too,' said Emilia crossly, sitting herself gingerly on the wooden bench. 'In the gutter press.'

'No, I don't read those sort of papers,' said Vanessa. 'On the other hand, I do know that Philip's up to mischief with a woman at Heartsease, because everyone for miles around is talking about it.'

'What?'

'It's a small world here, and Philip does seem to be behaving very badly. Lisa makes a good impression, you know, and then there are the children . . . And carrying on with this woman right under his wife's nose; it isn't very classy, Emilia.'

Emilia would brook no criticism from Vanessa or anyone else about her only son, and she told Vanessa so at some length, not hesitating to point out Lisa's many shortcomings and wickednesses.

'So it's Lisa's fault, is it?' said Vanessa, her eyes on the apple tree beyond Emilia, as she wondered whether it needed some attention. 'She's brought this on herself by being too independent and not paying enough attention to Philip? As well as being successful in her own right, and not looking after the children properly?'

Emilia sniffed.

'For someone who lives in London and prides herself on being up-to-date, you're very old-fashioned,' said Vanessa severely. 'Look at my Caroline, runs her business, has a happy marriage, is bringing up three happy, healthy, independent-minded children. That's the way women are these days.'

'Caroline's different.'

'That's because she isn't married to Philip. If she were, you'd disapprove of her as much as you do of Lisa. Honestly, your son marries a lively, funny, intelligent woman, overflowing with charm, who produces delightful children, and all you can do is complain about her.'

Vanessa rose and snipped off some dead heads with sharp efficiency. 'I'm glad to say that Caroline's mother-in-law is a very pleasant woman, who is very fond of Caroline and admires her for what she does.'

Emilia sat stunned. She had come to Vanessa for support and sympathy, not for a shower of cold water.

'Well!' she said.

'Well, nothing,' said Vanessa. 'Come along, we'll go back up to the house, and I'll show you my walled garden on the way. Then we can have lunch, and I can tell you one or two things about this floozie of Philip's. And I hope to hear more. I may live in the sticks, but my young keep me in touch with the outside world, and from what I hear, I think you need to be very, very careful there.'

CHAPTER 43

Dinner at Heartsease was an uncomfortable meal. Everyone was there, except for Alec and Polly, who refused to sit down and eat with the enemy. 'We'll have supper in the kitchen, Mum,' Alec said firmly.

Strange, thought Lisa. Alec usually made a big fuss about eating with the adults, and that always set Polly off on her refrain of 'It's so unfair, just because he's older . . .' And here they were, very polite and pleasant, saying that they'd prefer not to dine with the others, and Maria didn't mind, she'd said she didn't mind, and they were going to eat with her.

'And with Jarvis,' said Polly. Polly got on well with Jarvis.

'I suppose Harry will be eating here, as usual,' said Maria, consulting a huge Spanish cookery book with an intent expression on her face.

Guy curled an elegant lip. 'So he says, although he's going to get the sharp edge of Victor's tongue again, I wouldn't be surprised. And Mr Sermion, a poet, I understand, is dining tonight. The one who's staying with Sybil, her godson. Sybil asked if he could come to dinner at the Hall, because she wants to work this evening. She's finishing another book.'

'A wicked book,' said Maria with relish. She thoroughly approved of Sybil, whom she regarded as a highly civilised older woman of the old style. The discovery that this distinguished, good-looking woman wrote historical porn had come as a shock, until Maria had settled down to read one of Sybil's works; since then, she had regarded Sybil with something akin to awe.

'It keeps the wolf from the door,' said Guy. 'There's many a widow in her position and at her age would be very hard up, or needing handouts from the State; one gathers she makes a good living from her books.'

'It is because people in this country are so immoral, and they buy these books,' said Maria, who had read them all, and was longing for a new one to appear. 'Is Don here for dinner also?'

'Yes,' said Guy. 'He comes to be amused.'

'Amused?'

'Oh, yes, he thinks the men hankering after Claudia and all the troubles they cause are very funny. Personally, I find it very objectionable to have to watch them.'

'Be glad you are the way you are, and not susceptible to the lures of whores like this Claudia.'

Guy looked pained. 'Even if I liked women, Claudia wouldn't be interested in me; I'm not rich or famous enough.'

Maria made a clucking sound, indicative of strong disapproval, and returned to the pages of her book. Paella Alicantina, she said to herself. Possibly, possibly . . .

'Sit here, Emilia,' said Victor, glaring at Claudia. 'Fanny, you come and sit next to me as well, on the other side. Lisa, you sit there. Where are the children?'

Lisa explained, and earned another dark frown from Victor; he liked to survey the whole establishment from his place at the head of the table. He immediately lost interest in the placement, merely directing a further hard look at Claudia, who slipped in beside Philip before anyone could stop her, and turning his attention to the aromas coming from the sideboard.

'Smells good, Guy. What's Maria been up to?'

'A Spanish dish,' said Guy, whipping the covers off, and depositing a huge and steaming bowlful of paella in front of Hester.

'Excellent, excellent,' said Victor. 'Are those mussels I can see?'

They were, but before Hester could answer him, the air was punctuated by a large belch followed by the unmistakable rumblings of a fruity fart.

'Those children,' roared Victor, rising to his feet, napkin, bread and spoon flying in all directions. 'They've got a whoopee cushion, no wonder they didn't want to eat with us. Lisa, Philip, this is too bad. Can't you control your children?'

Silence.

'I hardly think . . .' began Emilia.

And then the crack of another fart, coupled with some violent belchings.

All heads turned towards Claudia. Whoopee cushions were forgotten; it was all too clear who was the source of the exuberant sounds.

Lisa stuffed her napkin into her mouth, and bent down as though hunting for Victor's scatterings. Only Don noticed; the others were watching Claudia, who with a final terrible belch, rose from the table and dashed from the room.

Philip, Harry and George all leapt to their feet, appalled, but quite ready to run to help the loved one.

'She must be ill,' said Philip, heading for the door. 'Mussels . . .'

'Sit down.' The voice rang out, stopping the men in their tracks.

They look so funny, thought Lisa, trying not to go off into another fit of laughter. Like schoolboys caught by the matron for stealing tuck, or smoking in the dorm. And who would have thought Hester, gentle Hester, could sound so commanding? She was always calm and quiet and collected, so that one tended to forget she was Victor's sister. These Cordovans were nothing if not effective.

'Sit down,' Hester said again, in a quieter voice which was still not to be argued with. 'If Claudia has been taken ill, she'd rather be by herself. She certainly won't want you three hanging around the lavatory bowl with her.'

'Hester!' said Philip, deeply shocked.

Hester took no notice, but began to ladle the food out on to the plates. 'This will get cold, and Maria will be offended if we don't do it justice. Claudia didn't touch a mussel, so nobody need have any worries about the food.'

Reluctantly, the three men slunk back to their places. 'An allergy, do you think?' said Harry.

'Probably stuffing too many acid drops before dinner,' said Lisa before she could stop herself.

Victor gave a great guffaw. 'Good one, Lisa,' he said, restored to geniality. 'Now, Hester's quite right. Leave the woman alone. Hester will go and see if she needs anything after we've had dinner. I never heard of wind being an emergency. Except for the person who has it, of course,' he added.

Harry shot his father a look of pure hatred.

'As for anyone being allergic to the sight or smell of anything in Maria's cooking, absolute nonsense.'

CHAPTER 44

'Leave them to it,' urged Don, taking Lisa's coffee cup from her. 'If they want to lurk around Claudia's windy door, baring their teeth at each other, then so be it. Where are Alec and Polly?'

'Gone to bed,' said Lisa. She sounded surprised. 'Well, not exactly. Hester's lent them a portable TV, and they're watching a film in Alec's room.'

Don's eyebrows rose. 'After nine in the evening? Aren't you alarmed about their moral well-being?'

Lisa laughed. 'I do keep an eye on them, Polly particularly, because she has nightmares. They're watching some American comedy, quite harmless. I know, because I saw it in London when it first came out. Some naughty words, but nothing they haven't known since nursery school.'

'Oh, wicked world,' said Don. 'In that case, stroll over to my house with me. It's a beautiful evening, I have champagne, part of my business, you understand, and we can sit in the garden and look at the sea. Or the vineyard, whichever you prefer.'

Lisa hesitated, but not for long. She felt carefree for the first time in a long while, and Don was right, it was a wonderful evening. Warm and full of dusky scents; it would be life-denying not to be out on such a velvety summer night.

'And you can tell me just what you gave Claudia, and how.'

'Me?' said Lisa. 'I'll just go and tell the children that I'm going out. Hester will look after them if they need anything.'

'And are you going to tell Philip you're going out?'

'I don't suppose he'd be interested.'

Lisa and Don walked along the footpath towards the vineyards and his house. It had originally been a farmhouse, he told her, as they moved among the trees, catching tantalising glances of the shimmering sea. Then it had been turned into a gent's res, sometime in the eighteenth century.

'At the time of the gothick revival, judging by the pointy windows and castellated parapets,' said Don.

'Charming,' said Lisa, thinking about Claudia.

'Yes,' said Don. 'Now we're alone, do tell. Just what did you slip Claudia? And how?'

'In that revolting yoghurt she's so fond of,' said Lisa, with a touch of smugness. 'And I'm not sure what she's taken exactly. I got it from . . . from a friend. Quite harmless, she promised, but look at the gratifyingly dramatic and incapacitating results.'

'Some fiendish laxative, one may guess,' said Don. 'I bet no one has ever done anything like that to her before.'

'Many would have liked to, I'm sure,' said Lisa.

'Better not let her discover you're to blame,' said Don. 'She'd have you hopping round the pond and croaking before you could draw breath. Were you discreet?'

'Very,' said Lisa. She frowned slightly. 'I only hope Maria doesn't get blamed for it.'

'If nobody else is afflicted, and she alone has eaten the yoghurt, then the blame will fall on the supermarket, or on the hapless milkman who delivered it.'

'Oh, dear.'

'If you're worried about the milkman, forget it,' said Don cheerfully. 'Hubert is his name, and he is of an evangelical leaning. He thoroughly disapproves of Claudia and her wanton ways; if she has a go at him, he'll read her a sermon about fallen women and the flames of hell.'

'I like the flames of hell,' said Lisa.

'Do you like champagne?' asked Don, refilling Lisa's glass.

'Not usually,' said Lisa. 'I don't like any fizzy drinks, they make my nose tingle.'

'Fizzy drinks!'

'I like this, though,' said Lisa. 'Delicious. Pure nectar.'

'Good,' said Don. 'It's excellent, I was sent a case from France, from the man who makes the wine.'

'Did you do him a favour?'

'We're old friends.'

They sat in silence, Lisa revelling in the pink clarity of the dusky light, which warmed the stones of the house behind them and lent a magical lustre to the landscape.

Don was content to watch Lisa. He loved women, as he loved good wine, and Lisa was a delight to his eyes.

She toyed with the glass in her hand. 'When you sit here, in this peace, you wonder why you live in London and work so hard and never, ever, just sit and look and reflect.'

'Do you need to live in London?'

Lisa considered. 'It's my home, and it's where my work is. And where else would I live? At Maffick, in the Fens?'

'What a terrifying thought.'

'Maffick has its charms. It's wonderful at Christmas, and in the spring, sometimes, and the children love it in the summer. But it's work, work when you're down there. However much money you spend on it, and however many professionals you have in to do things, there's always something that needs attention.'

In a minute, thought Lisa dreamily, he's going to kiss me. How nice.

He did, and it was.

And then, thought Lisa, pushing first one and then the other sandal off her feet, and relishing the warm stone underfoot, we're going to wander inside, to see the house.

Which was a treasure, furnished and decorated in a way which bore witness to Don's eccentric tastes, penchant for travelling and deep pocket.

'Look at this merry fellow,' cried Lisa. 'What is it?'

'Who,' said Don. 'Not what. He's Greek, a little Herm.'

'It looks like Harry.'

'Mmm,' said Don.

And now, thought Lisa, with a surge of wicked joy, we're going to find a room with a sumptuous bed, and he's going to make love to me.

And she was right.

'Wonderful,' she said sleepily, a little later.

Don propped himself on one elbow and looked down at her. 'What is? The champagne?'

'Oh, life,' said Lisa, noticing once again how characterful his nose was. She stretched an arm to pull him down. 'Wonderful,' she said again.

CHAPTER 45

Fanny had retired to her room in a thoroughly bad mood. Urged on by Victor, she had had a long and pointless conversation with Salvatore after dinner.

'No, I know I'm not an expert on Roman building. I appreciate that, but I do think . . .'

Salvatore wasn't having Fanny thinking. 'My dear, it is a matter of painstaking attention to tiny details. You must have learned this as an undergraduate, even if you learned nothing else. It is amateur to look at some pieces and declare them to be Roman, and original. If they were, which is extremely unlikely, then they will certainly have been brought to England from Italy in the eighteenth or nineteenth centuries.'

Fanny was dogged. 'Salvatore, there are all kinds of reasons . . .'

Salvatore brushed this aside, he didn't want to listen to any of Fanny's reasons. 'I have consulted with Dr Quelper, and she agrees with me entirely.'

Fanny was hopping from foot to foot. 'Salvatore, how can you describe them to Dr Quelper? You haven't seen them yourself.'

'No, but the moment you say, a figure like this, and such a bench and part of what might be a font and so on and so on, I know exactly what you have, and so does Dr Quelper. Now is there anything else, my dear? I'm really very busy at the moment.'

'Only some extensive Roman brickwork,' said Fanny sullenly. 'And tiles. Only I'm no doubt wrong about that, as well.'

Salvatore's voice took on a different tone. 'Bricks, did you say? Now, that could be very interesting. Are you sure they're Roman?'

'I know what a Roman brick looks like, I've handled a lot of them in my time, and as far as an amateur can tell, these are Roman bricks. Used in a flue, by the way they're discoloured.'

'Just lying around? I hope you haven't disturbed them.'

'Oh, I've gathered them all up in the washing basket, and carried them off to store in the garage,' said Fanny viciously. 'Loads of them.'

'Fanny!'

'No, of course I've left them where they are. The area is very heavily overgrown, but it seems to me that there were quite extensive buildings there. A hypocaust, it could be. But, of course, I wouldn't know. The ground is very up and down, lots of subsidence over the years. That's why so much brickwork is exposed still in place.'

'Years?'

'We're talking centuries,' said Fanny wearily. 'Now will you come and see for yourself? I know it's a long way, but you travelled all the way from Cambridge to see the kiln at Heartwell House, and that's nothing to what might be here.'

'Ah,' said Salvatore, not liking to point out that finds made by important television reporters were quite special to the dedicated archaeologist.

'Fanny, I will do my best. Meanwhile, please ensure that your host does not disturb the site at all. This is most important.'

Click.

'Why don't you tell him yourself?' said Fanny into the dead telephone.

Don was not the only member of his family to have his mind on lustful ends. Victor was in his study, catching up with some work; all this excavating took up a lot of time and energy. He grew bored, and restless, it was far too fine and beautiful a night to be sitting at a desk. Perhaps Fanny would join him for a drink. It was late, nearly midnight, but that didn't bother Victor.

He tapped on Fanny's door.

No reply.

Was she asleep?

He carefully turned the door handle and swung the door open. The glistening sunlight of the day had given way, not to darkness, but to the sultry light of a full moon. Light streamed from the window across the pale rugs on the floor. The curtains were still pulled back, the bed disordered but empty.

Victor took a quick look in the bathroom. Fanny must only

recently have come out of it. Victor sniffed appreciatively. Nice perfume, what was it?

Lisa could have told him, because she had given it to Fanny, in London.

'All your things gone with that fearful woman; you must have this, Fanny.'

'Nostalgie,' said Fanny, reading the label. 'Lisa, I couldn't, this is so expensive, and I never use smellies in the bath.'

'Why ever not?' said Lisa. 'It'll do you good. And it's not a scent I can use, it's too young for me. It was a present.'

From Rory, she didn't say, who always managed to convince himself that even the most mature of his girlfriends were hardly out of their teens.

Victor looked at the rumpled towel on the rail. So where was Fanny? Not here, in any case; very well, he would find her. He went back into the bedroom, glancing out of the window as he made for the door.

Ha! Who was that, sloping off across the lawn? Too slight a figure to be any of the men, not shifty enough to be a skulking reporter.

Fanny?

He would go and see.

Fanny was on a brick hunt. Having retired tearfully to bed, she started to fret. Why did Salvatore treat her like a fool? Why could she never make herself clear? Was she wrong about those bricks?

No,' she said out loud, pushing back the covers. Her book fell to the floor with a thump. She ran across the room and snatched up her silk robe from where she had left it draped over a chair. It was another present from Lisa, 'No, please take it, Fanny. I bought it in a sale, such a mistake, I can't wear it, I look like a vampire in pale green. But with your hair, it's perfect.'

Fanny loved wearing it, although she worried that she was exploiting the silk worms of the world. She felt dashing and luxurious in it; she had never felt like that in her ethnic cotton wrap, bought from a market in India.

No one was about, and Fanny made her way on light feet down the back stairs and out past the kitchen. All was quiet and dark in there; kitchens were strange, she thought, the way they died at night, like an unlit stage set. A thought struck her, and she went into the stable, now used as garage and glory hole, to search for a torch. She remembered seeing Jarvis put one back in there. Sure enough, there it was, recharging in its socket.

Fanny padded along the terrace and across the grass to the wilderness wherein were holes and bricks.

Victor, following, went into the wilderness wherein was Fanny.

Yells of fear rent the air, a beam of light flashed through the darkness of the undergrowth.

'Victor!' Fanny was squealing with fright. 'There's something in there, I heard it.'

'I expect it was me,' said Victor, enfolding her in a hug that might be called comforting but was a lot more besides.

Fanny hardly noticed. 'It wasn't you, you came the other way. It was crashing about. I think it was a wild boar.'

Victor burst out laughing. 'A wild boar?'

'Big and strong and wild,' said Fanny. 'It was!'

'A game bird,' said Victor fondly. 'A pheasant can make a lot of noise. Or a rabbit perhaps.'

Rabbit, indeed, thought Fanny, who had come to the conclusion that Victor was a bit of a wild boar himself. He was unquestionably big and strong, and there seemed tonight to be a touch of wildness about him as well.

They sank into the rich loamy soil for a very enjoyable few minutes of consolation. Then Victor got to his feet. He held out his hand to Fanny, and pulled her up. 'Come,' he said. 'There are more comfortable places for us to be together.'

I don't think I should be together with you anywhere, thought Fanny. She had strong views about not carrying on with married men. Did this count as carrying on?

Certainly.

Ah, but was Victor really married?

More than most men.

This is not a moment for frivolous thoughts, Fanny told herself, as she refastened her silk robe, and tried to keep up with Victor's more majestic stride. She didn't altogether like being hurtled along beside him like a small dog in a crowd.

When Gerry left her, she had sworn she would love him and him alone; that she would never let another man get close to her, in any way.

Too bad. Gerry had been doing quite a lot of close contact; was she going to live the life of a nun?

'No, I'm not cut out to be a nun,' she said firmly.

That stopped Victor in his tracks. 'Nun? What are you talking about nuns for?'

'Just something that came into my mind.'

'Then I think we had better get it out of your mind as quickly as possible, dear heart,' said Victor, alarmed. 'Where are you going?'

'In through the back,' said Fanny. 'I came out this way. No one will see us.'

Victor was very put out. 'I am not slinking up the back stairs of my own house, whatever next? We shall go in the normal way. Besides,' he added, 'no one will see us, because everyone's asleep.'

Little did he know.

They shrank back into the shadows as voices approached. Hard for Victor, who wasn't designed to shrink anywhere.

'Harry,' he said furiously, as the two men went past, arguing, and their voices faded into the distance. 'And that damned poet of Sybil's.'

Inside, the soft sound of Hester's feet could be heard coming along the passage to the hall. 'Quick,' said Victor. 'Up the stairs, as fast as you can. Wait for me, third door on the left.'

'Victor,' said Hester, unsurprised at meeting her brother at this time of night.

'Just been out for a breath of fresh air before I go to bed,' said Victor.

Hester gave him a keen look. 'And where's Fanny?'

'Fanny?' said Victor. 'Asleep, I suppose.'

'Turn out the light when you go upstairs,' said Hester serenely, and went on her way to lock up at the back. The tower door would have to remain unlocked, what with Lisa still with Don, and Philip on the prowl. She hoped that he wouldn't lock it if he went to their room first. He mightn't realise at first that Lisa wasn't back, and when he did notice, would he think to go down and unlock the door? Being a man, probably not.

There was little she could do about it, Hester told herself after a moment's thought. Pondering, she went to the kitchen to have a drink with Maria.

Fanny was waiting, trembling, at the top of the stairs which Victor had just plunged into darkness. 'Victor,' she breathed.

'What?' he said into the gloom. 'Fanny, why aren't you in my room?'

'I couldn't remember which one you said. I went into one, but I don't think it was yours, there were some very rude hangings, behind covers.'

'No, no, that's Aimée's room,' said Victor. 'My daughter, you know, away at the moment. Pretty room, though, if you share her tastes.'

'Oh,' said Fanny, thinking what a strange father Victor was. He opened a wide door at the end of the landing. 'In here,' he said. He closed the door behind him, and swept the waiting Fanny off her feet, dropping her down on the huge four poster bed.

'Now,' he said, unbuttoning his shirt.

At last, Fanny with nothing on. At last, Fanny lying there in the moonlight, every curve delectable, with utterly satisfactory breasts. Victor gave a cry of joy, and lunged.

'Oooph,' said Fanny.

Gerry was a smallish man.

CHAPTER 46

Hester knew exactly where she'd find Philip. Yes, there he was, pretending to be interested in the stonework of the old stable.

'I've come to bring a brew for Claudia,' said Hester. 'And a yoghurt, which she felt might settle her stomach. Perhaps you'd like to go and tuck your children up.'

'I expect Lisa will have done that,' said Philip, hating to leave the field free to Harry and George, who might be anywhere, ready to dash in and offer Claudia every kind of sympathy and assistance. And hating himself for feeling guilty about not wanting to say goodnight to his children.

'Lisa isn't back yet, and Polly was looking for you,' said Hester, making for the stone steps that led up towards Claudia's quarters.

'Where's Lisa gone?' said Philip, but Hester didn't respond.

He raised his hand to rub his eye, which was bothering him a good deal. Eye socket, rather, he thought gloomily. The doctor said it was a good sign, healing nicely. But it felt sore to him, and was often acutely painful. He hadn't looked at it yet, that was something he couldn't quite bring himself to do.

He had had no intention of having a glass or any kind of artificial eye. If a puckered eye socket bothered people, that was their problem. False eyes always looked so false in his opinion. A master at school had a glass eye, and it had terrified everyone. Mind you, that might have had something to do with it being bright blue while his own one was a murky grey.

One brave wag had asked him why he had a blue glass eye when his own were grey, and had been given very short shrift. 'My other eye is blue,' the master had said frostily. 'You must be blind yourself if you think it's grey. And you're gated for the week.'

'Sir! What for?'

'Impertinence. Gated for two weeks, for questioning a punishment.'

Philip climbed the stairs to Polly and Alec's floor without enthusiasm. Two pairs of eyes looked at him with wary defensiveness.

'Hester says your mother's not here, I can't think why not, so I've come to say goodnight.'

'We're fine,' said Alec in his most chilly tones. 'We don't need to be tucked up, we can take ourselves to bed.'

Philip looked at the pair of them. There had been a time when bedtime with their father was a highspot, a time for terrible jokes and much wild romping, which invariably ended with all three of them in a heap on the floor.

No danger of that now, he'd never seen such unnerving, still politeness.

'Goodnight, Daddy,' said Polly, marching past him to her own room, without looking at him.

'Night, Dad,' said Alec, standing by his bed, clearly waiting for his father to go.

'Don't read too long,' said Philip at last.

Alec just stood.

Philip tried again. 'Do you know where your mother's gone?'

'To see Don's vineyards,' said Alec, still standing.

'Goodnight, then,' said Philip, giving up and shutting the door behind him.

Bloody children, he said to himself as he hurried back down the spiral steps. He still had to be careful with steps, his single eye was apt to let him down when it came to judging distances. He made it down without mishap, and headed as a sailor to a lodestar, back to the old stables. Lisa was at the vineyards? She probably wouldn't be back for some time. And it meant that Don wouldn't be hanging about. For once.

Guy was off to Heartsbury after dinner, he'd heard him talking about it to Victor, so he wouldn't be there, inconveniently, just when he wanted to have a moment with Claudia. That only left Hester.

Oh, joy. There was Hester talking to George and Harry. If she was taking care of them, she'd be elsewhere.

Finally.

At last.

Time alone with Claudia. With blissful, fascinating Claudia.

Philip almost ran towards the old stable.

'Claudia.'

No reply, no sounds of life.

She couldn't have gone out, not in that brief time he had been with the children? Could she?

'Claudia, are you there?'

Philip was pressed against Claudia's door. Like a beastly tomcat on the prowl, yowling for a mate, he thought for one clear and bitter moment before his mind fogged over again with inchoate and uncontrollable desire for her.

He remembered another bedroom door, early one Sunday morning, when he had arrived at the tiny mews house in London which Lisa shared with a friend. His arms were full of roses, and Lisa had laughed and laughed as he strewed them at her bare feet.

That lovely laugh again, he thought. The liveliness of her sparkling eyes. Her beauty, not perfect to others, but perfect to him, and her tousled hair, her faintly flushed skin. He had swept her off for a day on the river; a punt, a hamper, and hours of drifting bliss. As usual, he had asked her to marry him, and, as usual, she had refused him.

'I'm too young to marry anyone,' she had insisted. 'I don't want to settle down.'

'We don't have to settle down. We can travel, wander the world, live wherever we want.'

'You have your work,' she had pointed out. 'And I need to work, too. And as for travelling, you don't need to be married to do that. Lovers travel, not husbands and wives. How staid those words are, husband and wife. All luggage and the first sitting for dinner and turning in early to be sure of getting a good night's sleep.'

Then it had been Philip who laughed and laughed. 'Oh, Lisa, you? You'll never be staid.'

And she isn't, thought Philip, as he stared at the closed door.

CHAPTER 47

Philip was convinced that Claudia had recovered from her attack and stolen out to meet either Harry or George. Or both, for all he knew, he thought bitterly, feeling hurt and frustrated. In which case, where would she have gone?

It came to him in a flash. Aimée's room. He had been in there with Claudia, overseen by the watchful Guy, who had no wish at all to show Claudia the famous tapestries.

Claudia was enchanted by them, declaring that she wanted to buy them for herself.

Guy was shocked at such vulgarity. 'They aren't for sale,' he said stiffly. 'Not now, nor ever likely to be. They've been in this house for generations. It's not like a picture, a hanging.'

'Picture,' said Claudia, suddenly remembering something. 'Oh well, never mind. There must be others, that are for sale. Or I suppose one could get them copied. Philip, aren't they just the loveliest things?'

Philip didn't like to disagree, so he made mumbling noises. He could appreciate the artistry, but he wasn't sure that art as frank and licentious as this was what he'd choose to have in his room. 'A little obvious, perhaps,' he said.

Claudia gave him a languorous look. 'Darling, so fusty, it's your generation, of course. Lots of talk about the sexual revolution and so on, but underneath, you're all Victorians, aren't you?'

Guy, his face rigid with disapproval, asked if Claudia had seen all she wanted because if so, he would replace the covers which hung over the tapestries while the room was decorated, and get back to his duties. Claudia reluctantly followed him and Philip out of the room, talking loudly about some of the scenes depicted.

Philip had been quite thankful when Alec and Polly appeared from nowhere, nodding to Guy, and eyeing Claudia with hostility.

Now he was sure that Aimée's room was where Claudia would choose to take a lover. Or two lovers, he reminded himself, gritting his teeth. His stomach gripped by spasms of rage and apprehension, he headed along the passage and through the doors which led from the old stables to the main house.

Up some stairs, along several passages, down some stairs, and there he was, on the landing. He hesitated for a moment, and then crossed to Aimée's door. He listened outside, feeling that he spent far too much time these days outside doors, begging to be let in.

Humiliating, when you came to think about it.

No sounds. He stealthily opened the door and peered in. It was dark in there; this room was on the other side of the house from Victor's, and the moonlight hadn't reached it yet. But there was enough light for Philip to see the ghostly hangings, and to be sure the room was empty.

He went out, hugely relieved. Then, as he was about to go silently back the way he had come, he heard some familiar and sinister noises. They were coming from that room, there. Whose room was it?

His inner voice told him that there was no way he should open the door and look in. His baser, more daft self moved him forward before he could stop and think about it. He flung the door wide open with a dramatic 'Ha!'

He was right, there were two people there, in bed. In flagrante. Only not Claudia.

Victor let out a cry of rage and hurled himself out of bed. 'Bloody man,' he shouted into the landing, before slamming the door shut and locking it with many imprecations.

Fanny was lying, huge-eyed and petrified, the covers drawn up to her chin. 'Who was it?'

'Philip,' growled Victor, climbing back into bed. 'The man's mad. Completely mad.'

Philip was aghast. Such appalling manners, how could he behave like this? Bursting into his host's bedroom, good God, whatever next?

Then anger rose in his turbulent breast. What on earth was Victor up to? Well, he knew what Victor was up to, it was perfectly obvious what Victor was up to. But that was Fanny in bed with him. Seducing a girl young enough to be his daughter, grand-daughter even. No, not grand-daughter, but it made little difference. It was gross behaviour; unseemly, and immoral.

And what of Julia? In strictly legal terms, she might not be his wife, but in the eyes of the world, they were a married couple. This wasn't fornication, it was adultery.

Indignation swelled in Philip, as he made his stealthy way back to Claudia's room. There he was, at a door once more. Philip had never felt meaner-spirited or hated himself more than he did tonight.

'Claudia?'

This time the door did, finally, open. A grey, unknown face peered blearily out at him.

'Claudia?'

'Oh, bugger off, Philip,' the apparition said wearily. 'Leave me alone, for God's sake. Go and have a wank and get some sleep.' Then to the noise of a terrible belch, the door was slammed in his face.

'Claudia,' said Philip in disbelief.

The torments of his night weren't over. He went on slow feet to his tower, feeling that for the first time in several months, he would welcome the warm, familiar arms of his wife.

And what did he find?

No wife.

Philip looked at the pristine bed. The covers on his side had been turned neatly back, Lisa's were still drawn up. He clattered down the stairs and looked into the other two rooms. Alec was asleep on his back, his sheet kicked off, his arm hanging down by the side of the bed.

Philip tiptoed into the room and manoeuvred him further on to the bed, his arm now beside him. He straightened the sheet, and pulled it up around him. Polly was asleep too, across the landing in her room, curled tightly round a stuffed elephant, her thumb in her mouth.

Philip felt a sharp pang, of desperate love for his children, and of jealous fury; where was Lisa? What was she doing?

Philip crept back to his room, and lay in the moonlight, waiting, waiting, for Lisa to return. He finally fell asleep, alone, and never stirred when Lisa stole into the room as dawn broke.

Lisa was asleep in her turn when Philip woke.

He coughed. Quietly, and then at full volume.

No effect.

Then he gave her a nudge in the ribs. Lisa gave a happy snuffle and turned over before sinking back into what was clearly a deep and blissful sleep.

'Shit,' said Philip, quite loudly, and got out of bed. He stamped across the floor, and then disappeared down the pair of steps into the bathroom, leaving the door open and making a good deal of noise, what with splashing, opening and shutting the cupboard several times, singing loudly and tunelessly while he shaved and clashing several bottles together.

He peered back into the bedroom. Lisa was still fast asleep. Thoroughly disgruntled, he dried himself, with many mutterings, and then pottered around their room getting dressed.

I suppose if Polly called out, she'd be awake in a second, he thought crossly.

Then, miraculously, the phone rang. Lisa twitched and murmured something. Philip picked up the phone. 'Hello?'

Toby's refined tones came down the line. 'Philip? How are you? Good, good. Is Lisa there?'

Now he had every reason to wake her up. She blinked at him in an endearingly owlish way before putting up a lazy arm and taking the receiver. 'Toby? Oh. When did he get in touch? And this mysterious client, no names,' she added in a whisper, with a quick look at Philip, 'is demanding the picture back if he won't sell it? All right, Toby, leave it with me. Everything else all right?'

Philip watched her as she chatted for a few minutes about work before putting the receiver back and sliding down into the bed again.

'And just where were you last night?' he demanded quickly, before she fell back into her slumbers.

'I went over to Don's house.'

'And did you have a good time?'

Lisa yawned. 'Yes,' she said, her eyes closing.

'Wake up,' said Philip furiously. 'Lisa, you weren't here when I came to bed.'

'No,' said Lisa.

'That was late.'

'Was it?' Lisa sat up. 'And where were you last night, if you came to bed so late? As if I need to ask. Did you have a good time with Claudia?'

'Claudia was ill, as you know.'

'I thought she might have made a speedy recovery.'

'She was extremely ill, if you want to know,' said Philip stiffly. 'She could eat nothing but a carton of yoghurt . . . Now what have I said?'

Lisa had gone off into peals of laughter, pulling the sheet over her head in her merriment.

'You may think it funny . . .'

'Poor old Philip,' said Lisa, mockingly. 'Off you go, primed for action, and there she is, glued to the loo. What a let down.'

More laughter.

'You're as crude as you're ungenerous,' said Philip with immense dignity. 'What's happened to you? You used to be, well, so full of warmth. Loving.'

'What's happened to you, Philip? All that wit and affection?'

'I haven't changed at all.'

Lisa was feeling too good-humoured to have an argument with Philip. Besides, it was no good arguing with Philip, he was too logical, and rarely lost his temper. His control came from years of living with Emilia, Lisa had always believed; you'd have to watch yourself with a mother like that.

On the other hand, she couldn't resist a few apposite remarks. 'You have. I suppose it's hitting fifty, and seeing your wonderfully organised life stretched out behind you.'

'Fifty? What's special about fifty?'

'Nothing,' said Lisa. 'Just bimbo-time, the last gasp before you become a man of gravitas. Fifty's "Oh-my-God-what-have-I-done-with-my-life?" time.'

'Bimbo?'

Now, thought Lisa, that really has struck home.

'Claudia is not a bimbo.'

'Young tart time, then,' said Lisa.

Philip was about to open his mouth, this was the moment he had been waiting for, when he was going to tell Lisa that he had fallen in love with Claudia, and that he couldn't live without her. That could they, please, arrange an amicable and civilised divorce and go their separate ways.

And in one of those strange, increasingly frequent time-slips, he was suddenly in Venice, fifteen years before. The light reflected from the water outside made patterns on the ceiling. In the bed with gold ends lay Lisa, eating an enormous breakfast. She always woke up ravenous, 'I must have something to eat now, this very minute.' She was planning a day of ecstatic art viewing.

Philip found he was enjoying the art as much as she did, though he wasn't sure whether it was the beauty of the paintings or Lisa's passionate reaction to them that gave him so much pleasure. She would lie on the floor of churches, on her back, to look at the ceilings, quite oblivious of the other visitors tripping round her.

And then, quite suddenly, she was wildly hungry again, and it was time for a delicious, leisurely lunch in some remote back street of Venice, where Lisa had sniffed wonderful cooking smells on the previous evening's walkabout. And then the hotel, for warm hours of intense afternoon love-making, before Lisa needed something to eat, now this very minute, before she set off on another trail, just one more picture she must see, this very day, she couldn't live another hour without seeing it.

'Lisa,' he had said, embracing her as they stood on a bridge over a murky canal. 'Lisa, I can't live without you. Exist, yes, live no. Please marry me.'

'I'll live with you,' offered Lisa.

'We practically live together as it is. No, I want to marry you, formally, properly, for all the world to see.'

'If I marry you, I'll have to become respectable,' said Lisa. 'No more the art student, but instead the soignée wife of a successful man. All those stuffy people.'

'Which stuffy people?'

'I'm sure all your business friends are stuffy.'

'Have you met any stuffy friends of mine?'

'No, because you keep them hidden from me.'

'It's because there aren't any, what would I do with stuffy friends?'

'All right, then,' said Lisa. Just like that.

Have I ever been happier than at that moment, wondered Philip. They had bought a ring in Venice, a handsome jewel from the Renaissance; Philip wanted nothing ordinary for Lisa.

Lisa broke into his thoughts as she slipped out of bed and went to the bathroom. 'I think what happens to men as they get older,' she said sadly, 'is that they forget how to be themselves.'

CHAPTER 48

It was a morning for phone calls.

'Emilia?' called Hester, popping her head into the sitting-room where she found Emilia with a cup of coffee and *The Times*. No lounging about in the sun for Emilia.

'There's a phone call for you, you can take it in here.'

It was Vanessa, big with news. Emilia's coffee grew cold as she listened, a look of growing horror coming over her face.

'Well!' she said finally. 'I do agree, not all the money in the world would make up for that kind of behaviour. How truly shocking. And is this publicly known?'

Vanessa's voice quacked some more. 'I see,' said Emilia. 'Am I going to do something about it? I most certainly am. Although,' she went on in a stern voice, 'I'm not quite sure what. Or how.' She became brisker. 'No, you're quite right, Vanessa. This mustn't be allowed to happen. No, I'm very grateful to you, one would much rather know.'

Emilia didn't hear the soft, almost imperceptible click on the phone just before she finished the call. She would never have suspected that Guy was listening in for all he was worth, ear glued to the extension in the kitchen. Hester knew quite well to check no-one was listening in before she spoke about anything more private than a call to the butcher or the hairdresser for an appointment.

In the kitchen, Maria and Jarvis waited with bated breath for Guy to finish.

'Well?' said Maria, as he hung up and came back to the table.

'*Well*!' said Guy. 'Just listen to this.'

CHAPTER 49

Lisa hummed as she showered. Polly and Alec came tumbling into the bedroom, shouting and talking about their plans, yes, she would come and see the stallion, the one only Alec could ride, later on that day.

'Now, shoo, I want to get dressed,' said Lisa as she came out of the bathroom.

First, breakfast. She was astonishingly hungry, she hadn't felt hungry like this in the morning for years.

Then she had to find some papers she'd brought with her and phone Toby back with one or two details.

After that, she must find Fanny, to tell her about her Harriety, now once more threatened; was there no end to Claudia's misdeeds?

Then she would spend a good long time with Polly and Alec. She stretched vigorously, and yawned, before seizing her brush and subduing her hair into some order. She wouldn't see Don today, he was off to London. She didn't mind at all. Which proves I'm not in love with him, she told her reflection, but she knew that already. Although it would be very easy to fall in love with him, such charm and such panache as a lover, she thought appreciatively.

But it was time to put away her toys, however delightful. This was time to think and behave as an adult.

If there weren't the children, would it be different?

Possibly. But they were there, thank goodness, and they came first. Lisa rose from the oak stool, designed, in her opinion, for midget-bums of an earlier time, and went forth to greet the day and its tasks.

Fanny's mind was elsewhere, and Lisa found it difficult to get her to think about the painting. Fanny was obstinate. It was her painting, if the man at the gallery knew that, then he couldn't let Claudia take it away, Fanny was sure about that. So she'd worry about it later.

'No, Fanny,' said Lisa. 'We have to do something about this now.'

That was a mistake; Fanny promptly collapsed in floods of tears.

'Fanny!' said Lisa, quite sharply. 'Pull yourself together, there's no point in crying.' There rarely is, she thought to herself; it was a mystery to her the way Fanny so easily gave way to tears.

'It's just that the painting was my mother's, and when I think of her not being here any more, then I'm so unhappy.'

'Then you must want to keep the painting, because it will remind you of your mother.'

More wailing. 'If she was alive, the painting would still be on her wall.'

'Yes,' said Lisa, with as much patience as she could manage, 'but she's dead, and the painting will shortly be hanging permanently on someone else's wall, unless you do something about it. And quite apart from any sentimental reasons you have to want the picture, it's worth a lot of money, Fanny. You can't lose a valuable thing like that simply because you can't bear to think about it.'

They were sitting in the library; Lisa had almost had to drag Fanny in there to talk to her. Fanny wanted to be outside, among her holes, preferably in Victor's company. She didn't in the least want to be indoors facing up to unpleasant tasks.

She looks about twelve, thought Lisa, exasperated, as Fanny sat on the edge of her chair, tracing a carving on its side with one finger, and with a very mulish expression on her face.

The door opened.

'Philip,' said Lisa, surprised.

He looked at Fanny. 'Crying again?' he said dispassionately. 'What's up?'

More sobs.

'Really, Fanny,' said Lisa. 'You'll make yourself ill; you must be dehydrated, the way you carry on.'

'Has she always been this lachrymose?' enquired Philip, coming into the room and shutting the door behind him.

'I don't remember it,' said Lisa.

'Shock, I expect,' said Philip. He crouched down by Fanny's chair. 'Here, have a hanky, and tell me what's up.'

'It's my fault,' said Lisa quickly. 'There's a problem with a picture which belonged to her mother. Someone took it, and it's at Oliver's. Cl . . . that is, the person who got hold of it, wants the gallery to sell it for her. They aren't too keen, and so this person is going to collect it to sell elsewhere.'

Philip stood up, and propped himself against the table. 'Oliver can't sell it if he knows the ownership is disputed. It could get him into a lot of trouble. All Fanny has to do is contact him, say it's her picture, and tell him she wants it back. He'll need some proof of ownership, of course, but that shouldn't be difficult. Is there an original invoice, or an insurance document? What papers are there relating to probate?'

Fanny bit her lip, still hiccuping, and looked at her feet.

'It hasn't been included as part of her mother's estate,' hissed Lisa. 'Fanny, was it ever valued, or insured?'

'I don't think so,' said Fanny finally. 'Not in writing.'

'Then we have a problem on our hands,' said Philip.

This was the Philip of old, thought Lisa, giving him a swift look. Cranking his mind back into gear, how bored he must have been all this time.

'Where are your mother's papers? No, don't start up again, it really doesn't help.'

'In a bag, in my room,' said Fanny.

Philip turned to Lisa. 'Do you know which room she's in? If we send her to fetch the bag, I bet she'll scamper off.'

'Sure to,' said Lisa, who could see Victor planted on the lawn, talking to Jarvis. 'She's in the yellow room, on the second floor.'

'What kind of bag?' Philip asked Fanny.

'A Dingles carrier,' said Fanny in a whisper.

'Keep her talking,' said Philip over his shoulder.

'Fanny,' said Lisa urgently, as soon as Philip had gone. 'Philip will help you get the picture back, he's very good at that kind of thing. But you mustn't let him know that it was Claudia who pinched it.'

'No?'

'No,' said Lisa.

'All right, I won't then,' said Fanny. 'Can I go back outside now? I was just going to clear another hole, and it looks as though there are lots more bricks.'

'When Philip's had a look through your mother's papers,' said Lisa.

'Does he need me for that?'

'He does.'

Alec was trying to stay cool and grown up, while Polly danced and frisked round her mother. 'Daddy's already there, talking to Geraghty.' She shot a dark look at her mother. 'Horrible Claudia's there, too, looking green. Harry's with her, and George is mooching about as well.'

'Quite a crowd,' said Lisa brightly, as she joined the others. Philip looked surprised to see her, but said nothing.

'Which is this horse, Alec?' Lisa asked.

Alec pointed silently to where the stallion stood under a tree, his fine head up, his lovely liquid eyes surveying the scene.

'Darling, he is beautiful,' said Lisa, impressed.

'Ho,' said a deep voice behind them. 'Here you all are. I wanted to know if any of you has got a Polaroid camera? I did have one, but God knows where it's gone. Even Hester hasn't got an idea where it is.'

'I have,' said Alec, not taking his eyes off the horse for a moment.

'Excellent, excellent. Ah, that's the horse Philip's going to buy. James will be down in a few days, he can fix it all up then.'

'Is he really going to buy him?' said Alec, delighted.

'Yes, yes,' said Victor. He raised his voice. 'Isn't that so, Philip? You're buying this horse?'

Philip nodded.

'It's a good buy. A generous present, but you won't regret it. After all, who better to spend your money on than your son.'

'Son?'

'Alec. I hear he rode him, well done, Alec. He won't let anyone else on his back.'

'Oh, I'm not buying him for Alec.'

'Not exactly, Dad,' said Alec. 'I mean not for me, precisely, but for us, and he'll live at Maffick. And I can ride him.'

Philip looked into the middle distance. 'Probably not,' he said shortly. 'You'll have to ask Claudia, it's going to be her horse.'

'I don't like anyone but me riding my horses,' said Claudia, quick to protect what she considered her interests.

The look on Alec's face cut Lisa to the heart. She moved

forward instinctively to shield him, to hide his naked disappointment from the others. It's like a tableau, she thought, looking at the motionless group of people. Philip was still gazing into the distance; the groom looked at his feet; Victor, a thunderous frown on his face, was staring at Philip; Claudia was ogling Philip with a pleased little smile on her pale lips; Harry was gazing dotingly at Claudia.

And Polly?

Polly suddenly sprang to life and hurled herself at her father, fists flailing. 'You can't, you can't. It's Alec's horse, you can see it is. Horrible Claudia shan't have him, she shan't.'

'Polly,' said Philip, winded. 'Polly, let me explain.'

'You can't explain. You just want to give it to horrible Claudia because you want to leave Mummy and go and live with her.' Then she whipped round and practically spat at Claudia. 'You only want the horse because he's valuable, you don't care about him like Alec does. And you think you want Maffick, and . . .'

'That is *enough*,' Philip's voice cut through the air.

How funny, thought Lisa through her fury. He sounds weary, not angry.

'It's true,' said Polly, slipping away from her father's restraining hand. 'She does want Maffick. She's got a book, and she gloats over the pictures. Only it's not like that,' she shouted at Claudia. 'It isn't often sunny, and it isn't smart. It's shabby and bits of it are falling down, and the rain comes in all over the place. There's only one smart room, which Mummy's having done up. You would hate it there. It's cold, and the neighbours are all mad. And they'd hate you.'

Philip winced, thinking of the Clewerths and the Tomkins. They might be bowled over by Claudia's extraordinary charms. Or they might not. He didn't think Claudia would find them charming at all.

The hell with it. You loved people for themselves, not to please friends and neighbours. Look how those very families had eyed Lisa with doubt and wariness. Especially after Emilia had driven out to the Fens to gather them all together and express her strong disapproval of her daughter-in-law to be.

Lisa hadn't cared a bit, and now they flocked to Maffick when Lisa was there; not that Lisa had made any attempt to please or ingratiate herself with them. She was the way she was, they could like it or not like it, it was nothing to her. He had always approached life in the same spirit; that was why he had been so instantly taken with Lisa.

Life could not be dictated by the Clewerths and Tomkins.

Lisa knew exactly what was going through Philip's head. She was so annoyed with him, so enraged by his treatment of Alec, that she felt no sympathy for him at all. *I hope he takes Claudia to Maffick, and that a large lump of masonry falls on her and squashes her flat,* she thought viciously.

Meanwhile, there was something she could do. Dimly, she remembered that the stud at Heartsease wasn't James's entirely. 'Victor,' she said. 'Do you own any of this Arabian? A couple of legs, or a tail, something like that?'

Victor, who had looked as though about to explode, simmered down. He cocked a knowing eye at Lisa. 'Ah, clever you,' he said. 'I believe I do.'

'And *you* haven't agreed to sell him to Philip?'

'No.'

'Then I'd like to put in an offer for him.'

'Done,' said Victor promptly. 'I'll get on to James right away, and tell him it's all fixed. He'll be delighted when I tell him about Alec.' Another glare at Philip. 'He likes a horse to go to the right owner.'

A shriek of protest from Claudia.

Philip simply turned and walked away.

Harry went over to his father, furious and expostulating.

Claudia turned to George for comfort, but George was in another world. The paddock, the feuding families, the horses, had stirred together in his mind. He looked at Claudia with blank eyes, and then wandered slowly off, talking to himself.

'Bloody, bloody poetry,' Claudia yelled after him.

Lisa put her chin up. 'Pure Billingsgate, my dear,' she said to Claudia. 'Have you ever thought of taking elocution lessons?'

CHAPTER 50

This satisfactory solution put Victor in an excellent humour, increased further by Alec's producing a battered Polaroid and offering his services as photographer to the excavation.

'Although it isn't much of an excavation,' grumbled Victor. 'Fussy Fanny won't let me touch a spade or trowel, says it won't impress Salvatore unless it's untouched. I'm not so sure I want to impress this Salvatore, lacks pep if you ask me. Very slack, these academics, I must say. I think he's got a boyfriend up in Cambridge, idling away the summer vacation in a very inappropriate way when he could be digging here.'

'Girlfriend, don't you mean?' asked Alec after a moment's thought.

'What?'

'Dr Buonamici? Isn't he a man? Wouldn't it be a girlfriend?'

'Oh, I doubt it,' said Victor, who had taken a dark dislike to the absent doctor. 'I doubt it very much. Little boys, even, I wouldn't be surprised. Magazines delivered to his door in plain brown covers, all that kind of thing.'

'Victor,' cried Fanny warningly. 'Salvatore isn't a bit like that.' Fanny should know, she had had a violent crush on him in her student days, when he had come to her rescue after a particularly tricky assault from Dr Quelper.

'Oh, Alec's old enough to know how people carry on,' said Victor, reluctant to admit he might have made some injudicious remarks. He became brisk. 'Now, enough of this chatter, what a pair of time-wasters you are. Let's get down to work.'

Fanny and Alec exchanged aggrieved glances and headed for the bricks.

The much-maligned Dr Buonamici was eating a sandwich at his desk in Cambridge when the fax machine gave a shrill yelp and juddered into action. Wiping some eggy crumbs from his elegant beard, he rose from his seat and went to have a look.

He stared at the upside-down foggy images as they rolled slowly out. Who was this from? Where was it? Good God, from Fanny Jenson, that women who had been pestering him about a putative Roman site, and what was his name? Victor Cordovan, that was it.

Maggie Quelper heard the sudden frenzy of activity in Salvatore's office and bounded in to see what was going on. She stood at the door in astonishment as Salvatore flew about his room, opening and shutting desk drawers, filing drawers, cupboards.

'What's up?' she asked. 'The Inland Revenue after you?'

'No,' cried Salvatore. 'A find! Such a find.'

'Where?'

'Heartset.'

'Not the one that idiotic girl's been blathering about?'

'Yes, indeed. Blind, I've been blind. She *told* me, but I knew better, I didn't listen, I didn't think, I didn't put two and two together. Or rather I did,' he said, stuffing a camera into a natty shoulder bag, 'but I made three. It should have been five!'

And with a final cry of triumph, he was gone.

'George!'

George was walking about the sunken garden in a moody trance. His poetic impulse was spent, a poem, of sorts, was there in a notebook, but he felt no sense of relief or achievement.

'George!' Fanny called again.

George looked up to see Fanny standing at the far end of the sunken garden, taut and grubby in shorts and a brief top. She waved at him. 'You aren't doing anything,' she said. 'Come and help.'

'I'm thinking.'

'Oh, nonsense,' said Fanny. 'Manual labour, that's what you need, take your mind off things.'

'Poetry . . .' began George.

'Pooh,' said Fanny. 'You aren't pondering lines of poetry, you're having a good bout of self-pity about Claudia.'

'Claudia,' said George softly.

'Yes, I can tell, because you look like a sad sheep. Now, buck up and make yourself useful. And don't tell me I don't understand, because, believe me, I do. It was my Gerry your Claudia took off with, remember? Mind you, I've found solace, that helps.'

The solace was commanding operations with much gusto. 'Got to get all these dead leaves and so on out of the way before this chap gets here,' he explained to George.

'It looks revolting,' said George, peering down gloomily at the damp, dark earth.

'Townee,' said Victor with genial contempt. 'Do you good to get your hands dirty. Give you an appetite for dinner.'

That touched another nerve. 'I don't suppose I'll be having any,' he said morosely. 'Sybil's still wrestling with her climaxes, it's the pub for me.'

'And an excellent meal you'll get there,' said Victor. 'Still, not as good as Maria's cooking. You must have dinner here. I'll tell Hester we'll be one extra.'

George flushed. 'No, no, I'm fine, I wasn't fishing for an invitation.'

'Didn't think you were, but can't have Sybil's godson out in the cold. That's settled. Now, you'll have to use your hands, strict orders from Fanny. Minimal disturbance, you see, just getting the top layer off.'

CHAPTER 51

'Hester! Victor!'

Julia's imperious voice rang through the house. She was a tall, golden woman, with an operatic air about her.

Doors flew open. Victor emerged from his room, dripping wet and stark naked. Guy came flying from the direction of the kitchen and Hester hurried in from the garden.

'Better get back to your room, Pa,' Don called up to his father. 'You might frighten the natives.'

'Don! Did *you* bring Julia?'

'Yup,' said Don. 'I was in London, and I'd dropped in to see Uncle Gray. I'd only been there half an hour, when Julia rang, telling him to come and collect her from the airport. Gray wasn't too keen; he has some big legal thrash on tonight, and thought he mightn't be back in time. So I nipped out to Heathrow and drove Julia back here.'

'You've put on weight, Victor,' said Julia.

'Ah,' said Victor, disappearing.

Julia dropped a cool kiss on Hester's cheek. 'I've brought you back some Swedish herbs,' she said.

'Thank you, Julia. I hope you enjoyed Sweden. You'll want to have a shower and change before dinner, so I'll tell Maria to wait.'

'Just family for dinner?' asked Julia as she started up the stairs.

'The Mafficks are here,' said Don. 'Including Emilia,' he added darkly.

'Of course, you said. I shall be pleased to see them.'

'And there's Fanny, I told you about her as well, Julia. The archaeologist, she's here to look at one or two finds.'

'You said Victor had been doing some digging, yes,' said Julia. 'Nothing too destructive, I trust.'

Hester and Don looked at each other.

'All in a good cause,' said Don. 'I'll nip back home now, and bring up a few special bottles to celebrate your homecoming.'

Julia's eyes narrowed as she watched Don leave. 'He's very light-hearted.'

'Vines are going well,' said Hester absentmindedly.

'Anyone else?'

'Sybil's godson, George. Do you remember him?'

'I do indeed,' said Julia, appreciatively. 'A very attractive young man.'

'And a guest of Harry's. A young woman.'

'I see. Harry's at home with Zoë, I suppose. Not long for her to wait now.'

The phone rang before Hester could reply.

Hester crossed the hall to the little table set beside the door. 'Hello? Oh, Zoë, it's you, we were just talking about you, Julia's here, she wondered how . . . No, I'm afraid Harry isn't here, he went to Bath. He didn't tell you he was going? Oh, that's too bad of him. I'm sorry, I didn't catch that. Not feeling at all well? Oh, Zoë! Hold on.'

Julia was nearly at the top of the stairs, but she came down with remarkable speed for a big woman and seized the phone. 'Julia here.' She listened for a moment. 'I'll be right over.'

She replaced the receiver and turned back to Hester. 'Is the car in the garage?'

'Oh, bother, Jarvis was cleaning Victor's car today, and he's only half way through. Yours went in for a service, of course we weren't expecting you back quite so soon.'

'No, I heard rumours, and so I cut my journey short.' Julia was back on the phone. 'Don? Please come back to the Hall. I have to go to the Lodge. Right now. Yes, I'm afraid so.'

There were disapproving faces in the kitchen.

'It's quite wrong,' said Guy, in tones of deep disapproval. 'Taking off to Bath with a hussy, when his wife's about to have a baby.'

'Why should he do such a thing?' Maria's eyes were dark with sympathy for Zoë, and disgust for the ways of men.

'He said he felt sorry for her, she'd been ill, and nobody was concerned about her.'

'Ill! She was just suffering from a laxative.'

'No one knows where he's gone,' said Guy, shaking his head. 'Hester's rung round the cinemas, but no luck.'

'She is a bad, bad woman, to take a young woman's husband away at such a time.'

'It's very wrong of Harry to take her,' said Guy tartly. 'Hark, I hear the phone.'

They waited, and then heard Hester's steps hurrying along the passage. She came into the kitchen at speed, to announce that Zoë had to go into hospital, at once, and that Don was taking her and Julia. 'No time to wait for an ambulance, Julia says.'

It was a subdued party which gathered before dinner. Victor had rung the hospital three times, and his fidgets were driving Hester into a most unusual state of irritation.

'I know, Victor, Harry should be there. But babies are born every day of the week without their fathers being there.'

'That's all right when no-one knows who the father is. Obviously, there are times . . . well, men in the navy and so forth. But none of this excuses Harry's behaviour. A first baby, and early. Zoë could be in danger. She needs her husband there. Has her mother rung back yet?'

'You asked me that five minutes ago,' said Hester. 'No, there's no reply from her number.'

'Damn her, what's the matter with these people? Doesn't family count for anything these days?'

Lisa and Emilia found themselves in agreement for once, finding Harry's careless and selfish behaviour unforgivable.

'Of course husbands were never present at the birth when I had Philip,' said Emilia. 'Not there in the room with you. But they were at the clinic or hospital, even Charles was, and he was the most thoughtless of men.'

'I was very glad that you were there when Alec was born,' Lisa said to Philip. 'You spend such ages just waiting, like a slab of meat, and no one talks to you.'

'You had a very bad time with Alec,' said Philip shortly. 'I trust that everything goes easily for Zoë.'

Victor stamped over to the door. 'I'm going to ring the hospital again,' he said.

'No, Victor.' Hester was firm. 'If there were any news, Don would ring.'

At that moment the phone rang. Everyone was silent as Hester fended off Victor and picked it up. 'Don? Oh, good, good. Half an hour? She'll be so pleased.'

'Well?' said Victor.

'They've got hold of Harry; he finally answered his mobile phone, and he's driving straight to the hospital.'

'Better late than never,' said Victor.

The phone rang again, and this time he got to it before Hester did. 'Oh,' was all he said, and then, 'Philip, it's for you.'

Philip raised an eyebrow, but took the phone. 'Yes.' He listened for several minutes, his face expressionless.

I know what it is, Lisa thought. It's Claudia, saying come to Bath and get me.

'No,' said Philip. 'I can't drive. Because of my eye.'

Everyone in the room heard Claudia's disgruntled and carrying tones rattling down the line. 'Such a bore, that eye of yours. Aren't you ever going to be able to drive again? It's very inconvenient. Please get someone else to pick me up, then, would you?'

Philip held the receiver in the air. 'Any volunteers?'

Silence.

'Sorry,' said Philip. 'Nobody seems able to come. I suggest you get a taxi.'

'A taxi! That will cost a fortune.'

'Have it on me,' said Philip, in a most unloving way. He very carefully put the phone down. Then he walked across to the window, his back to the company.

'Excellent,' said Victor.

'Yes,' said Hester quickly. 'Excellent news, that Harry is on his way to the hospital.'

Fanny and George slid into the room. 'I'm sorry if we're late,' said Fanny. 'Only, it seemed a bit of a family do tonight. We wondered if we should go out.'

'No, no,' said Hester. 'Zoë's baby is arriving sooner than expected, so we're at sixes and sevens.'

'Oh, poor Zoë,' said Fanny. 'I thought . . . That is, someone said that Victor's . . . that Julia was back?' She flashed a quick look at Victor.

'She is,' said Lisa. 'But she's gone to the hospital with Zoë.'

'Oh. Oh, I remember, she's a doctor, isn't she?'

'That's right,' said Hester. 'No, don't sit down, because dinner's ready; I'll go and tell Guy we're all here.'

Julia looked thoroughly at home in the hospital. 'Really, Harry,' she said, in ringing tones. 'Did you have to come in that ridiculous get-up?'

Julia hated Harry's dramatic biking clothes, from his black helmet to the big leather boots with silver wings painted on them.

Harry had never got on with Julia. 'I dumped the car at the office and borrowed a bike,' he said, sounding a trifle sullen. 'Where's Zoë?'

'They're examining her. No, leave her be, you can see her in a minute.'

'Is she all right?'

'That's what they're finding out. She's certainly in labour, it's just a question of how long it's likely to be.'

'It's three weeks early,' said Harry, running a hand through his hair. 'It's too soon.'

'There's nothing you can do about it,' said Julia. 'Her waters broke, and once that happens, the baby has to be born.'

'Was she alone at home, when that happened?' said Harry. 'Or was Mrs Slubs there? Or you?'

'Why should I have been there?' Julia's voice was very sharp. 'She was alone, and she was very frightened. Childbirth is terrifying, especially the first time.'

Harry shifted from foot to foot, feeling about fourteen years old.

In Julia's opinion, Harry had behaved like a fourteen year-old. 'You had no business to be away like that, for the whole evening. And out with a woman! What were you thinking of?'

Harry looked at his stepmother with barely concealed hatred. He didn't say a word.

There was nothing to say.

CHAPTER 52

Lisa woke early, listening to an unfamiliar drip, drip, drip.

Rain.

Poor Victor, she thought, that would make a mess of his holey terrain. She slid further under the bedclothes. It was very early still, no need even to think about getting up. Beside her, Philip, who had been so silent all yesterday evening, was soundly asleep. Lisa yawned, and fell asleep herself.

She was woken a second time by sounds of running water. Philip must be up. He came back into the room, sitting down on the bed with his usual thump to put his socks on. He saw that she was awake, and got up. 'I didn't mean to wake you,' he said. 'I'm going to London.'

'London?'

'Yes, I'm taking Fanny up to Oliver's, we must get that picture back. Is there anything you want me to bring back?'

Lisa was still half asleep, and puzzling as to why Philip should be so concerned. She asked him.

'Poor kid,' he said with uncharacteristic sympathy. 'She's had a rotten time, with her mother dying, and then that fuss with her boyfriend.'

Fuss, huh? thought Lisa. But she was surprised. Two-eyed Philip would have had little time for Fanny's misfortunes. 'Old enough to get herself sorted out, she should find herself another job and get back into things,' that would have been his comment.

There was another surprise to come. 'And best to get her out from under Julia's nose,' he said.

Goodness. 'When will you be back?'

'If you don't need anything, it'll be straight there and straight back.'

'How are you going?'

'Fanny's driving me.'

He vanished, leaving Lisa with a bemused and amusing picture of Philip rattling up to London in Fanny's disreputable Deux Chevaux. Do him good, she thought. I must get up, she told herself with another yawn. I've got a lot of work to catch up on.

Lisa went back to sleep.

Sleeping, she missed the excited hubbub which greeted the return of a triumphant Julia, bearing tidings of the newest Cordovan.

'Wake up, Mummy, wake up,' said Polly, jumping on to her bed, and tugging at her head. 'Zoë's had her baby, it's a girl, and it's going to be called Xanthe.'

'Xanthe,' said Lisa, struggling to sit up. 'How pretty.'

'And you're to get up right away,' said Alec, tossing her wrap on to the bed, 'because there's going to be champagne for breakfast, Victor says.'

'For everyone, even us.'

'So hurry up.'

'Where's Daddy?'

'Gone to London,' said Lisa.

'Good,' said Polly. 'I hate him.'

By the time they had crawled through the streets of London to Oliver's gallery, Philip felt that he needed another night's sleep, and probably a visit to the dentist as well. His wound throbbed, and he demanded a glass of water as soon as he set foot inside the gallery.

Oliver looked at them with disapproval. He knew Philip slightly, through Lisa, but in his country clothes, Philip looked very far from being a prosperous and successful man, such as Oliver's customers generally were. And as for this girl with him! Oliver shuddered as he looked at Fanny's functional but well-worn jeans and old sweatshirt.

Such a pair would not make a good impression on any passers-by, or visitors who had come inside to have a look. Oliver ushered them rapidly into the rear of the gallery, gave Philip a drink of water, and asked, quite curtly, what he could do for them.

'You have a picture which belongs to this young lady,' said Philip. 'A Harriety. My wife has spoken to you about it. She wants to take it with her now.'

Oliver's countenance became extremely foxy. 'Ah, yes, I remember, Lisa did raise some matter concerning the painting.

However, there is no question of this person taking the picture away.' He gave a slight laugh. 'I've never seen her before, and as far as I know, she is not the owner.'

Fanny sniffed.

'Now you've done it,' said Philip. 'First of all, let's have a look at this painting.'

'Why?'

'I want to make sure that you've got it here, and that it's the right one. Now, there's no point in being obstructive. My wife's been a very good customer of yours over the years, and Miss Jenson here is a relation of hers.'

Fanny gave him a startled look, but didn't say anything; she was too busy trying not to cry. It had finally occurred to Fanny that Philip didn't like her to cry, and he was being so kind and helpful. Personally, she could see that the whole trip was a waste of time. This was hopeless. It was clear to anybody that this little man wasn't going to hand over her picture. Not if he'd had dealings with Claudia, who was far richer than Fanny, and probably much nastier.

Oliver reluctantly summoned a minion and asked her to bring up the painting. 'Of course,' he said, 'if you were interested in *buying* the painting . . . perhaps as a gift for this lady?' Oliver had read the papers, he knew that Philip had a young thing in tow, although Fanny seemed to him to be a most inappropriate choice for a man of distinction and substance.

'Oh!' Fanny gave an exclamation of joy and darted forward as the assistant heaved the painting on to the easel. 'That's it,' she said. 'It's my mother's painting. Oh, thank goodness it's all right.'

'Miss Jenson!' Oliver was affronted. 'No painting in our care is other than in good condition. All right, indeed!'

Fanny hastened to reassure him. 'I didn't mean you, but I couldn't be sure what that horrible woman had done with it, she might have squashed it in the back of her car, or anything.'

'The owner of this painting,' said Oliver emphasising the word owner, 'is someone with a good deal of experience with paintings and valuable objects. There is no way she would mishandle a work of art.'

Fanny was becoming cross. 'She is *not* the owner of this painting. This painting is mine. It was given to my mother by Harriety himself.'

Oliver had never heard a more unlikely story in his life. 'My client informs me that the painting was given to her family by the artist some years ago.'

'She's a liar. Goodness, couldn't you tell that just by looking at her?'

Oliver ignored this intemperate remark. He turned to Philip. 'You perhaps have some papers relating to the picture Miss Jenson claims to own? Which can prove it is indeed this canvas? Or not, as the case may be.'

'Of course,' said Philip, not batting an eyelid. He took out a sealed brown envelope from the capacious inside pocket of his mac, and handed it to Oliver. Then he strolled over to the picture.

Oliver went to his desk; he wouldn't dream of opening an envelope with his bare hands. He had a silver paper knife, where was it? He made a tsking sound of irritation; for some reason, it wasn't on his desk. 'One moment, please,' he said, disappearing into his own private regions beyond the rear room.

'Quick,' said Philip to an astonished Fanny.

He grabbed the painting, and shot through into the main gallery. 'Open the door, please,' he said to the assistant, and such was his authority that she did so without hesitation.

'Oh, and I seem to have Oliver's paper knife,' said Philip, dropping it by the door. 'Please give it back to him.'

'Don't run,' said Philip to Fanny. 'Don't attract attention. Just go ahead, and open the car.'

Philip had thoughtfully directed Fanny to park several right and left turns away from the gallery. 'I don't think he'll come after us,' he said, as he tucked himself with difficulty into the passenger seat.

'He will,' said Fanny, her hand trembling as she reached for the ignition. 'I know he will.'

'Not he,' said Philip. 'He's on very shaky ground, and he knows it. He'll get back on to that client of his, the thief, and ask a few questions before he makes a fuss.'

'But she isn't there,' said Fanny.

'How do you know?' said Philip, bracing himself on the dashboard as Fanny took a wide corner.

'Because she's at Heartsease Hall,' said Fanny with a loud wail. 'It was Claudia who stole my painting.'

CHAPTER 53

Refreshed by a substantial if late breakfast, and feeling highly pleased with her part in delivering Victor's first grandchild, Julia decided to spend her first morning back at home walking the bounds.

Hester tried to dissuade her. It was inevitable that Julia would discover what Victor had been up to, but it would be pleasant if it could happen in stages.

Julia was having none of it. 'I know it's raining, Hester, I can see that. It rained a lot in Sweden, too, let me tell you, and I took my exercise there in the normal way. A brisk walk every day, and it would do Victor good to follow my example. I know he's a big man, but he's looking portly.'

'I gather Zoë has no baby clothes,' said Hester cunningly.

Julia was tempted, but no, she didn't need to alter her plans. 'After I've been round and seen how everything is I shall drive to Salisbury and do some shopping there for Zoë's baby. Where's Jarvis?'

'He's gone to pick up your car,' said Hester, relieved that she had had the forethought to get Jarvis out of the way, at least for the time being. Jarvis had a long list of Victor grumbles which he was longing to share with Julia.

'I shall start in the rose garden,' said Julia.

Hester winced.

'The roses should be quite lovely by now.' She poured herself another cup of coffee. 'Hester, what's that terrible screeching noise?'

'That? Oh, it's the peacock,' said Hester.

'None of our peacocks sounds like that. What's the matter with it?'

'It's a new peacock. A white peacock. Victor saw an advertisement for one in a magazine.' She didn't have to explain further.

'Just a single male? That seems very cruel.'

'No, no, there are peahens as well. But the peacock has a feud going with Electra, and he's very noisy when she's about.'

'That cat is never about,' said Julia. 'She does nothing but sleep. It comes of having her neutered; it's most unnatural.'

'Ah,' said Victor, coming blithely into the dining room. 'There you are. Are you going down to the clinic?'

Victor was very pleased with life, and he was glad to have Julia back. Fanny was all very well and quite delightful, but on the other hand, there was something about Julia which made the night hours particularly rewarding.

He didn't look so pleased when Julia announced her plans. 'Not the clinic on my first day back,' she said. 'I'm not due there for another ten days. I'm going to take a stroll in the garden and see how everything is coming on.'

Victor looked wildly at Hester for support, but she ignored his pleading eyes and merely clanked the lid of the coffee pot in a warning way. 'We won't be many for lunch,' she said. 'Philip and Fanny have gone to London, Harry presumably will be at the hospital . . .'

'He will if he knows what's good for him,' said Julia grimly.

'. . . and George is taking Claudia off to the seaside.'

'Excellent,' said Victor. 'Bit of peace and quiet for a change.'

The peace and quiet was at that instant shattered by the roar of an engine as a car shot up the drive. Julia cocked an ear. 'Are we expecting visitors?' she asked.

'It's probably the fish man,' said Victor.

'Does he drive a Morgan?' asked Hester, who was looking out of the window.

There came a peal on the doorbell, which was never used. Birds flew up out of the climbers creeping over the ancient porch, the peacock started up again, and loud Spanish cries could be heard from the kitchen.

'Rowdy fellow, whoever he is,' said Victor. 'Wonder what he wants.'

Guy came into the dining room, with Salvatore, in a state of great excitement, close on his heels.

Julia rose, frowing. Victor loomed. 'Who are you?' he said.

'I,' announced the visitor, 'am Dr Buonamici. And you are Victor Cordovan. I must congratulate you. Even from those very poor faxes, I can see that you have made a major, major find. Now, take me to the site immediately if you please. My colleague, Dr Quelper, is following me down with a full team.'

CHAPTER 54

Lisa wasn't worried at first when there was no sign of Polly at lunch-time. She knew that nothing would keep the two children away from the ever-increasing troop of archaeologists, students, pressmen and inquisitive locals.

'The little girl?' said an archaeologist, dragging his mind back to present day matters. 'If she's the one with dark hair, I saw her setting off on her pony some time ago. Down the road, that way, I think she went. I can't be sure, mind.'

Lisa felt annoyed with Polly, who wasn't supposed to ride out alone on the road. Of course, she'd be all right, but there were a lot of strangers about. She wondered where Alec was, and found him, inevitably, in the dining-room, bolting down a quick tea before returning to the diggers.

'Nope, haven't seen Pol for ages,' he said. 'Not since before lunch. She hasn't been with us.'

'Go and see if she's in her room, Alec, will you, please.'

Alec was about to protest when he saw Lisa's face. 'She's probably there sulking,' he said, taking an apple to sustain him on his journey.

'I hope so,' thought Lisa.

'Not there,' said Alec returning more quickly than seemed possible. He was panting, and held out an envelope. 'Um, this was on her bed. It's addressed to you.'

Lisa, her heart thumping, tore open the letter. She read it with growing horror, and looked blankly at Alec, feeling as though everything was happening in slow motion.

'She's run away, Alec,' she said, in a quite unfamiliar voice. Alec came over to her and put an arm round her.

'Let me see.' He scanned the messy lines and sighed. 'I thought so. She's been so upset by Dad, and you know . . . Oh, bugger, where can she have gone?'

239

'Alec, language,' said Lisa automatically. 'Oh God, Philip's in London, I don't know when he'll be back. I'm not sure what I ought to do.' She couldn't think clearly, as she knew she must. Alec vanished, leaving her feeling frighteningly alone. I should ring the police, she told herself. That's the first thing to do.

Alec was back again, this time with Hester. Then Don was there, organising, arranging, calming her and Alec.

'No, Lisa, you aren't going off to look for her. Victor and Julia are seeing to all that. You must stay here; she may ring. Now listen, she's perfectly all right. She can't have gone very far, even on her pony. If she isn't back soon, we'll contact the police.'

'She could have had an accident, we'd never find her in all these woods and valleys around here. Or she might have gone to the sea. And a child, alone, she's so vulnerable if someone sees her.'

'If someone sees her, they'll tell us, and then we'll know where she is,' said Don with infuriating good sense. 'And there's no shortage of searchers, all those university types swarming all over the place in boots and shorts. If they can find Romans, they can find Polly.'

The hours wore on, broken by the terrifying return of Polly's pony, who came trotting back alone. Nobody noticed him at first, since Geraghty and his lad were out scouring the hills for Polly. Then Maria spied the pony placidly tugging at the grass, and she ran to tell Lisa.

Lisa, who had been controlling herself admirably, broke down. 'Oh, my God, no!'

Hester was brisk. 'Sssh, Lisa. Now, stop it. Carrying on like that won't help Polly. Now *listen*. That pony hasn't come back because he's thrown Polly off. You can see for yourself.' Hester almost dragged the frantic Lisa out to where the pony was standing munching on the verge of the drive. 'Look,' she said. 'The reins have been knotted on his neck so that he wouldn't catch his leg in them. And the stirrups have been run up the leathers. She's a good girl, your Polly.'

Philip found her there when he got back from London. She had buried her face in the pony's neck, and was trying desperately not to cry.

Philip hurled himself out of the car, and behind him, Lisa could see Fanny's shocked face.

'Don told me,' he said, putting an arm round her. 'She can't

240

have gone very far. She was out on the pony? And he's come back. Now, you can see for yourself that this pony hasn't been ridden hard at all. My bet is that she's been pottering about along the lanes, not sure of where to go. Lisa, why has she run away?'

Lisa valiantly blew her nose, now full of pony hairs, and handed him the letter which was crumpled up in a tight ball in her hand.

'I see,' he said finally. 'Where's Mother?'

'Over with that Vanessa friend of hers,' said Lisa. 'She's on her way back, though.'

'Into the house with you,' said Philip. 'I'll see to the pony.'

'No,' said Lisa. 'I feel better out of doors. Only, it's so quiet.'

There was indeed an uncanny stillness about the place. The rain had stopped, and insects were buzzing to and fro. A bird let out a stream of trills, but there were no voices, no signs of movement. Everybody was out, looking for Polly.

Except for Claudia. She and George had been stopped by a party of searchers on their way back from the sea, who asked if they'd seen Polly. George had then summarily dumped Claudia, telling her to walk the rest of the way, while he set off to help look for the child.

Claudia had declined to join the foot contingent, dismissing their concerns with visible scorn.

'What a cow,' said a freckle-nosed student. 'Fancy not caring about a lost child.'

'Come on,' said one of her companions. 'With any luck, she'll get lost, too, only we won't go looking for her in a hurry.'

Now she walked disconsolately up the drive, her face brightening when she saw Philip. 'Darling,' she said. 'Just the man I wanted. There's nobody here; everybody is out fussing about that tiresome child, as if she wasn't just hiding to draw attention to herself. Philip, I need to go to Heartsbury, there are one or two things I must get. You can take me.'

Emilia had driven in the back way and she came round the corner of the house at that very moment.

'Well,' she said, giving Claudia a frosty look, but otherwise ignoring her. 'Philip, Lisa, is there any news? I always knew that Polly was a headstrong child, but whatever is she thinking of?'

Without saying a word, Philip handed her the letter which was by now almost in shreds.

Emilia smoothed it out as best she could, and read it with growing horror. 'Why, the poor child,' she exclaimed. 'And I know who's to blame. For this, and a lot besides.' Her eyes narrowed, and she swung round to Claudia. 'It's all your doing. I know all about you.'

'I doubt that,' said Claudia, without interest.

'What about that business with your brother, then? I've just heard the details from Vanessa Rackrent. Scandalous! Shameless! Your own brother!'

Claudia shrugged, a bored expression on her face.

'Incest,' shrieked Emilia, infuriated by Claudia's indifference. 'I'm talking about incest. There, what do you say to that?'

Philip and Lisa exchanged horrified glances, while Emilia glared at Claudia like a hawk with its prey.

Claudia was quite unconcerned. 'You couldn't ever understand about someone like me,' she said contemptuously. 'You belong to an old, dead world, you have no concept of sexual freedom, and you're full of tired value judgements. Old women like you can't accept that the family is a relic, a thing of the past, a clapped-out code.'

'Oh, shut up, Claudia,' said Philip. 'You talk such balls.' Then he froze.

Inside the house, the phone was ringing.

CHAPTER 55

George was the hero of the hour.

Lisa and Philip had hurled themselves into the car to make the short journey to Heartsbane, where George had taken Polly when he had found her sitting disconsolately under a large oak tree.

She had been pathetically glad to see George. 'I've got blisters on my feet,' she said. 'Can I sit in front?'

'She's fine,' George told them on the phone. 'Sybil's given her a huge slice of chocolate cake, a particular favourite, I understand, and she's quite happy. And very relieved, I feel.'

Lisa tumbled out of the car and flew into the house. 'Polly, oh Polly,' was all she could say. Philip followed her into the cottage, banging his head on a beam, and wincing.

Polly was contrite, because she could see at a glance just how worried Lisa had been, but she wasn't that contrite. 'I still hate you, Daddy,' she said in a small voice.

'No, you don't, Polly,' he said, ruffling her hair. 'How about you and Alec going down to Maffick after all?'

'Not if horrible Claudia's going to be there,' said Polly, her face shadowed.

Philip knelt beside her. 'Polly, I promise you that we are going to leave Heartsease the very minute we can, and that I'm never going to see or speak to Claudia again.'

Polly eyed him warily. 'Are you sure?'

'Quite sure. Word of a Maffick. Now, we've trespassed here long enough, so let's get you home. Alec won't be happy until he's seen you for himself.'

Claudia was alone in the sitting-room, looking decidedly peevish.

'There's a fax come for you,' said Guy, in his chilliest tones.

He didn't wait for the thanks which wouldn't be forthcoming, but sped to the kitchen to report the news. 'It's from a man in

Switzerland. I think it must be that rich man Claudia was with before, the one who had to go into a home.'

'Another fool,' said Maria.

'It said he was being let out, and would Claudia marry him.'

'No!' said Maria.

'Never mind, such good news for all of us. The Swiss are welcome to her, and Switzerland is a good long way from Heartset.'

'And from London,' said Maria. 'What relief.'

Lisa was waylaid by Don as she flew backwards and forwards from the car, loading up suitcases, bags of hastily assembled possessions, children and Philip.

Don held out both hands to take hers. 'You're off, then.'

Lisa smiled warmly at him. 'Yes. It's best, I think.'

He kissed her on both cheeks, very gravely, and then drew her closely to give her a lingering kiss on her mouth. 'Goodbye, my dear.'

Lisa rested her face for a moment on his shoulder. 'Thank you.'

'Thank *you*,' said Don.

POSTSCRIPT

Lisa stood on the balcony, watching the sun dance on the water in the canal below.

Emilia had been very po-faced when Philip announced that he was taking Lisa to Venice. 'The children will be at Maffick, it's all arranged.'

'Venice? In July? Philip, it'll be impossible. The heat! The smells! The tourists!'

'We'll survive,' said Philip firmly.

'But why does it have to be Venice?'

'Because it does,' said Philip. 'There's always the Lido, for a refreshing swim.'

'The Adriatic!'

'Are you going to Maffick with the children?'

'They don't need me,' said Emilia huffily. 'Now you've invited George and Fanny . . .'

'That's Lisa's doing,' said Philip, laughing quite in his old way. 'She's matchmaking. Do go, Mother, it will do you good.'

'I hope they're all driving her mad,' said Lisa, leaning back against Philip with her eyes shut, basking in the morning warmth.

Philip put out a hand to touch her cheek. 'Well, *carissima*, what's the plan for today?'

Lisa's eyes opened, and her face lit up. 'Philip, there's this picture, a Tintoretto, in the Anticollegio. *Ariadne and Bacchus*, I simply must see it. Now, immediately, this very morning, quick, before the crowds get there; I can't wait another day.'